Also by Kathleen Fuller and available from
Center Point Large Print:

The Promise of a Letter
Words from the Heart
The Teacher's Bride
The Farmer's Bride
The Innkeeper's Bride
A Double Dose of Love
Hooked on You
Matched and Married
Much Ado About a Latte
Love in Plain Sight

**This Large Print Book carries the
Seal of Approval of N.A.V.H.**

Sold on Love

A MAPLE FALLS ROMANCE

KATHLEEN FULLER

CENTER POINT LARGE PRINT
THORNDIKE, MAINE

To James. I love you.

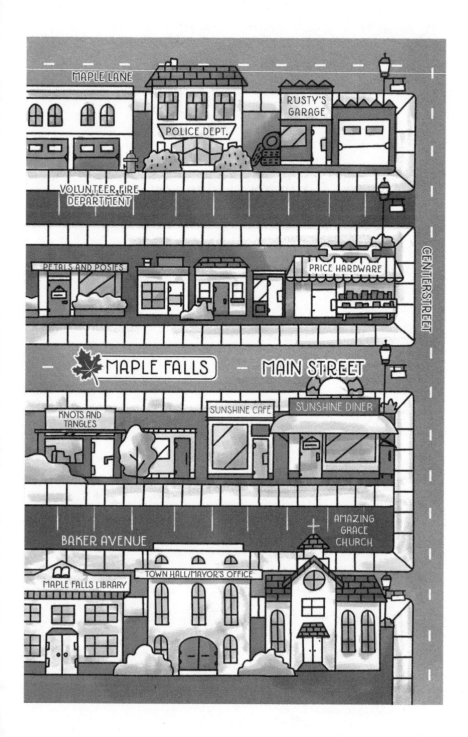

Chapter 1

*N*o . . . *no* . . . *For the love of* . . . *NO.*

Harper Wilson groaned as her Mercedes shuddered to a halt. Unbelievable. She banged the heels of her hands on the steering wheel, then twisted the key in the ignition. Nothing. Three more turns. Yep, her baby was dead.

She grabbed her phone, stepped out of the car, and slammed the door shut, grimacing against the blast of muggy midday heat. But that was nothing compared to her rising panic. In fifteen minutes she was supposed to show a potential client a seven-acre plot of land nearly three miles down this dusty road. In just a few hours she needed to be at Amazing Grace Church for Anita and Tanner's wedding. She was a bridesmaid—again—for one of her BFFs, and normally she would already be at the church helping out with whatever needed to be done. But Olivia, Anita's perfectionistic maid of honor, had things under control for the bridal party. Since Anita's mother was controlling everything else, Harper had decided she could sneak in this showing.

She looked at her cell. Zero bars. "Great. Just great," she muttered, holding the cell away from her, then up in the air. After turning around in a circle, she finally saw a bar appear in the upper corner of the screen, but only if she held the cell above her head while she stood on one foot, her narrow four-inch heel sinking into the soft ground of the dirt road. Quickly she searched for the familiar number, then hit it with her thumb.

"Hiya, Harper." Rusty Jenkins's low, affable drawl came through the speaker.

"Thank God you answered," she said, not daring to move and lose the precious service bar.

"Did ya break down again?"

She sighed. "Of course I did."

"Dang it. All right, I'll come get ya and tow ya back to the garage. I'm sure sorry about this, Harper. I thought I'd fixed her up for good this time."

"It's okay, Rusty." She gave him her location, then hung up and tried to call her client, only to lose her balance and drop the phone onto the dry dirt. "No!" She grabbed it and searched for service. Nothing. Held the phone above her head and stood on one foot again. Zip. Now beads of sweat were running down the side of her face.

Yuck. The only time perspiration was permissible was when she was working out or playing for the church softball team. But dripping sweat while standing next to her stupid car? Ridiculous.

She opened the door and sat on the driver-side seat, the hem of her peach-tinted silk sheath dress rising above her knees. Bad idea. The cream-colored leather interior was stifling.

8

She grabbed her Louboutin Paloma bag—a luxury purchase to celebrate her first real-estate sale seven years ago—and exited the car. She fished for her makeup bag inside the purse, then pulled it out, quickly unzipped it, and found the small rectangular mirror inside. One look at her reflection had her cringing. Her perfect coiffure, meticulous makeup, and optimistic disposition were all wilting under the scorching sun.

Who gets married in August anyway? Anita and Tanner, that's who. And while Harper was just as happy for the two of them as she'd been last summer when her friends Riley and Hayden had gotten married, summer weddings in Arkansas were peak insanity.

As she waited for Rusty to pick her up, she dabbed at her face with a tissue and scrolled through the emails already downloaded on her phone. Six messages from prospective buyers surfing property websites on the internet. *Good, good.* For the past six months the local real estate had taken a downturn, which was one of the reasons she didn't want to cancel today's showing. Thankfully her business was still in the black, and she wanted to keep it that way.

She then scanned the email reminder of the final committee meeting for the ALS Foundation gala and auction happening in Hot Springs the last Saturday in October. *Oops.* She'd already missed the last few meetings due to work. This was her third year volunteering for the gala, although she'd attended them for the past five years—once with Anita's brother, Kingston. She made a mental note not to schedule anything for that evening.

The rest of the emails weren't urgent, and she decided to wait to answer them until after the wedding reception was over. She glanced at the time on her phone. If Rusty arrived in five minutes or less, she'd still have time to meet the client and not be late for the wedding. *Please, Rusty. Hurry.*

As if on cue, his tow truck appeared in the distance, clouds of dirt flying behind it. She tossed her phone into the Paloma and hurried to the middle of the road to flag him down. When he halted a few yards away, she met him on the passenger side. "Perfect timing," she said after he rolled down the window. She poked her head through the opening. "Can you do me another favor?"

His easygoing grin reappeared. "Sure."

"I'm meeting two clients farther up the road. Could you take me there?"

"After I hook up your car?"

"No, before."

Confusion entered his eyes. "All right," he drawled. "Climb on in."

Relieved, she opened the door, barely noticing the light-blue towel draped over the seat. She sat down and pointed straight ahead. "They should be there already."

Rusty put the truck in gear and drove for a few minutes until they saw a dark-gray sedan parked on the side of the road. Only then did she realize she'd left her phone and purse in her car. She pulled down the visor and checked her face. The air-conditioning in the truck had helped her cool off a bit, but she still shone with perspiration. "I look awful."

She felt a tap on her shoulder. When she looked down, she saw Rusty's huge hand holding out a clean white paper towel. "Thanks," she said, then dabbed her damp skin a few times before opening the door. "Wish me luck."

"But Harper—"

She shut the door, pasted a smile on her face, and walked to the middle-aged couple standing by the sedan. The smartly dressed woman fanned her face with what looked like a brochure as the man wiped his brow with the back of his hand.

"Hello," she said when she reached them, extending her hand. "Harper Wilson. Goodness, it's a hot one today, isn't it?"

Both of them looked her up and down, the man with more interest than the woman, who quickly gave him an elbow to the ribs. The woman glanced at Rusty's truck behind her. "Is something wrong with your car?" she asked.

"Nothing major." *I hope.* The last thing she

needed was a huge repair bill. "Now, let's talk about this jewel of a property. Isn't it an absolutely perfect place to build your retirement dream home?"

Rusty sat in the cab of his truck, cool air blasting through the AC vents and muted classic rock playing through the scratchy radio speakers. He'd set the volume on low, but he could still hear the Eagles singing "Desperado" as Harper led the couple to the field on the opposite side of the road, the grass dry and brown from the hot sun.

He was surprised she hadn't wanted him to hook up her Mercedes to the tow lift right away. Anita and Tanner's wedding started in less than two hours, and they had invited him. He glanced down at his navy-blue dress pants. When Harper called, he'd been halfway done putting on his fancy clothes. But an emergency was an emergency, and this wouldn't be the first time he'd had to stop what he was doing to tow someone. He'd thrown on his work shirt, jumped in the truck, and come here. Hopefully whatever Harper was doing wouldn't take long. He didn't like being late.

Rusty glanced at her again. Judging by her sleek, form-fitting dress, her high-heeled gold shoes, and her blond hair piled high on her head, she was going to the wedding too. He reckoned she might be in the wedding party since she and Anita were good friends. Or maybe it was just another day for Harper Wilson. She was always dressed fancy.

"Desperado" faded into Journey's "Faithfully," and he leaned back against the seat. He'd gotten to know Harper somewhat over the past year since her Mercedes had started giving her—and him—fits. Although he'd been working on cars and trucks in some capacity since he was a kid, his grandfather, Russell Jenkins Sr.—"Senior" to everyone who knew him—the first owner of Rusty's Garage, had rarely tackled foreign automobiles. But Rusty liked a challenge, and he wasn't about to let the Merc get the best of him. Besides, it cost a pretty penny to tow the car to the nearest Mercedes dealer in Little Rock, and he liked to save his customers an extra expense if he could.

He continued to watch Harper and the couple as they talked. The sun beat down through his driver-side window, and the outside-temp gauge on his dash read ninety-five degrees. With the humidity it felt hotter than that. But Harper looked as cool as a fall day, seemingly unaffected by the heat. A few minutes ago had been the first time he'd see her flustered, or even sweat. She was gorgeous and elegant, he had to admit. Miles out of his league. Or she would be if he was interested in her that way.

He wasn't dumb, though, and he knew better than to even open his mind to the idea. Harper was sheer class. Rusty was a grease monkey who lived for working on cars. They existed in two different universes that only collided because her Merc was probably a lemon—although he wasn't going to tell her that. Not until he tried everything he could to fix it.

As the minutes continued to pass, he grew a little concerned. He considered exiting the truck and insisting she and her clients quit their discussion before they ended up with heatstroke.

Finally the couple got into their car, and Harper hurried to his truck. How she walked so quickly in those heels, he'd never know, but she had a wide smile on her face when she opened the passenger door.

"Yes!" she said, pumping her fist before she sat down on the towel he'd laid out for her. His tow truck was old but in good condition, and he tried to keep it as clean as possible. But there were a few coffee spots on the seat, and he hadn't wanted her to sit on stained upholstery.

"Good news?" he asked as he waited for the sedan to turn around and pass.

"Absolutely." Her cheeks and the tops of her shoulders were bright red. "They're ready to sign the contract on Monday!"

"Congratulations." The gray sedan passed by, and Harper waved.

"Lord knows I needed this sale." She leaned against the back of the seat and closed her eyes.

He didn't have a clue about real estate, but he did know how to run a business. From her comment, it sounded like she might be in a lean time. Fortunately, lean times were few and far between for his garage.

Rusty turned the truck around and headed for her car. When they reached the Mercedes, he hopped out and went to work hooking it up while Harper retrieved her bag from the driver's seat. She waited in the tow truck's air-conditioned cab until he finished.

A few minutes later, sweat poured down his back and over his face as he hooked up the last chain. Today was a scorcher. He jumped inside the cab. "Mind if I turn this up?" He pointed to the air conditioner.

"Please do."

He turned the knob to full blast and let the cold air hit him. *Ahhh.*

"Here." Harper held out the roll of paper towels for him. He grabbed it, tore off one, and wiped his face. "Thanks."

But her attention was focused on her phone screen. He put his truck in gear and took off. "Want me to drop you off at the church?" he asked.

"Hmm, what?"

"The weddin's startin' in about an hour."

She stopped typing, then gasped. "I didn't realize the time! I'm going to be late!"

"I'll take that as a yes." He accelerated as fast as he safely could and headed for Amazing Grace Church while Harper yanked a mirror and a glittery bag out of that huge purse of hers.

"The Lattes are going to kill me for this," she muttered.

He glanced at her. "The who?"

"Lattes. It's the temporary name of our little group of friends. Me, Anita, Riley, and Olivia." She pulled out a small, red-tipped wand of lipstick and smoothed it over her lips. "If I'm late, Olivia will never let me forget it."

"She seems like a nice gal. I reckon she won't be that hard on you."

"There's a drill sergeant underneath that innocent librarian veneer, trust me."

He hadn't spent enough time in the library to know anything about Olivia other than she was in charge in some capacity. "We'll be there soon," he assured her. "You won't be late." *Not that late, anyway.*

"First you show up in record time to tow my car, then you stay while I conduct business, and now you're making sure I get to Anita's wedding on time." She turned, her ruby-red lips forming a brilliant smile. "How you haven't been snatched up by some girl yet is a mystery to me."

"Aww, I ain't all that." Truth be told, his single

status was a mystery to him too. He didn't want to be single. More than once he'd put himself out into the dating scene only to have his heart stomped on like a wood floor in a country bar each and every time. After his last date, he'd given up on women entirely. "I could say the same for you," he said, turning into the Amazing Grace parking lot.

"No time for romance. Or much of anything else."

Before he could wonder what she meant by that, they were at the church. As soon as he pulled up in front of the building, she opened the door and hopped out, dragging her big bag with her. "Thanks again."

"No prob—"

The door slammed shut.

"—lem." He watched her rush inside, more of a habit his grandmother had drilled into him when he was growing up than paying attention to how good she looked in that dress. Well, yeah, he was noticing that too. He wasn't blind. Harper Wilson was something else. Gorgeous, smart, and she obviously cared about her business. He just hoped she didn't overwork herself. It was never a good idea to wear yourself out.

He towed her Merc to his garage, unattached it in a parking space near one of his two work bays, parked the tow truck in its spot, then jumped into his pickup truck and headed home. It was too late for him to attend the ceremony, but he could make it to the reception.

A short while later, he whipped his truck into his driveway, ran into the house, and took a quick shower, making sure he got all the grease he could from underneath his nails. Then he wrapped a towel around his waist, went to his room, and looked for a shirt to go with his pants. What shirt went with navy blue? He looked at the four shirts that didn't say *Rusty's Garage* on them. One was white with long sleeves, the other three short-sleeved plaid. Too hot for long sleeves. That narrowed down the choices a little.

Senior's ringtone, a country song from the sixties, trilled from his phone as he pulled the green-and-white plaid one off the hanger. "Hey, Senior," he said, putting the phone on speaker mode and setting it on his bed. "What's up?"

"Not a dang thing," his grandfather said. "Other than chasing after your niece and nephews."

Rusty grinned as he slipped on the shirt. "I reckon it's the other way around." His sister Amber had four children under eight years old. But his grandfather still had some kick left in him.

Senior laughed. "And you would be right."

"I hate to cut this short, but I have a weddin' to get to."

"Anyone I know?"

"Tanner and Anita."

"Oh, that's right. Them two were just gettin' together when I moved to Amber's. You takin' anyone special with you?"

Rusty finished fastening the last button and started tucking his shirttail into the pants. "Just me, myself, and I."

"Well, shoot. I was hopin' maybe you'd found a young lady you were sweet on."

"Nope." *Not in the plan.* "Are we still on for next week?"

"Yep. Can't wait to get back to Maple Falls for a spell. Don't get me wrong. I enjoy livin' in Little Rock. Found a good church to attend, and it gives me time to spend with my granddaughter and grandbabies. Austin's a fine sort too."

"He sure is." His sister had hit the jackpot when she married him. Not any husband would agree to have his wife's grandfather move in with them, but he'd been just as enthusiastic as Amber when she proposed the idea to Senior. Rusty also approved, even though he missed his grandfather at the shop and at the home they'd shared together. The only person who took convincing was Senior—a lot of convincing. But now that he was settled, he seemed content.

Except when it came to driving. Rusty steeled himself for what Senior was going to say next.

"Don't worry about pickin' me up," his grandfather said. Rusty mouthed his next words along with him: "I don't wanna be no bother."

"You're not a bother." Rusty's pants slid to his hips. It had been a while since he'd worn them. Riley's wedding last year, now that he thought about it, and he'd lost some weight since then. He grabbed his belt and threaded it through the loops.

"I can still drive, you know."

He buckled the belt on the last notch. The pants were still a little loose, but now he didn't have to worry about his trousers dropping to the floor. "We've been through this." *Thousands of times.* "You don't see well enough to drive."

"I see fine," Senior grumped. "What does that doctor know anyway?"

"He's one of the top ophthalmologists in the state. So when he says you can't see well enough to drive because of macular degeneration, you need to listen to him. He knows his stuff."

"Hmmph. You and Amber are stubborn, you know that?"

Rusty grinned. "Can't imagine where we got that from."

"Fine. I'll let you pick me up next week," Senior said. "I'll also let you get goin'." His tone brightened. "Who knows, maybe you'll find that special lady you can't live without at the weddin'."

"Yeah, right," Rusty muttered.

"What's that?"

"See ya next week." He hung up the phone

before Senior had a chance to make any more comments on his love life—or, more accurately, lack of one.

He went into the bathroom and looked in the mirror. *Tie or no tie?* He decided against one. No need to have a cloth noose around his neck in ninety-plus-degree weather, especially when he couldn't really knot one anyway. Besides, who would he impress? He knew everyone in town and had worked on most of their cars at one time or another. Senior had started him in the garage at age eight, and by the time he was twelve he'd been able to take apart and put back together an engine faster than Senior could.

He grabbed a comb and tried to force his wiry, wavy red hair into a decent style as he thought about Riley and Hayden's wedding again. He'd danced with Anita at the reception. Tried to, at least. He could fix a car in his sleep—except for Harper's Mercedes, apparently—but he had two left feet when it came to dancing. Fortunately, Tanner had cut in before Rusty broke one of Anita's toes . . . and the rest was history. Now the two of them were getting married, and he was still . . . single.

His hair stuck up around the edges; he was in desperate need of a trip to the barber. Oh well. He shoved his feet into his barely worn dress shoes, grabbed his sports jacket and keys, and went to his car, shaking his head as he thought of Senior's words. The chances of him finding a special lady today were exactly zero. In fact, he was starting to think she didn't exist.

Chapter 2

I can't believe you were late."

Harper glanced over her shoulder at Olivia, who had muttered the words under her breath. "I'm sorry," she whispered.

"This is Anita's special day," Olivia said, her brow knitting together. "She was worried you wouldn't show up."

Harper stared straight ahead, gripping her bridesmaid's bouquet as they lined up for the bridal party procession. The peach, mint, and teal roses were beautiful, but she couldn't enjoy them through the guilt. She hadn't meant to be late, and if it hadn't been for Rusty, she might have been tardy for the ceremony. Still, she didn't appreciate Olivia scolding her, even though she had expected it. And deserved it. "I said I was sorry," she whispered out of the corner of her mouth.

"Ladies, can this wait?"

She turned to Kingston, the groomsman she was paired up with. Even with her high heels, she had to look up at him. Anita's pediatrician brother was flawlessly handsome in his light-gray suit and teal tie. With their blond hair and almost matching blue eyes, more than one person had already said Harper and Kingston were a striking pair. But there was zero spark between the two of them. He was more like her brother—if she'd had one. He was also right. Now wasn't the time to apologize or argue.

"Sorry," Olivia said.

Harper couldn't help but glance at her. She and Lonzo, who was Tanner's best man and younger brother, both stood at attention, staring straight ahead. *Like I should be.* Following their cue, she smiled as the sanctuary door opened.

She waited as Anita's sister Paisley and her husband, Ryan, entered the sanctuary behind Riley and Hayden, the other members of the bridal party. Kingston tucked her hand in the crook of his elbow, and they proceeded down the aisle.

As expected, the ceremony was perfect. Anita's mother, Karen, was already crying before Olivia and Lonzo reached the front of the church, and Harper saw a sheen of tears in her husband, Walter's, eyes too. Even Kingston showed a little emotion, the muscle in his jaw jerking as Anita and Tanner said their vows. Not unexpected since the two of them were very close.

"You may now kiss the bride."

Harper grinned as Tanner took his bride into his arms and kissed her sweetly. And that was that. Anita was now Mrs. Tanner Castillo, and Harper was thrilled.

She met up with Kingston again, and they walked back down the aisle. Feeling calmer, she enjoyed standing in the reception line and visiting with everyone as they congratulated the couple and their bridal party.

"My stars, look at the two of you." Erma McAllister, Riley's grandmother, stepped in front of her and Kingston. She leaned over to Bea, Peg, and Myrtle—three women from the Bosom Buddies group, otherwise known as the BBs, who stood beside her—and said, "They look straight out of a fashion magazine, don't they?"

Bea, Olivia's aunt, nodded. "They sure do." She leaned forward and whispered, "Maybe you two will be the next ones to get married."

Harper laughed. The idea was preposterous. Even when the two of them had gone to the gala together year before last, it had been as friends. She glanced at him, expecting him to find the comment as humorous as she did. Instead, he stood looking at Olivia for some reason, his expression the exact opposite of humorous. Olivia didn't seem to notice.

"That's the thing about weddings," Harper said, turning her attention back to the older ladies. "We all get a chance to clean up for a change."

Erma leaned forward. "Pretty *and* modest. I like that. We'll keep you." She winked at Harper.

"I'll keep you, too, Ms. McAllister." And then, to squash any possible ideas the BBs might have of her and Kingston ever being a couple, she added, "Trust me, I'm not getting married any-time soon."

"That's what they all say." Erma winked at her, and she and her friends moved on.

When the wedding party finished with the receiving line, it was time to head to the Maple Falls community center for the reception. Since the center was only a few blocks from the church, everyone took their own car.

Wait . . . Her car was in the shop.

She saw Kingston head for the door. "Can you give me a ride to the reception?" she asked.

"Sure."

"Thanks. I just have to get my purse." She hurried to the third-grade Sunday school room, grabbed her bag from the child-sized semicircle table at the back, and met Kingston at the front of the church.

He held open the door for her. For the second time that day, the oppressive, damp heat almost took her breath away. What she wouldn't do for crisp fall weather. But cooler temperatures were at least a month and a half away. *Horrific heat it is.* "I really appreciate this," she said as they crossed the parking lot. "My car broke down again."

"That red Mercedes?" Kingston slipped off his suit jacket and loosened his tie. "Nice car."

"It's not nice to me," she grumbled. "When I bought it two years ago, it ran fine. Now it breaks down as soon as I get it out of the shop."

"Who's working on it?"

"Rusty." She dangled the handle of her Paloma from her fingers.

"It's in good hands, then." The Audi was already running by the time they reached it. "I'm sure he'll figure it out," Kingston said, walking to the driver-side door. The doors automatically unlocked.

"I hope so. I love that car." Harper got into his vehicle and immediately felt relief. "Ah, air-conditioning. I love you too."

Kingston pressed the starter, and soon they were on their way to the community center. "I can't believe both of my sisters are married," he said as they turned out of the church lot.

"That means you're next."

He chuckled, but it sounded a little strained. "Stop sounding like my mom." He paused, then said, "Like I told her, I'll get married when I'm ready."

Had she hit a nerve? "Okayyy."

"Sorry." He grinned, back to his all-American male persona. "Weddings seem to give folks carte blanche to tease the single people. I've been to three since June. It's getting a little old."

She could totally relate.

The community center came into view, and as he turned into the lot she saw Rusty's emerald-green pickup truck parked near the back, the words *Rusty's Garage* displayed on the passenger-side door. She sure did owe him one.

She wasn't sure how she would pay him back, but she'd figure out something.

"Thanks again for the ride," she said when they were out of the car.

"Anytime." Kingston smiled, as if he hadn't been even a smidge irritated a moment ago.

As they walked inside the hall, the last of Harper's tension faded away. The community center was almost as old as Maple Falls, and not only did it double as a social venue and gymnasium, it was also an official polling place and used to host the annual Maple Falls talent show, although that had gone by the wayside almost half a century ago. The expansive room was beautifully decorated in Anita's wedding colors, and soft lights shone everywhere, from the peach and teal candles in clear globes flickering on the table centers to the numerous strands of clear white lights draped on the walls.

"Oh, there's Mom," Kingston said, gesturing to Karen, who stood by the dessert table in animated conversation with one of the caterers. "Uh-oh. She looks ready to pop off."

Karen Bedford was legendary for micromanaging and getting her nose out of joint if things didn't go strictly as planned.

"How can you tell?" Harper asked. "She looks fine to me."

"That's the calm before the storm. Better go rescue that guy."

"Good luck." She watched as Kingston moved to stand beside his mother. When he lightly placed his hand on her back, Karen's flailing hands went to her sides. Another crisis averted.

Harper turned around, needing to find the rest of the bridal party before they wondered where she was—only to walk straight into something solid.

"Oof." Rusty took a step back, raising up his palms. "Sorry."

"No, I'm the one who's sorry," she said, a little embarrassed. "I didn't see you there."

"I didn't exactly make myself known either."

"Then we'll call it even." She took stock of his outfit. Due to her love of clothing and fashion, she normally paid attention to what others wore. But she never judged. Everyone had their own sense of style, and Rusty's currently resembled thrift-store comfort. Nothing wrong with that, but there was comfort and then there was . . . whatever this was. His cobalt-blue suit jacket sat tight around the shoulders but loose around the middle and barely escaped clashing with his navy-blue pants. She'd noticed—especially since she and the Mercedes had spent so much time at his garage lately—he'd slimmed down over the last year. Only now did she realize how much. His baggy work shirt and jeans hid a lot, but it was clear that his dress clothes were way too big. The green-and-white plaid shirt was a nice pattern—for golf pants. And she had to resist the urge to pat down the cowlick sticking up on the right side of his head.

None of these things were horrible. Just messy, in a clueless kind of way.

"Harper!" Riley called out from a few feet away, motioning for her to go to the bridal table in front of the stage. The heavy burgundy velvet curtains that usually hung there had been replaced with layers of sheer fabric, also covered in lights.

Harper glanced around and saw that most of the guests had already found their seats. "Gotta run," she said, moving quickly past Rusty. Then she called out over her shoulder, "Save me a dance, okay?"

"Uh, okay."

But she barely heard him as she took her place next to Olivia. "I know, I know," she said, sitting down between her and Paisley. "I'm late again."

Olivia reached out under the table and grabbed her hand. "I'm sorry I snapped at you," she said. "I've been a little crabby lately."

Relieved, Harper squeezed her friend's hand. "It's all right. I was late, and I deserved it." She started to tell her why, then decided against it. Putting her job before her BFFs wasn't a good look. She also felt bad that she hadn't noticed Olivia being crabby at all up until today. Usually the Lattes met once a week at Knots and Tangles, but she hadn't been able to meet with them lately due to, of course, work. That wasn't good either.

"Everything worked out great, though." Olivia's strained expression softened as she glanced at Anita and Tanner. The two sat close together, their heads touching as Anita spoke into his ear. "They're both so happy. And I'm happy for them."

Harper nodded. "Me too." She shoved business out of her mind. Tonight she was going to enjoy herself and her friends. Work would have to wait.

Rusty was experiencing déjà vu. Or life on repeat, to be more accurate. He was babysitting the punch bowl again, like he'd done during Riley and Hayden's reception last year. But unlike the weak beverage they had served, the margarita drink in this bowl packed a little punch—pun intended.

He took a sip from his small clear glass and watched everyone dancing. This was his third drink, and apparently that was the charm, because he was starting to feel the effects. Not bad ones, just a mellow sensation going through him as he spied Harper and Kingston slow dancing together.

"Save me a dance." Her request had surprised him, but he hadn't taken it seriously. She had her pick of partners, and at the moment Kingston

was her choice. He'd seen them walk into the community center together. He had to admit they looked good together, like one of those celebrity couples from the magazines he kept in the small waiting room at his garage to help his customers pass the time. Once the bridal party introductions were finished, Harper and Kingston hadn't parted ways and continued to dance during the next song. Which was fine by Rusty. *Whatever makes her happy.*

"*Psst.*"

Rusty turned to see that Jasper, the town's oldest resident and one of Senior's good friends, had appeared next to him. "Hey, Jasper," he said. "Want some punch?"

"Shhh." He moved closer to him. "Keep your voice down, will ya?"

Leaning toward him, Rusty asked, "Why we whisperin'?"

"I'm trying to be incognito."

"Why?"

Jasper gave him an exasperated look. "Never figured you for the nosy type."

Eyebrows raised, Rusty turned away and finished off his punch.

"Fine, since you're buggin' me about it." Jasper moved close enough to Rusty that he was almost leaning against him. He was several inches shorter than Rusty and at least half his size. "I'm avoiding *her.*"

Rusty's gaze followed the direction Jasper pointed. "Myrtle?"

"No. The battle ax next to her."

His eyes widened. "You're hidin' from Ms. McAllister?"

"Avoiding. There's a difference, boy."

Jasper was clearly ducking behind him, so Rusty figured the old man had his words mixed up. "Why are you hidin'—er, avoidin'—her?"

"Because she is the bane of my existence."

Rusty turned to face him. "The what of your what?"

"Don't draw her attention. Oh drat. Too late." Jasper grabbed a cup and handed it to Rusty. "I'll take that drink now."

Rusty filled the cup halfway and handed it behind him.

Slurp!

"Hello, Rusty." Erma grinned as she reached the table. "Manning the punch bowl tonight?"

That sounded a little pathetic. "Just observin' the festivities," he said. A tad better, but not by much.

"I see." She craned her neck to peek around his shoulder. "Observing all by yourself, then?"

"Uh . . ." There were very few things Rusty outright hated. Lying was one of them. But he didn't want to upset Jasper either. Who knew standing by the margarita bowl would put him in such a pickle?

"Don't bother fibbing, Rusty," she said. "I know that old coot is right behind you."

"Who you callin' an old coot?" Jasper moved to stand next to Rusty. He weakly slammed his empty glass on the table.

"If the suspenders fit . . ." Erma crossed her arms.

Rusty's lips twitched. Jasper was rarely seen without his suspenders.

"I will not be aspersed by you." Jasper lifted his chin.

While the idea of learning a new vocabulary word was a little interesting, the fire in Erma's and Jasper's eyes was not. "I best be gettin' along—"

" 'Aspersed.' " Erma rolled her eyes.

"Yes. Aspersed."

"All I did was ask you to dance. Then you ran off like the scaredy cat you are."

Jasper scowled. "I ain't afraid to dance."

"Then prove it."

"If it'll get you off my back, then I will."

Erma smiled as if she'd won a secret lottery jackpot. She held out her hand.

Groaning, Jasper trudged around the table.

"Slower than molasses flowing upriver," Erma mumbled, but she was still grinning.

"We'll see who's slow." As if he'd suddenly found the pep in his step, he grabbed her hand and practically dragged her behind him onto the dance floor.

Rusty wondered if he was the only one who noticed Erma's hand fluttering to her chest. He shook his head and smiled.

"Ready for that dance?"

He looked up to see Harper standing in front of him. And then something weird happened. His mouth went dry at the exact same time his palms grew damp. What in the world? It wasn't as if this was the first time he'd seen her today. But it was the first time he'd reacted like this. That punch was stronger than he thought.

She tilted her head, her blue eyes filling with slight confusion. Then she brightened and walked around the table to stand next to him. She slipped off her heels and pushed them under the table with the side of her foot. "Ah, that's better. My feet are killing me in those things."

"I, uh . . ."

"Is there something wrong?"

"Um . . ." He took a step back. "I didn't think you were bein' serious. About the dance."

"Of course I was. I love to dance." And in much the same way Jasper had led Erma out on the dance floor, Harper took his hand and gave it a slight tug.

Not wanting to look like he was being dragged away, he walked beside her. "Celebration" was playing, and Harper lifted up her arms and started to dance.

"I'm not a great dancer," he said, moving his

feet from side to side in what he hoped was some kind of rhythm. He suspected he looked more like a bull hoofing on a hot plate, though. At least he wasn't stepping on her toes. Maybe he should have taken off his shoes, too, but it was too late for that.

She took his hands, and they both moved their arms back and forth like they were playing a crooked game of London Bridge. Then the song switched to one with a slower tempo. Gratefully, he started to release her hands and go back to the punch table where he belonged. But in one smooth move she placed his hands on her slim waist, moved closer to him, and put her hands on his shoulders.

Wow.

"I can't thank you enough for bailing me out today," she said, the music low enough that he could hear her clearly. "I owe you one."

Ah. That was the reason she asked him to dance. "Just doin' my job," he said. "You don't owe me anythin'."

"I figured you'd say something like that." She smiled, rested her wrists on his shoulders near his neck. "Thanks again anyway."

The soft music played in the background, and they stopped talking. He breathed in her perfume, a heady scent he hadn't noticed when he picked her up earlier. He was noticing it now, along with how his hands almost spanned her waist and the soft, silky feel of the fabric of her tight dress. *Nice. Very nice.* Now all he had to do was not step on her—

"Ow!"

"Sorry!" He jumped back, dropping his hands. "Are you okay?"

"I think so." But when she stood on both feet she winced.

Oops. He'd been so focused on how good she felt in his arms that he hadn't paid attention to his clumsy feet. What if he'd broken her foot?

Without thinking, he swept her up into his arms.

"Rusty, what are you doing?"

He didn't answer as he took her outside the gym to one of the folding chairs in the hallway and set her down gently. Then he knelt in front of her. "Which foot is it?"

"I'm fine, really . . ."

Rusty looked up at her. "Are you sure? I can get some ice for it."

She held up her left foot in front of him, wiggling her toes, the nails polished white.

"See? I'll live."

He leaned back, breathing out a sigh of relief. "This is why I don't dance. I always step on someone's toes. Or feet. Mostly both."

"You just got my big toe." She put her foot down and grinned. "I appreciate the chivalry, though. It's not every day a girl gets whisked away in a man's arms."

Now that he knew he hadn't damaged her, he felt his cheeks redden. "Sorry. That was a bit much, huh?"

"A bit." But she was still smiling. Then she leaned over and ruffled his hair.

The gesture was an innocent one, but his mouth felt like the Sahara again. *Time to lay off the punch.*

Harper stood up. "Thanks for the dance, Rusty. It was fun." She gave him a little wave and walked back into the gym, her limp barely noticeable.

Slowly he rose, still floored by what had just happened. He'd never literally picked up a woman in his life. He'd never gone completely cottonmouthed with one, either, and that included all of the dates he'd been on. Not that he'd had a lot of them. But none of those women had been as nice as Harper. And he had to be honest—they weren't as beautiful either. They were pretty, though. He thought most women were, in their own way. And he was never one to be hung up on looks anyway. But Harper was an absolute knockout.

Nuts. He had to stay away from that punch. It was making him think things . . . feel things . . . he didn't want or need.

He paused, then started to go back inside, only to stop himself. He'd made an appearance, had a chuckle at Erma and Jasper's expense, and had a mostly humiliation-free dance with Harper. No need to hang around any longer. He could spend the rest of the evening working on his classic GTO, something he hadn't been able to do much of lately. Besides, no one would notice he was gone anyway. Not a pitiful thought. Only a factual one.

Rusty turned around and walked outside, then made his way to his truck. When he opened the door, he slipped off his jacket, caught a whiff of Harper's perfume, and smiled.

"We saw Rusty carrying you out of the gym."

"What was all that about?"

"Are you keeping something from us?"

Harper turned away from the hazy mirror in front of her and stared at her BFFs. Anita, Riley, and Olivia had followed her into the women's bathroom, and like most things in Maple Falls, it needed a makeover. Earlier she'd apologized to all three of them, then added two more apologies to Anita for almost ruining her special day. And because they were the best friends in the world, they'd all forgiven her.

Apparently they were also the nosiest.

She leveled her gaze at Riley. "No, I'm not keeping anything from you." Then she looked at Anita. "Rusty stepped on my toe. And that, Olivia, was why he carried me out of the gym."

"He tends to do that," Anita said, tucking a

strand of her long auburn hair that had escaped from her updo behind her ear. "I had a bruise on the top of my foot from our dance last year, but I never told him about it."

Harper turned around and checked her false eyelashes. They were fine, but she needed something to do or her friends might see how inexplicably unnerved she was. Not because Rusty had picked her up, although that was pretty awesome. He had a rock-solid torso, something she'd noticed when they were slow dancing together.

Ah, that slow dance. Up until he stepped on her toe, she had felt . . . Well, she wasn't sure what she'd felt. Only that it felt good. *Maybe we can dance again.*

But when she and her friends went back to the reception, he was nowhere in sight. She went to the beverage table and slipped on her heels. Jasper stood there, looking grouchier than he usually did at wedding receptions, although he never missed a single one. "Have you seen Rusty?" she asked.

He shook his head. "Not for a while."

"Okay, thanks." She went to the entryway of the community center and stepped outside. Now that the sun sat lower in the sky, the heat wasn't as bad, although still oppressive. She searched for Rusty's truck and didn't see it. He'd left.

She was surprised at the bit of disappointment

she felt. It wasn't like she hadn't danced with other men before at these things. At Riley's wedding she'd hit the floor with a number of guys, both married and single. She'd even slow danced with Jared, the unmarried pastor of Amazing Grace. And of course Kingston at Riley's reception and twice this evening. She liked dancing with him because he was an exceptional dancer, having been forced by Karen to go to cotillion when he was a kid. But while those dances had been fun, she'd never *felt* anything. She wasn't even sure she'd felt anything with Rusty.

Or had she?

As if he'd read her thoughts, Kingston approached and held out his hand. "Dance?"

Harper opened her mouth to say yes, but nothing came out. She cleared her throat. "Um, not right now. I hurt my foot a little while ago while I was dancing."

"Oh. Want me to take a look at it?"

"No," she said, waving her hand. "I'm sure it's fine."

He nodded. "You should probably stay off of it to keep it from swelling." He eyed her feet. "I'm sure those heels aren't helping."

Her toe barely hurt, but she nodded anyway. "Thanks for the advice, Dr. Bedford."

"Anytime. Just save me a dance at the next wedding." Then he gave her a sly grin. "Maybe you'll be Maple Falls's next blushing bride."

"Hey, I thought this was a no-teasing zone."

"No teasing *me,*" he said. "You, on the other hand, are fair game."

She smirked. "Laugh it up, Chuckles." As she slipped off her shoes, she spied Olivia sitting by herself at the bridal table. "Olivia's free. Why don't you dance with her?"

A strange look crossed his face. "Uh, sure."

She watched him slowly walk over to the table, then pause before he reached Olivia. Olivia looked up from the nearly empty plate in front of her. Her big brown eyes widened even more as Kingston said something to her. She looked down at her lap.

Huh. That was weird. She'd never seen Olivia and Kingston act so strangely with each other. Now that she thought about it, she'd never seen the two of them together other than in a group— usually at church when Kingston wasn't working or on call, or during a few softball games last season when he would show up to cheer on the team. Harper had only made the first two games of this season before dropping out to deal with her sinking sales, but Olivia had still played. Was something going on with them?

Finally Olivia nodded and followed Kingston onto the dance floor. Three couples seemed to simultaneously surround them as the DJ played the latest pop song. Soon almost everyone was dancing, and all Harper could see was the top of

Kingston's blond head bopping back and forth.

She picked up her shoes and went to sit at the bridal table again. Olivia and Kingston. Nope, that would never happen. They didn't have anything in common, and probably the only person in this room who was more entrenched in singledom than her and Kingston was Olivia.

The moment she sat down, her phone buzzed. She glanced at the message flashing across the screen.

Hey, Harper. It's Jack. Call me.

She froze, reading the text again. Only one person named Jack had her phone number, and she couldn't believe she'd forgotten to block his. Not after what he'd done to her almost three years ago. Then again, she hadn't expected to ever hear from him again.

Harper grabbed the phone and dropped it into her purse. She'd deal with the text later—by erasing it and then blocking his number so hard the cell tower would topple over. On his head.

I wish.

She yanked back her thoughts. This wasn't the time to stew about him. She'd let Jack ruin enough of her life back then, and she wasn't going to let him ruin tonight.

But as she watched the reception wind down a little, fatigue suddenly hit, and she realized how exhausted she was. It had been a long day. An exciting and lovely one for her friends, and a fruitful one for her, professionally speaking. Also an unexpected one where Rusty was concerned. She thought back to their slow dance. The way his big hands had lightly rested on her waist and how broad his shoulders were as she wrapped her arms around them when he carried her out of the hall. Harper Wilson didn't swoon—and this was Rusty, anyway, and she wouldn't ever swoon over him. Yet those few moments in his arms had been . . . bliss? No, surely not that. Just a nice dance with a nice guy. Nothing special about that.

Still, she couldn't help but smile.

Chapter 3

Two months later

*H*onk!
Rusty moved his head from underneath the GTO's hood and saw a red Mercedes approach his garage. He groaned as he heard the knocking sound coming from her engine. Nuts. He'd thought he'd fixed Harper's car for good back in August. He should have known the car wouldn't surrender so easily.

He wiped his hands on a rag, left the small, separate building next to the two garage bays where he housed the GTO, and walked over to the space where Harper had parked the Merc. The shop had closed an hour ago, and he'd decided to work on his baby for a little while before going home. Senior was coming for another visit next week, and he didn't want to ignore his grandfather while he worked on his car. He also didn't want Senior helping him either. This was his project, and he wanted to do all the work himself. Senior wouldn't understand, and more than likely he'd be offended.

"Oh good, you're still here," Harper said as she exited the car. "I was just going to drop off my car and leave you a note if you weren't." As usual, she looked like a fashion model in her charcoal-gray long-sleeved shirt, matching flared pants, and, of course, black high heels. She also wore a black leather jacket and a black, gray, and white plaid scarf around her neck to ward off the October chill. "Aren't you cold?"

He glanced down at his short-sleeved work shirt. "Naw. I like cool weather. Easier to work in." He tapped the top of her car's roof. "So what's got her so wound up this time?"

Harper sighed and threw up her hands. "No idea. It's been driving fine up until an hour ago. I left my office to go meet a client, and the engine light came on. By the time I got here, there was a banging noise coming from inside."

"More like a knockin' sound."

"You could hear that?"

"Yep. Mind poppin' the hood for me?" When she did, he lifted it. Took a look around at the engine, checked all the cables. From first glance everything appeared okay. He could tell this was going to be another mystery. "Don't suppose you can leave her here with me again?"

"I figured I'd have to anyway." She sighed. "My dream car is turning into a nightmare. But I'm not ready to give up on it." She paused. "Are you?"

"Nope. I'll stick with her as long as you need me to."

" 'Her.' Never thought of my car as a girl before."

"Of course she is. Just look at her." He ran his hand over the hood. "Refined. Classy. Sexy." *Just like her owner.*

Wait. Where had that thought come from? He hadn't seen Harper since he'd fixed her car after Anita's wedding, but there'd been a few times shortly afterward when he thought about their dance. Not lately, though. When Harper Wilson was out of his sight, she was out of his mind.

"Hmm. I never thought of her as sexy either. I can see it now, though." She smiled, but he could tell it was strained.

"I'll get to her first thing in the mornin'," he assured her, then frowned. "Just remembered that Hank borrowed my rental car for tonight. I can call him and ask him to bring it back so you can use it."

She hesitated. "That's okay. I can call an Uber."

"No need to do that. I'll carry you home."

"Are you sure? I don't want to be a bother."

"Don't worry. It ain't no bother at all." Maple Falls was such a small town that he often took his customers home when they had to leave their cars. Harper technically didn't live in Maple Falls, but she was just on the outskirts, and that was close enough.

"Thanks so much." She bent over to get her purse and briefcase out of the car.

Now that's a view—

He shifted his gaze to the ground before she

caught him staring. It was hard not to, though. The last time she'd picked up her Merc after he *thought* he'd fixed it for good, he'd had to smack Percy, his only full-time employee, upside the head to get him to stop staring at her. "What was that for?" Percy had said, rubbing the side of his bald head as Harper drove away.

"You're being disrespectful."

"Look who's talking," Percy grumbled. "I seen you watching her, too, Mr. Goody Two-shoes."

Rusty hadn't been aware of that at the time, but he was now. He moved to stand in front of the car and pretended to inspect the headlights.

"I think I got everything," she said as she stood. Then she frowned. "Are you sure you don't mind driving me home? I forgot it was Friday night. I don't want to mess up your plans."

He almost chuckled at that. Tonight he was doing what he did every Friday night—work on his car, then head home. "I reckon I can make some room in my *busy* schedule. Give me a sec to wash up. You can wait in the office if you want."

"I'm fine here." She pulled her cell phone out of her jacket pocket, instantly absorbed in whatever was on the screen.

Rusty hurried to the small bathroom in the back of the garage and washed his greasy hands, checked his fingernails, and scrubbed them again. As he dried off, he looked in the mirror. He faced this reflection every morning when he brushed his teeth and ran a brush haphazardly through his hair, but only now did he notice how sloppy he looked. His grease-stained ball cap with the *Rusty's Garage* logo sat backward on his head to keep his bangs out of his eyes, and his beard was out of control. He took off the cap, but that made things worse—revealing all his wild red hair plastered against his head. He tried to finger-comb it into some sort of decent style but failed. Oh well. Harper had already seen him, anyway, and all he was doing was taking her home.

He shut off the light, locked up the garage, and went to his second, smaller garage where he worked on the GTO and turned off the radio. After locking that door, he got into his truck and went to pick up Harper.

She climbed into the front seat, the phone pressed to her ear. "I understand that the Tarpin Road house isn't suitable, but would you be interested in seeing something else?" she said into her cell. "There are six five-bedroom listings in this area. I can make appointments for you to go see them." She set her briefcase and purse on the floor and softly shut the door. "Oh. I see. Well, if you change your mind, you can call me at any time, day or night . . . Thank you . . . Bye-bye." She hung up the phone, then tossed it into her purse. "Shoot."

He shifted his truck into Drive, and they headed toward her house a few miles outside Maple

Falls. He'd never been there, but he'd filled out enough paperwork for her Merc that he had her address memorized. After a few minutes of silence, he asked, "Everythin' all right?"

"Yeah. At least it will be. I hope." She leaned against the seat and closed her eyes. "It's been a long week."

Since she didn't seem in the mood to talk, he turned on the radio, keeping the volume low as he found a soft-rock station.

"I think you're the only person under forty who still listens to radio instead of a playlist," she said.

"Oh, I listen to those too. But sometimes I just turn on the radio and see what's playin'." Soon she was humming to an Air Supply song. "You like the oldies too?" she asked, her eyes still closed.

"Yep. Senior liked playin' classic rock in the garage, and G'ma listened to adult contemporary at home. I ain't heard this song in forever and a day, though."

"Me either. I'm usually on the phone when I'm in the car. And by the time I get home, I just crawl into bed. But when I do listen to music, it's usually the old stuff."

He glanced at her. She had opened her eyes and turned her head so she was looking at him, still relaxing against the seat. "Who's your favorite group?"

50

"Toto. Eighties are my jam." She grinned. "What about you?"

"The usual. Some Zepplin, Rollin' Stones, Skynyrd."

Her cell rang and she hurried to grab it. When she looked at the screen, however, she frowned and set it in her lap. "I don't hear from her in three weeks, and now she decides to call me," she muttered.

"Who?" He asked without thinking, then added, "Sorry. None of my business."

"It's okay. Madge—er, my mom. She must have been on another one of her trips with my dad and"—she made air quotes—" 'forgot to tell' me."

"You can call her if you want. I won't eaves-drop."

Harper shook her head. "She can wait." When the song switched to REO Speedwagon's "Can't Fight This Feeling," she said, "Can I turn it up? I love this song."

"Sure."

Neither one of them talked for the next few minutes. When the song finished, Harper finally spoke. "I'm sorry I pulled you away from work."

"You didn't. The garage closed over an hour before you arrived."

"But you were still working on a car."

He grinned. "That's my car."

"Really? What is it?"

51

"A 1967 GTO convertible. Been fixin' her up for about a year now."

"Ah. Does it run?"

"Not yet. There's still plenty of engine work to finish. Once that's done, I'll tow it to a body shop in Hot Springs, and they'll work on the exterior and give her a paint job. While she's there, I'll have the seats reupholstered, and then when she comes back from the body shop, I'll finish up the interior." He paused and glanced at her. "Sorry. Don't mean to bore you with car talk."

"Not boring at all. I don't know anything about cars, obviously. What color are you going to paint it? Or her."

"Haven't decided. Probably blue or gold."

"I'd go with red."

He laughed. "Of course you would."

They'd listened to two more songs and a commercial by the time he pulled into her driveway. He put the truck into Park and said, "Here ya go. I'll let you know about the Merc on Monday."

"Okay." She looked at him. "Thanks for the ride, Rusty."

"No problem."

She opened the door and reached for her purse and briefcase. Then she paused and faced him again. "Have you had supper yet?"

"No."

"Me either." After another pause she added, "I could fix us something."

Rusty shook his head. "I don't want you to go to no trouble on my account."

"Hey, you brought me home. The least I can do is feed you. Unless you have plans for supper already."

"Just a leftover meat loaf sandwich waitin' for me at home."

"I can do better than that." She stepped out of the truck and shut the door, then waved him in to follow her.

Well, he was hungry. And what he didn't tell her was that the meat loaf was on its third day, and he wasn't the one who'd made it. Bea Farnsworth had brought it over when she'd picked up her twenty-seven-year-old Lincoln Continental Tuesday afternoon. Bea was an excellent cook, and the meat loaf was delicious, but after three days in a row he was eager for something else.

He shut off the engine and followed Harper inside. The interior of her house was as he expected it to be—a large front room connected to an open kitchen, all in shades of white and gray. Everything was spotless and looked brand new. The exact opposite of his old house.

"Make yourself at home," she said, dropping her keys into a crystal bowl on a small glass table near the front door. "I'm going to change into something more comfortable."

As she disappeared down the hallway off the kitchen, he glanced around at the white leather furniture, then at his jeans, craning his neck around so he could see if he had any stains on his backside. Not wanting to risk it, he sat down on one of the wooden barstools surrounding a large marble island in the kitchen. Not the most comfortable seating, but better than possibly leaving a butt-shaped grease stain on her upholstery.

His palms grew damp again, and this time he couldn't blame alcohol like he had at the Castillo wedding. Why was he reacting like this? He and Harper were having a meal together, that's all. Probably a frozen one, or maybe even ordering in. She didn't seem the type to cook, and he couldn't imagine her cutting onions or peeling potatoes in expensive clothes and high heels.

"There. That's *so* much better."

Rusty spun around on the barstool. When he saw Harper, his mouth dropped open.

She pushed up a pair of thick-lensed glasses on her nose. Her face was scrubbed clean of makeup and her hair sat in a messy bun on the top of her head. She gestured to her light-blue sweatshirt and black yoga pants. "Welcome to my Friday-night outfit. What you see is what you get."

All he could say was, "Wow."

Harper stilled. She'd hesitated to change her clothes and remove her makeup, including her false eyelashes. No one except for her best friends ever saw her this dressed down. Even her mother hadn't since the day Harper moved out of the house six months after she'd graduated from college. But her eyes were dry and scratchy from her contacts, and frankly, she was getting tired of the fake-eyelash trend. She also didn't want to ruin any of her nice clothes by spilling or splashing food on them while she cooked. Besides, this was Rusty, who wasn't exactly the epitome of fashion himself. And what she'd told him was true—this was her Friday-night outfit. More often than not lately, her favorite one of the week.

But his reaction set her off-kilter, and she was unexpectedly nervous. "Is that 'Wow, you look great' or 'Wow, what a mess'?"

"Definitely great."

That not only made her smile, but now she was completely relaxed. A welcome change from the stress of the past few days. *More like the past four months.*

He tilted his head. "Didn't know you wore glasses."

"I've worn them for years." She padded over to the fridge in her pink flip-flops and opened the door, then pushed up the plain black frames. "Since second grade." Grabbing a bottle of Riesling, she added, "Would you like a drink?"

"No," he said quickly. "I'm, uh, driving."

She reconsidered the wine and put it back in the

fridge. "Let's see. It's been a while since I had a chance to get groceries, but I think I can cobble something together. How about minestrone soup with crusty bread?" She grabbed a bottle of red wine and a wedge of Parmesan cheese and set them on the counter.

"Minestrone . . . I ain't sure I've had it before."

"Do you like vegetable soup?"

"Sure do."

She opened the freezer. "Then you'll love this."

"Need any help?" he asked.

"Can you operate a cheese grater?"

Chuckling, he said, "I reckon I can manage."

Soon she had water boiling for shell pasta while Rusty grated the Parmesan cheese. She sauteed some garlic in olive oil, added some onion and carrots, then put them all in a big pot with beans—frozen green and canned pinto—and two cans of Italian-seasoned tomatoes. Whatever leftovers she had would last her part of next week.

When she turned around, Rusty had a nice, neat pile of shredded Parm in the small blue ceramic bowl she'd given him. She washed her hands in the sink on the island, then grabbed the small remote on the corner of the island counter and turned on the sound system. The same soft rock station Rusty had had on in the truck played in the background.

As the soup and pasta cooked and the oven

preheated for the bread, she poured two tumblers of iced tea and handed one to Rusty before sitting down next to him.

"Thanks." He took a sip. "Nice and sweet."

"That's the way I like it." When he tilted his head at her again, she said, "What?"

"I'm plum surprised, that's all."

"That I can cook?" She set the glass on the countertop.

"Well, yeah."

She moved to sit cross-legged on the stool. "I don't mind cooking. I just don't have time for it. I'd rather bake anyway. Breads, cakes, cookies. If it's a carb and you can bake it, I'm there. I can't remember the last time I baked anything, though. Years, probably."

"Too busy?"

She nodded and thought about the past week. Not only had it been long, but it was also lousy. Another reason she couldn't wait to get out of her real-estate clothes. She'd lost three sales over the past two days, and while the market had picked up a little since August, she'd only made one sale.

And then there was Jack. After she'd blocked him on her phone, he tried to reach her through social media. She blocked him there, too, but not until after reading his last message: *I'm sorry about what happened between us. Can we talk?*

She couldn't hit the Block button fast enough. That was after Anita's wedding, and she hadn't heard from him since. Until this morning. He had called the office, and fortunately she'd been out showing a property to a client—the client who had just called her and changed her mind about purchasing a house.

"You've got that look again," he said, breaking into her thoughts.

Her gaze focused on him. "What look?"

"The one you had when you were on the phone earlier. Same as the one that showed up on your face when Madge called."

"Ugh." Although thinking about her mother was better than musing about work or what she was going to do about Jack if he didn't leave her alone. A tad better, but she'd take it.

He ran his thumb across the edge of the white-and-gray marble countertop. "I'm sorry she hurt your feelings."

"She didn't." Harper jumped up from the chair and rushed to the stove, where she gave both the soup and pasta a stir.

"Sorry." He took a big swig from the tea. "I shouldn't have assumed that."

Harper blew out a breath and turned around. "Don't apologize. Honestly, my feelings aren't hurt exactly, but . . ." She leaned against the counter. "How can parents forget their children exist?"

His head jerked up. "When you find out the answer, let me know. I haven't talked to my folks since I was eight."

"You haven't?" Her brows shot up. "Oh, Rusty, I'm so sorry. I had no idea."

"Not everyone does. Just a few people who grew up here."

One thing she knew about the lifelong citizens of Maple Falls was that they could keep a secret if they set their minds to it. She'd found that out when Riley's wayward mother had shown up a little more than two years ago, then disappeared just as quickly. Before that she hadn't heard a peep out of anyone about the woman. "I'm sorry I brought up a sore subject."

"Oh, I ain't that sore." He shoved back his long bangs, but they fell to the sides of his face again, almost obscuring his eyes. "Not anymore. Senior and G'ma did a good job raisin' me and Amber. Better than our parents could have. Junior—that's my dad—never sat still much. Didn't like bein' stuck in the garage. Really didn't like it when my mom got pregnant with Amber when they were still in high school. They had the shotgun weddin' and all that. By the time I was born three years later, Junior up and left us and Arkansas. Last I heard, he was livin' in a camper and writin' a travel blog."

"You didn't try looking him up?"

He shrugged. "Why would I? I never knew

59

him, and I barely knew my mom. She met someone else with a kid and kept droppin' us off
with Senior and G'ma. Next thing I know, she's
married and moved to Chattanooga."

"That's awful."

"It ended up all right. Senior and G'ma were
the best. I miss G'ma, though. When she died,
it was tough on all of us, especially Senior. But
he's livin' with my sis now and happy as a pig in
a wallow."

She chuckled. Rusty's southern drawl was as
thick as it was charming.

The timer dinged for the pasta, and she got up
and strained it, then added it to the soup. After
putting a loaf of French bread into the oven to
toast, she removed bowls from the cabinet and
started to set them on the table.

"I can do that for you." Rusty got up and took
the bowls from her.

She couldn't remember the last time she'd
eaten at her kitchen table for supper. She and the
Lattes had gotten together a few times for Sunday
lunch here, but they usually congregated around
the island while they ate takeout or something
Tanner had prepared and sent with Anita. Her
cooking skills weren't anything near his, but she
could make a decent soup.

Rusty set the table while she added the finishing
touches to the soup, and when everything they
needed was on the table, they started eating.

"This is good," he said, dipping a piece of bread in the minestrone.

"Glad you like it. It's a good way to use up leftover veggies."

He wiped his mouth with a paper napkin. "I'll have to remember that."

As they ate, silence stretched between them. Not exactly awkward, but also not the easy camaraderie they'd had before. She also figured that since he'd told her about his family, she should at least fill him in on hers. "Madge and Don have decided to 'find themselves.' "

He picked up his tea glass. "What does that mean?"

"I have no idea. When I was growing up, Don was always out of town. He's a retired pilot and used to fly out of Memorial Field a lot."

"Why do you call your parents by their first names?" he asked.

"I do that when I'm mad at them. Or frustrated. I'm both now." She glanced down at her bowl. "Not very reverent of me, I know. But right now they're driving me crazy. Actually, they always drove me a little nuts."

"How so?"

"Because Don spent so much time away from home, Madge mostly raised me. When I was in elementary and middle school, she was volunteer of the year—every year. And then in high school she worked as the school secretary."

"And that's a bad thing?"

"No. I just wish Don would have been home more. I think Madge resented him for leaving all the parenting to her. So I tried to make sure I wasn't too much trouble." An unexpected lump formed in her throat. "Anyhoo, that's the past, and now that Don's retired, they've been spending a lot of time together and next to none with me. It's like they don't want me to be a part of their lives anymore. Or they don't want to be a part of mine." She started to tear at the chunk of bread in her hands.

"Hey." He took the bread from her. "At least she called you."

"True. And I'll call her back, like I always do. Tomorrow. Or maybe Sunday. I'm feeling a little petty."

Rusty shook his head. "Can't imagine you bein' petty about anythin'."

"I can be cutthroat when I need to, especially when it comes to business."

"How's that goin'?" he asked, wiping the last of his soup with another slice of bread.

Harper sat back in her seat. "I wish I could say good, but that's not true. And if things don't get better—" Uh-oh. She hadn't meant to say that out loud.

His brow furrowed. "You won't be in any trouble, will you?"

"No, nothing like that." She put her hands in

her lap to keep from mutilating another piece of bread. Should she tell him about her long-term plan? He was so easy to talk to, and she'd already confided things about her family that she hadn't with anyone else, including the Lattes. Part of that was due to her busy schedule. The other part was that she didn't want to talk about how messed up her business and her family were right now. Madge had always kept her personal problems under wraps, and Harper naturally followed suit.

But for some reason she was okay with telling Rusty. "I want to close my office and open up a new one in Maple Falls," she said. "Specifically, in #6, the building next to Price's Hardware."

His concerned expression disappeared. "Downtown can always use new businesses."

"That's what gave me the idea. That and I spend a lot of time in Maple Falls anyway. Might as well work here too. I asked about renting part of the building, but the owner wants to sell, and his price is high. Too high, I think, but with the revitalization that's already happened on Main Street, he believes he can get what he's asking."

"Can he?"

"In my case, yes. I'm willing to give him an offer, but I also have personal reasons attached, so spending a little extra is acceptable. Back in the spring I was ready to buy it, then the real-
: market slowed down, and I lost some

clients." She clasped her hands together in a tight fist. She hadn't meant to let that detail slip.

"Business goes up and down. I've had some slow times myself."

"Exactly. I'll be okay." She relaxed her hands and lifted her chin. "Things will pick up soon."

He rubbed his chin. "Any way I can help out?"

She chuckled. "Not unless you want to buy a house."

"Afraid I don't, sorry."

"I wasn't being serious anyway." She waved her hand. "Don't worry, I'll be fine. I just have to work a little harder, that's all."

"Seems like you're already workin' hard."

She couldn't deny that. "You know how it is. I'm sure you've had to burn the midnight oil a time or two."

"Once," he said. "Three years ago. Percy was out sick for almost a week, and Senior had gone on vacation to visit an old friend in Oklahoma, so it was just me tryin' to get everythin' done. Told myself I'd never let that happen again. Hired Hank the next week. I work to live, not the other way around."

"What about the GTO? Isn't that work?"

He grinned, his slightly crooked teeth shining through that thick mountain-man beard of his. "That ain't work. That's fun. What do you do for fun?"

Lately, nothing. But she couldn't very well

tell him that. "Hang out with my friends. Go shopping. Um . . ."

"Bake?"

"Yeah. Sure."

"What's your favorite thing to bake?" he asked.

"Cupcakes," she said without hesitation.

"I've never been able to turn down a cupcake."

Her brow arched. "Is that a hint?"

"Maybe." He smiled again. "Guess I'd better be gettin' home," he said, pushing away from the table. "Bill Farnsworth is dropping off his '57 Ford truck for a tune-up in the morning. He's spiffin' it up for the parade."

"Parade? What parade?"

"The First Annual Maple Falls Fall Parade. It was Hayden's idea. He's tired of Mayor Quickel sittin' on his hands about bringin' back community events. After August's business meetin' when Quickel put off discussin' things again, Hayden contacted all of us privately, and we decided to do a small parade toward the end of October."

"I've been so out of the loop I had no idea," she said.

"It's small, just a short parade with a few antique cars. All the businesses in town are handing out Halloween candy to the kids. We haven't publicized it too much. Quickel's been gone for the past two weeks anyway on his monthlong annual vacation. What he don't know won't hurt him."

Harper nodded. She'd met Quickel twice, and he'd creeped her out both times. "That's for sure. Can I do something? Donate some bags of candy, maybe?"

"I'm sure you could, but you'll have to talk to Hayden about that."

She nodded. "He should run for mayor some-day."

"That's what we've all said." He looked at the dishes on the table. "I'll help you clean up."

Shaking her head, she stood. "That's what dishwashers are for."

"I wouldn't know. Never had a dishwasher."

"Really?"

"Yep." He picked up his dishes anyway and walked to the kitchen.

She followed. "I'm serious, Rusty. I'll get these. It's bad form to make a guest clean up after the meal."

"Yes, ma'am." He smiled as he said the words, keeping his gaze on hers.

When he didn't look away, she frowned. "Is something wrong?"

"No." But he glanced away as he spoke.

"Oh. I just . . ."

He looked at her again. "Just what?"

"Well, you were kind of staring."

His face—what she could see of it anyway—turned bright red. "Sorry 'bout that. I was just thinking how nice you look right now."

He had to be joking. "With no makeup, sloppy sweats, and my thick-lensed glasses?"

"Yep. You don't need makeup and fancy clothes to look pretty."

She couldn't help basking in his compliment, even though she had a tough time believing him. She remembered the last time Jack had seen her without makeup. He hadn't even tried to hide his shock—and that was the last time she'd let anyone other than her best friends see her barefaced. Except for tonight. "You're a nice guy, Rusty Jenkins."

His gaze dropped to the floor. "I get that a lot," he mumbled.

"I mean it. I'm glad we're friends."

" 'Friends'?" he said as if he didn't understand the word.

"Of course. I don't have just anyone over for minestrone, you know."

He chuckled, and they walked to the foyer. "I'll let you know about your car Monday," he said when she opened the door. "And I'll have Hank drop off Lois here first thing tomorrow so you won't be stranded here."

She'd forgotten all about her Mercedes. "Lois?"

"My rental car. That's what we call her."

"Oh, right. Thanks," she said, resting against the doorjamb. "And thanks for taking me home and staying for supper. I needed this tonight."

He grinned, and she wondered what his smile

67

looked like without the beard. "Me too," he said. "Good night."

After he left and she closed the door, she leaned against it. He really was a nice guy. Then the strangest thought came over her. *What if we were more than friends?*

She shook her head, laughing out loud at the thought. This was what happened when she was exhausted—her brain filled with foolish, out-landish ideas to distract her from the pressing problems in her life. And while she would love to kick back and say that she worked to live, right now she had to live to work or she wouldn't have a job.

Focus, focus. There would be plenty of time to relax after she made enough sales to buy #6. She just hoped it would still be available by the time she did.

Chapter 4

Rusty didn't turn on the radio when he got into his truck. Instead, he thought about what Harper had said about them being friends. Normally, hearing a woman say that to him—and they had, more than once, always after a date, and then he'd never hear from them again—would bother him. But it was good to hear it from her.

It wasn't as if he didn't have friends. Two, actually, now that he thought about it. He hung out with Percy sometimes after work, but Percy had gone through a divorce six years ago and had his kids every other day and twice a month on the weekends. Then there was Hank, the older guy he'd hired to work part-time three years ago. They occasionally had a drink together, and he'd gone over to Hank's apartment a couple of times to watch a football or baseball game. But when Hank got a girlfriend last March, that had stopped.

Up until tonight he hadn't realized how thin he was in the friendship department. Then again, he'd spent his free time working on the GTO or going to the lake when the fish were biting, along with attending the occasional church potluck and, lately, weddings. That had been fulfilling enough. Or so he thought.

But tonight had been nice. Real nice. And he was glad he'd gotten to know Harper better. He just wished she hadn't caught him staring at her, but he couldn't help it. She was a natural beauty.

More like breathtaking.

Cool it. He didn't need to think about how gorgeous she was. They were friends, and if he was stupid enough to even think about being anything else with her, he would ruin what they had. He was glad she hadn't been offended when he told her she didn't need the makeup and clothes she liked to wear. He hadn't meant for that to slip out.

His phone rang, and he hit a button on his dashboard. "Hey, Amber," he said as he entered the Maple Falls town limits. He hadn't talked to his sister in over two weeks, although that wasn't unusual.

"Hi, Rusty. How are you?"

He knew better than to tell his sister he'd just had dinner with a woman, so he said, "Good. Nothin' new happenin'." Nope, nothing new at all. "How's the family? Senior behavin' himself?"

"Of course not." Amber laughed. "Actually, he's doing great. The kids are good, and so is Austin. I do have some news, though."

"Lay it on me."

"Austin's been offered a job in Colorado Springs."

Rusty let that settle for a moment. "Really?"

"Yeah. He hasn't taken it yet, and we're still discussing things. It would be a big move, but good for his career."

He listened while she explained the job to him. She was right; it would be good for his brother-in-law. "I don't mean to sound selfish, but I'd miss y'all."

"We'd miss you too," she said softly.

"What did Senior say?"

"We haven't told him yet. I wanted to let you know first." A pause. "I don't think he'll want to move with us. It took forever to get him to Little Rock."

"I agree."

"If he won't, he'll have to come live with you again."

Rusty nodded. "That's fine. Don't worry, he always has a home with me."

"In *that* house."

He bristled at the derision he heard in her voice. "What do you mean, 'that house'?"

"You know exactly what I mean. It's a miracle that place hasn't fallen down already."

"It just needs a few repairs," he said.

"Now you're sounding like Senior," she scoffed. "I'm surprised you're still living there."

"Of course I am. I—we—grew up here."

"That's what I mean," she said. "Don't the memories bother you?"

He turned into the driveway and shut off the truck. He had great memories of growing up in Senior and G'ma's house. But there were some bad ones, too, mostly reminders of his parents' abandonment. Like the times he'd spent looking out the picture window and waiting for his mother to come back . . . then finding out she wasn't going to. Or seeing the sadness both Senior and G'ma had tried to hide after those rare phone calls they'd received from his dad, who never seemed to have enough time left over to talk to him and Amber.

He'd buried those memories, and others, so far down he'd forgotten about them. *Almost.* Talking to Harper about his parents had dug up a few, and now Amber was yanking the rest of them out.

"Just think about it," Amber said.

He blinked. "Think about what?"

"Finding a nice house for you and Senior. It would be a fresh start for both of you. I'll keep in touch and let you know what we decide about Colorado. Love you, little bro."

"Love you too."

He hung up, but he didn't get out of the truck. A new house? Living anywhere else hadn't crossed his mind . . . Wait. That wasn't exactly true. There was a time or two when he had thought about buying his own place. But that had been before going out on a date, when he'd been frivolous enough to think about the future he wanted, like the one Amber had. He wasn't jealous of her. Just the opposite. She was bucking their parents' trend of divorce and ditch. And like his sister, he wanted to do things differently than his parents had done. That meant getting and *staying* married and having a family.

Of course those thoughts had disappeared like smoke out of a chimney after the dates imploded, and now that future seemed like a far-fetched idea. He and Senior would be fine living here, just the two of them. They'd managed when Amber and Austin left, and they would manage when—or if—Senior returned.

He got out of the truck and went inside, not bothering with the lights. He was headed for the kitchen when his right foot went clear through the floor.

"What the—" He balanced on one foot as he pulled the other one out, then hopped over to the lamp on the end table near the couch. He flipped it on and checked his ankle. No harm done, fortunately. The floor, however, wasn't in as good shape. A gaping hole the size of his foot now sat in the center, the old green carpet torn where he'd stepped. G'ma had hated that cheap carpet when Senior had put it in more than forty years ago. But it had saved Rusty from a scraped leg, or worse.

He stared at the hole, then the peeling wallpaper, before moving to look at the ripped carpet.

The floorboard hung on by a nail and a prayer. Maybe Amber was right, and not just because of the cracked memory lane they both shared. Senior deserved better than this. Eventually he wouldn't be able to manage the staircase. And although he still had friends in Maple Falls, several of the neighbors who had lived on the street when he and G'ma were here had moved, either to live with their own kids or to a place for elderly adults. Three of them had passed away. Hadn't that been part of the argument to get his grandfather to move in with Amber? So he would have a better life in his golden years?

Rusty didn't cotton much to change, but sometimes it was necessary. He grabbed the ripped area of the carpet and pulled it back so he didn't forget about the hole and made his way to the kitchen. He was 110 percent sure Senior wouldn't go to Colorado if that's what Amber and Austin ended up doing. So it was up to him to convince his grandfather to move to a new home in Maple Falls. One problem, though—he didn't know the first thing about looking for a house.

Good thing he knew someone who did.

"I really don't have time for this, Erma."

Erma peered over her reading glasses at Madge Wilson, tamping down her irritation. When she'd seen Madge make a rare appearance in church last Sunday, she'd cornered the woman after

74

the service to get her to come over to Knots and Tangles under the ruse of giving her the pattern for the Bosom Buddies' charity project this year—baby caps and booties for the Changepoint Pregnancy Center in Hot Springs. Madge hadn't attended their weekly BB gatherings for weeks, and before that she'd only come once or twice a month. Erma sensed something was going on with her friend, and she wanted to get to the bottom of it. She'd finally convinced Madge to come over today. And even though Saturdays tended to be their busiest day, right now the shop was empty.

"This won't take but a minute," Erma said, pretending to thumb through a stack of patterns, even though she'd already set aside the one she needed before Madge arrived. "While I'm looking, catch me up on what's been going on in your life."

"Oh, you know. Things. Have you found the pattern yet?"

"Guess it's not in this stack." Erma pulled a box of papers out from underneath the counter. Riley kept everything organized in the shop they ran together, but when it came to old copies of patterns, her granddaughter knew better than to attempt to make rhyme or reason of them. "What kind of things?"

Madge tucked a strand of platinum-gray hair behind her ear. "My, aren't we a nosy posey."

Erma took off her glasses. "When it comes to my friends, yes. I am." Out of all the BBs, Madge was the least likely member of the group. Myrtle and Bea, along with Gwen, Peg, and Viola, had all lived in Maple Falls for decades, and Myrtle and Bea had gone to school with Erma way back in the day. Even Rosa Castillo, their newest member, had roots in Maple Falls. But Madge was different. She didn't live in Maple Falls, and she was younger than the rest of them except for Rosa. But Erma still remembered the day she'd showed up at Amazing Grace almost eight years ago, alone and looking lost, although she tried to hide it under a cool veneer. Erma had taken her under her wing ever since, but even she had to admit there were times Madge was a square peg in a round hole when it came to the BBs, and sometimes her frostiness could be off-putting. But they all still cared for her very much.

Madge narrowed her gaze, then sighed. "My daughter isn't speaking to me."

Now that was a surprise. She'd never figured Harper would be the disloyal type. "She's not?"

"I called her last week and then yesterday. Both times, no response." Madge's mouth tightened. "The nerve of that child."

"She isn't exactly a child, Madge."

Madge's chin lifted. "She's acting like one."

Erma walked around from the back of the

counter. "Let's get a cup of coffee," she said. "Anita keeps us well stocked."

"I really don't have time—"

"Please," Erma said, touching her arm. "You can spare a few minutes for a friend."

Madge paused, then nodded.

A few moments later they sat on the bright-green sofa in the back of Knots and Tangles. Riley was having lunch with Hayden, as she usually did if the store wasn't busy or she wasn't in the middle of one of her art projects or dyeing yarn. Erma and Madge had the whole shop to themselves, and Erma was glad they did. "Tell me what's going on."

Madge took a sip of her coffee. "Don and I are getting a divorce."

"Oh." The news wasn't that surprising, but the blunt way Madge delivered it sure was. Although Erma had only met Don a handful of times due to him often being out of town for his job, and he was quite friendly and charming each time, she'd sensed not everything was well between the two of them. Since Madge rarely brought him up in conversation, the BBs didn't either.

Maybe we should have.

"I need to inform Harper," Madge continued. "But I can't do that if she doesn't answer her phone."

"Why not meet her at her office?"

77

Madge rolled her eyes. "I shouldn't have to chase down my own daughter."

Erma was rarely at a loss for words, but this time was an exception. When Madge didn't say anything else, she couldn't remain silent. "Don't you think you should in this case?"

"A phone call is sufficient." Madge set her cup on the coffee table. "I appreciate your concern, but like I said, I have a lot of things to do. I'm meeting with a Realtor later today to discuss putting the house on the market."

"You're not using Harper?"

"I didn't think it was appropriate for her to sell the house she grew up in."

"Right." Erma winced. "Should have thought about that."

"I also have an appointment with my lawyer next Tuesday morning to hammer out details of the divorce. Don and his attorney will be there too. We'll be discussing the assessment and distribution of our assets."

Bothered by how clinical Madge sounded, Erma said, "Is there anything we can do to help?"

Madge rose from the couch. "No help needed. I'll be fine. This has been a long time coming. I should have left him years ago." She headed for the back exit to the small parking lot behind the store. "If you see Harper, tell her to call her mother."

"Madge—"

But she was already out the door.

Erma dropped back onto the couch. Oh, this wasn't good. Divorce, even when it was mutual, was never pretty. Fortunately, she'd never experienced it herself. Her parents' marriage had been good, and her own marriage to Gus was wonderful until his untimely death. She wished Madge wouldn't try to go through something so traumatic by herself. But the woman could be stubborn, and all Erma could do was pray she would change her mind and lean on her friends.

The bell rang above the front door. By the time Erma got up from the couch, Riley had entered the room. "Hey, Mimi . . ." She paused. "What's wrong?"

She was tempted for a moment to tell her about Madge and Don. But Riley and Harper were close friends, and Harper wasn't aware her parents were splitting up. No way was Erma going to be the bearer of those bad tidings. "Nothing, just my bum leg." She pretended to limp a little as she walked to Riley. "It's bothering me a bit today."

She'd broken it two years ago sliding into third base while playing on Amazing Grace's softball team. It had been the first game of the season too. But the accident had brought Riley back to Maple Falls, and her and Hayden together, so it was all worth it. And she wasn't exactly fibbing about the healed injury twinging, because when it rained it more than twinged. Today was a cloudless, sunny day, though.

Concern crossed Riley's face. "You should go home and rest, then."

Erma scoffed. "I only work here two days a week now. I rest enough as it is. If you'll excuse me, I have some paperwork to organize."

Riley crossed her arms. "Now I know something's up. You wouldn't be organizing something unless you were avoiding something else." She glanced at the two mugs on the coffee table. "Who stopped by?"

"Madge," she said. No reason to fib about that. "She dropped by to pick up the baby booties pattern." Which Erma had forgotten to give to her. Drat. Well, that gave her another excuse to see Madge, although she'd bring reinforcements next time. Madge Wilson could brush off one Bosom Buddy but not all of them.

Riley smiled. "I think it's wonderful that the BBs are going to donate to the center."

"Yep. I can't wait to start knittin' those tiny booties and caps." Erma smirked. "I might make an extra set or two and set them aside. You know . . . for the future."

"Oh no," Riley said, walking back to her studio where her yarn-dyeing equipment was set up. "Not this conversation again."

Riley didn't like having the "baby talk," as she put it, but Erma was willing to bring up the taboo

80

topic to keep her granddaughter from asking about Madge. Riley wasn't as much of a nosy posey as Erma, but even an innocuous question might require a protective layer or two of revisionist history, and lying about Madge wasn't on Erma's list of things to do today. "I have no idea what you're talking about," she said, innocently fluttering her eyelashes.

Riley pulled her medium-length bob into a short ponytail at the nape of her neck. "Sure you don't." She turned to Erma. "Like I've said many, *many* times, when Hayden and I are ready to have children, you'll be the first to know. Right now he's busy with the hardware store and the fall parade."

"Have I told you how happy I am that you're subverting Farley Quickel?"

"Numerous times." Riley shook her head. "Has he always been so unreasonable?"

"Ever since I've known him. And now that he's mayor, he's been unreasonable *and* insufferable. Serves him right that the people of Maple Falls stage a mutiny. For the sake of the town, of course."

Riley gave her a pointed look. "It's a parade, not a mutiny."

"Potato, potahto."

"It's not that either." Riley shook her head, but she was smiling, although it faded quickly. "Mimi, I'm serious about being busy. I have all this yarn to dye by Christmas, and if the fall parade goes well, Hayden has some other plans in the works."

"I'm intrigued." Erma raised a brow. "Like what?"

"Don't tell anyone," Riley said, lowering her voice. "He's thinking about running for mayor when Quickel's term is up."

"Oh, what a wonderful idea! He'll be an excellent mayor."

"He's just thinking about it," Riley said. "Don't go telling the BBs or anyone else, okay?"

"These lips are sealed." Erma made a zipping motion with two fingers across her mouth.

"Thanks. So you see why we can't even think about babies right now?"

"Riley," Erma said, forgetting about her limp and going to the granddaughter she loved so deeply. "When it comes to having a baby, there's never enough time, or the right time, or any other . . . reason." She almost said "excuse," but she stopped there.

"Mimi." Riley put her hands on Erma's shoulders. "This is between me and Hayden, okay?"

"Fine." Erma turned and headed up front. Riley was right: the decision to have a child was their business alone, despite how much Erma longed for a great-grandchild . . . or four. Even five. All right, she'd be happy with one.

She picked up the pattern for the baby cap and booties, then smiled. She'd make an extra set anyway and not tell Riley.

You never know when they'll come in handy.

Chapter 5

A h, ain't it good to be back home."
"You were just here three weeks ago,"
Rusty said to Senior as they entered the house.
"And I thought Amber's house was your home."

"It is. Sorta. But as nice as her place is, it don't hold a candle to Maple Falls."

Rusty set Senior's small suitcase on the floor as Senior walked into the living room. He hadn't heard from his sister since she called a week ago, and when he picked up Senior she'd been so busy sending him off and wrangling the kids that he hadn't had a chance to ask her if she and Austin had made a decision. What he did know was that Amber must have made Senior buy new luggage. The last time Rusty had picked him up, Senior had packed everything into his old army duffel bag that looked and smelled like it had seen much better days. Did that mean he was moving with them? Or was she just tired of him using that old duffel?

"What's for lunch, Rusty?" Senior said, heading for the kitchen.

"Uh, before you walk any farther—"

"Where did this dadgum hole come from?"

Rusty hurried to his side. Fortunately, Senior hadn't stepped into the hole and fallen down.

Between figuring out what was wrong with Harper's Merc and having an unexpected influx of customers this week, Rusty hadn't had a chance to repair the hole yet. Now he wished he'd taken the time to fix it before picking up Senior.

He guided his grandfather away from the hole to the kitchen. At least that floor was in decent shape. Barely. "The wood's rotted underneath the carpet," he said.

"I can see that." Senior sighed and sat down at the fifties-era kitchen table. "Those planks are only fifty years old. They should've lasted longer than that."

"They might have," Rusty said as he opened the fridge to make them both a sandwich for lunch. "If they hadn't been underwater three decades ago."

"Oh, right. That's why I put the carpet in. Got that for next to nothin', by the way."

Rusty nodded as if he hadn't heard this story at least a dozen times. A huge storm had flooded this part of Maple Falls back in the seventies, and once the house had dried out, Senior had laid the cheap, forest-green carpet over it. "Mustard or mayo?" he asked.

"If it's ham, mayo. If it's roast beef, mustard."

"Mayo it is." He quickly fixed them each a sandwich, poured a handful of ridged potato

85

chips on the side, and set the plates on the table, along with a bottle of grape pop for Senior and water for himself.

"You're lookin' good," Senior said as Rusty pulled out the chair across from him. "Slimmed down some more, I see."

"Some." He hadn't set out to lose weight last year, only to cut back on fast food and soda. In doing that he had lost almost twenty-five pounds. That, along with working steadily on not only his customers' cars but also the GTO, had been the contributing factors to shedding what his sister had always called his baby fat.

Senior took a bite of his sandwich. "Any day now some pretty girl is going to come chasin' after you."

Rusty rolled his eyes. "Can't we talk about something else? The shop?" *This house?* They had to talk about it sometime soon.

"You already caught me up on the shop," Senior said, "and I know better than to ask you what's goin' on in town. You never know nothin' important."

"You mean the latest scuttlebutt?"

"That's exactly what I mean." Senior picked up a chip, showing zero shame that he was interested in hen-party talk. "I'll get the real scoop from Jasper."

Rusty grinned. Senior could be worse than a tabloid when it came to gossip, and Jasper wasn't far behind. "Maybe he'll tell you about his dance with Erma McAllister."

Senior smirked. "Already heard about that on my last visit. Jasper wouldn't talk about it, though. He's got some explainin' to do. I never knew he was sweet on Ms. Erma."

"He didn't seem too happy when she asked him to dance," Rusty said.

"Oh, he was fakin' that, sure as Sunday. If he didn't wanna dance with her, he wouldn't have. I'm just wonderin' why he's being so cagey about it."

"You'll have to ask him." Now Rusty wished he hadn't said anything about Jasper and Erma, much less direct Senior to quiz Jasper again. But he'd do anything to interrupt his grandfather's dogged determination to discuss dating and marriage, even if it meant throwing Jasper under the bus. The old man could handle Senior's nosiness. "I do have something to talk to you about," he said. Might as well prime the pump sooner than later.

"Let me guess," Senior said, squinting at the label on the grape pop can as if he were having trouble seeing it. Then he looked at Rusty. "You wanna talk about Amber moving to Colorado."

Rusty stilled. "You know about that?"

"I'm goin' blind, not deaf." A quick wave of sadness crossed his face, only to disappear into a grin. "Walls sure are thin in those newfangled houses they build nowadays."

"So what do you think?"

Senior sat back in his chair and crossed his arms. "I think I ain't goin'. It's one thing to move to Little Rock, but half a country away? No, thank you."

"But what about the grandkids?" Rusty asked. "Won't you miss them?"

"Darn tootin' I will, but that's what airplanes are for." He uncrossed his arms and leaned forward. "I'm too old to put down new roots again. I ain't mad at Austin about this neither. From what I've gathered—"

"By eavesdroppin'," Rusty said dryly.

Senior rolled his eyes. "It's a terrific opportunity for Austin, and Amber is excited about goin'. Wish they'd come right out and tell me, though."

"They don't want to upset you."

"Like I said. Ain't upset." Senior grinned. "So when do I move back in here with you?"

"Uh," Rusty said. "That's what I needed to talk to you about. I'm, uh, thinkin' about selling the house."

"What house?"

"This one." He took a deep breath and waited for his grandfather to get upset.

"Okay." Senior crunched another chip.

He almost fell out of his chair. "What? You just said it was good to be home."

"I said it was good to be in Maple Falls. So as

long as you're stickin' around here, I'm fine. You are buyin' somethin' 'round here, right?"

"Definitely."

Senior glanced around the kitchen, his expression turning unusually somber. "Lots of memories here, but let's be honest. This place is barely standing."

"I could fix it up."

"You mean *pay* to fix it up," Senior said, smirking again.

"Yeah."

"Then you would be stuck here."

Rusty shook his head. "No, I wouldn't."

Senior adjusted his round silver-framed glasses. "I don't want you to put all your money into this old house. Just enough to get her sold. Then you can buy something bigger and better. Knowing you, I reckon you got a nice chunk of moolah set aside for a rainy day."

"I do, but . . ." He didn't understand his mixed feelings. Before this conversation he'd been willing to find a new place, and he'd expected Senior to put up a fight to stay here. Now he wasn't sure what to think.

"No buts. This house has served its purpose. It's time to let it go." Senior frowned. "I just wish you kids didn't have me hanging around your neck like an old bald tire."

"That's not true," Rusty exclaimed. "I would never think about you like that. Neither would

Amber. You and G'ma took care of us. Now it's time for us to be there for you. If you want to stay here, we'll get this house fixed up and stay."

Senior picked up his drink and took a swig. When he set it back down, he said, "What about when you get married? Have kids? This house was barely big enough for the four of us. You need to be thinkin' about the future, Rusty. I'll admit there was a time when your G'ma and I were worried that your parents' actions would sour both you and your sister on marriage. Avoiding the altar seems to be the thing with young folks nowadays. Honestly, in yours and Amber's case, it's understandable why you wouldn't want to."

"Obviously, Amber did want to get married," Rusty said.

"What about you?"

It was hard to admit how much of a failure he was at dating, even to his beloved grandfather. But he had to be honest with him. "I thought I'd have found someone by now. Got a couple of friends from high school who are already married, but they moved away right after graduation and found their spouses outside of Maple Falls. There's not too many single women here anymore."

None that want to date me, anyway.

"Do you feel tied to the town because of the shop?"

"No, not at all. I like Maple Falls. I don't wanna

live anywhere else. And I ain't tied down to work neither. I love my job."

Senior smiled. "I can't tell you how relieved I am, knowin' that my life's work is in good hands."

"Thanks for your confidence in me."

"No thanks needed. You earned it. And don't worry, son. You're a good, honest man, and one day you'll find a good, honest woman who will appreciate you."

"You're my grandpa," Rusty mumbled. "What else are you gonna say?"

"The truth. Now don't be such a Sad Sam. You've got lots of blessin's in your life, including me."

Rusty laughed. "That's true."

"So it's settled, then. You'll sell this house and find a new one."

"All right. I'm sure Harper can help me do that." At Senior's questioning look, he added, "She's a real-estate agent. I'll give her a call next week."

"Why not call her today?"

He paused, then nodded. There wasn't any reason to wait. "I will."

"Good," Senior said, a gleam appearing in his green eyes. "Now for the more important question: Is she single?"

"You're not gonna let up, are you?" Rusty said, rolling his eyes.

"Nope. Not until you're happy and hitched." His grandfather finished the last bite of his sandwich, then said, "I need to get unpacked. What time are you meetin' your agent?"

"I have to call her. I took the rest of the day off. Can I drop you at Price's on the way?"

"That would be dandy. Me and Jasper need to talk." Senior shook his head. "Ms. Erma. Who would have thought?"

Rusty got up and retrieved the suitcase from the living room, then took it to the bedroom at the back of the house. This room had been Senior's and G'ma's, then Senior's before he moved to Little Rock. Now it was Rusty's, but he had moved his stuff upstairs to his old room so his grandfather didn't have to deal with the steep staircase. He set Senior's suitcase on the bed and turned around as his grandfather walked into the room. "I'll let you get settled. Let me know if you need anythin'."

"I'm fine. Think I'll take me a catnap before we leave."

While Senior unpacked and took a little nap, Rusty went to the living room where his desk and computer were set up, making sure he avoided the hole. Relieved that his grandfather was on board with selling, he called Harper's number and wasn't surprised that she didn't pick up. He left her a message and hung up, then typed in the name of a real-estate website and began to search for houses. He figured he should have an idea of what he wanted before he met with Harper.

When the site loaded, he paused, the reality of what he was going to do sinking in. Spending a lot of money on a new house didn't bother him. He'd been building his nest egg since he was ten with the intention of buying an old car to fix up. He'd done that and sold it, along with three other cars over the years. The GTO was his fourth, and while he had planned to sell that one, too, he'd had a second thought or two about keeping it.

But the GTO sat in the recesses of his mind right now. He didn't cotton much to change, but Senior was right. Their current house was fine for just the two of them but too small for additional people. And while he didn't have any prospects on the horizon, he still hoped his grandfather was right about Rusty finding the right girl. *Someday.*

After clicking on a few houses, he saw a listing for land only. Twenty-five acres just outside Maple Falls. He clicked on the link and smiled. This was perfect. Tons of trees and privacy, along with a large, fully stocked pond at the edge of the property line. The listing described abundant wildlife, or the land could be transformed into a farm if the buyer wanted. And having a fishing hole right on his property? Jackpot. He and Senior both loved to fish.

He did some more searching, then printed out four listings to show Harper. He hadn't expected to be this excited about looking for a new place to live. Senior was right. He shouldn't be so down in the mouth. It was time to focus on what he had instead of dwelling on what he didn't.

Madge waited until midnight before she readied herself for bed. She clenched her jaw and started her evening routine—cleansing and moisturizing her face, brushing her teeth for exactly two minutes with her electric toothbrush, and smoothing lavender-scented lotion on her skin. Then she got into her empty king-sized bed, turned off the light, and put on her sleep mask.

But she was too irritable to go to sleep. Harper hadn't called her back . . . again. Her daughter was well past being childish and on to rude. Their relationship had been strained for a few years now, ever since Harper had opened up her own brokerage firm and become too busy for anything but work and her friends. Madge had been proud of her daughter's ambition and success, but she had also thought Harper had gone out on her own too soon. When she let her thoughts be known to Harper, her daughter had been upset. Oh, she'd hid it well. But Madge was her mother. A mother could always tell how her child felt.

Harper wasn't the only person she was irritated with. She was also mad at herself for telling Erma about the divorce last week. For so long she'd tried to hide the embarrassment over her failed marriage, and that was the main reason she had avoided the Bosom Buddies. But ten minutes with Erma, and she hadn't been able to keep her emotions and her secrets to herself. She shouldn't be surprised, though. Erma McAllister had a way of getting people to open up to her. Madge had seen it numerous times. Not because the woman was a busybody—although she did like to stick her nose in people's business sometimes. But she always had good intentions.

In this case Madge didn't care what her intentions were, and she wasn't about to return to Knots and Tangles or the Bosom Buddies anytime soon.

Dread formed in the pit of her stomach. This coming Tuesday she and Don would have their first meeting with their lawyers—something that was supposed to have happened earlier this week but had been suddenly postponed by his attorney. She wanted all this over with—telling Harper, hammering out the divorce details, and putting Donald Michael Wilson in her past. She'd been right about what she told Erma. Their marriage should have ended a long time ago.

Her phone rang, and she quickly pulled off the mask. Finally Harper had remembered to call. But when she picked up the phone and looked at the screen, she was shocked to see Don's number.

She stared at the digits. Should she answer it? They hadn't communicated in more than a month, and that had been fine with her. Why was he calling now? Probably wanting to reschedule their meeting with the lawyers again to keep her off guard. She was sure he was behind the postponement. That's how it had always been during their marriage. His needs and priorities came first.

Not anymore.

The phone stopped ringing. Whatever he had to say he could tell her voice mail.

She set the phone on the nightstand and started to pull down her sleep mask. The phone rang again, and Don's number once more appeared on the screen.

She snatched up the cell and answered it. "What do you want?"

"I didn't think you'd pick up," he said.

"I didn't the first time." She sat on the edge of the bed and pushed her bare toes against the plush white carpet in their bedroom. Now her bedroom, and it wouldn't be hers for much longer. "It's late, Don. Whatever you have to say can wait until Tuesday."

"No, it can't." A pause. "Madge, I don't want a divorce."

She stilled, and something deep inside her frozen heart started to thaw. She covered it in another sheet of ice. "You canceled the appointment with the lawyers, didn't you?"

"Yes, because I don't want to end our marriage."

"Too late."

"I still love you, Maddie."

She rolled her eyes. She'd hated his stupid nickname for her when they started dating years ago after they'd met at a bar in Little Rock. Not the classiest place to fall for someone, but that was exactly what had happened. The moment she'd laid eyes on Don, she'd loved him. Little did she know how much pain he'd put her through almost thirty years later. What a fool she'd been, giving up her goal of being an interior designer so she could become Mrs. Donald Wilson. A few years after they married, she became Harper's mother, and any thought of going back to school was off the table.

"Have you talked to Harper yet?" he asked.

"No."

He let out a frustrated breath. "Me either. She won't answer my calls. This is a good thing, though. I realized that we need to talk to her together, after we work things out between us."

"There's nothing to work out, Donald. I don't love you. I don't want to be married to you anymore. The next time we talk, it will be with our attorneys present."

"But Maddie—"

She hung up the phone before he had a chance to say anything else. Such as how sorry he was or that he would never hurt her again. Words she had heard over and over. Hurt her he had, although not physically. Or verbally either. They'd rarely fought during their long marriage. Maybe they should have. Then maybe he wouldn't have gone running into another woman's arms.

Two months ago she'd found out he'd had a long-term affair. They'd spent the last two years trying to reconnect, and he'd never said a word about being unfaithful. She was *done.*

The way she found out was so cliché she could hardly believe it was real. They'd been at a four-star resort in St. Petersburg, Florida, and had spent a lazy, satisfying morning in bed. Don was in the shower when a text buzzed in. She picked up his phone from the nightstand and read the text, thinking it might be one of his golfing friends from Hot Springs.

> Don, please answer me. I know you're not happy with Madge. You haven't been for years. But you were so happy with me. Call me. V.

When she confronted him, he insisted he'd ended things a year ago. "It's over, I promise."

"Then why is she still texting you?"

"I don't know. This is the first time I've heard from her since then."

She crossed her arms. "I don't believe you."

He grabbed his phone and handed it to her. "Go ahead. Check my messages. Then you'll see I'm telling the truth."

Madge turned away.

"I'm blocking her number now," he said, then tossed the phone on the bed. "She won't bother us anymore."

But the damage was done. She had packed her bag, left him in the fancy hotel, and caught an earlier flight back to Arkansas. When he returned to their house later, she told him to move out. Without a single word, he did.

Madge threw off her mask and turned on the light. She couldn't sleep now, the shame and horror of that moment washing over her like it had so many times in the past. That day had started so perfectly. All their trips had been wonderful, and she had believed that finally, after three decades, she had back the husband she'd fallen in love with. She should have known better, and his full confession didn't change her mind—not then and not now.

But she faced a life alone now, and she wasn't sure what to do. When her daughter was younger, they'd been inseparable, but that was mostly her doing. Madge had spent all of Harper's elementary and middle school years volunteering—PTA, classroom mom, party and dance chaperone. When Harper started high school, Madge got a job as the school secretary and quit after Harper's graduation. Three months later, Harper left for the University of Arkansas in Fayetteville, leaving Madge by herself, along with occasionally being Don's wife when he deigned to show up.

Where did all that effort leave her? By herself in a huge, empty house. She'd lost the will to engage with any of her friends, including the Bosom Buddies. And Harper was as distant as ever. It was painfully clear she was more like her father. Ambitious, driven, and too consumed with herself to make time for her own mother.

Making her way to the living room, Madge sat on the edge of the couch but didn't turn on the light. After the divorce everything would be different. She would have a new start and focus on herself for a change. If Harper wanted to be a part of her new life, that would be nice. But if she didn't . . .

Madge swallowed. If she didn't, that would be Harper's loss. *I'm moving on . . . with or without her.*

Chapter 6

Harper picked up the chai latte Anita placed on the table, her eyes never leaving her phone. "Shoot," she muttered. If the Sunshine Café hadn't been full of customers, she would have said a stronger word than that. Another sale lost, and this time through a text message.

> I'm sorry, Ms. Wilson. I can't meet with you later today. I've decided to put my plans on hold for the time being.

She set the latte back on the table, untouched. The cancellation didn't make sense. Harper had cleared her Saturday afternoon to help this client—*former* client—who had seemed so excited to buy her first home. And now she was canceling . . . by text? Not even a voice mail?

She shook her head. This was the worst three months she'd ever had as a real-estate agent. Up until this year she'd always been in the black with her business, even during slim times. Now, with each passing day she inched toward red. Never mind buying #6. She'd be lucky if she made enough to cover her office rent this month.

"Earth to Harper."

She glanced up to see Anita already seated

across from her. When had she sat down? "Sorry." She pressed the side button on her phone and set it next to the croissant that had also appeared in front of her.

"Everything okay?"

"Of course." She sipped on the latte, savoring the sweetly spiced drink and taking a few seconds to hide her frayed emotions. "I love that hairstyle on you, by the way."

"Thanks." Anita's amber-colored eyes shined as she touched the end of her side ponytail. Her old, cute pixie cut had completely grown out, and now her hair lay well past her shoulders. "It's something different from a plain old pony-tail."

"It definitely suits you." Harper smirked. "So would some fake eyelashes."

"Don't even go there." Anita laughed.

Harper grinned, knowing how much her friend hated those things, along with any kind of fancy makeup. Anita had a naturally fresh complexion, so she didn't need to worry about it. As for Harper, she'd worn foundation since she was in sixth grade, after her mother advised her to cover up her acne. Madge showed her how, and with some experimentation Harper had learned how to perfectly disguise every single blemish. Unfortunately, she still had to deal with a breakout here and there, even as an adult.

"I'm glad you're able to stop by today," Anita

said. "It's been a while since any of us have seen you."

"Work has been crazy. Pretty much all I do anymore is eat, show houses, make cold calls, and sleep." She pinched off a piece from one end of the croissant. She shouldn't have ordered it, but right now she needed something to soothe her nerves, and the buttery, flaky carb was doing the trick.

Anita patted her arm. "We're all missing you at Knots and Tangles. Riley also mentioned that your mom hasn't met with the Bosom Buddies in months either."

"That's Madge for you." She crammed the soft bread into her mouth, feeling a pinch of guilt that she still hadn't called her mother back yet. *Tonight, I'll call her tonight.* "How are things with you and Tanner? Still in newlywed heaven?"

"Yes," Anita said with a long sigh. "We did get into a huge argument a few days ago . . ." A dreamy look entered her eyes.

"Let me guess. You kissed and made up, right?"

She blushed. "Yeah, we did."

Harper laughed and took another bite of the croissant. "These are amazing," she said around a mouthful. "Where did you get them?"

"Rosa made them," she said, referring to her mother-in-law. "Now that she's stepped back from working so much, she's taken up baking, along with crochet. The woman can't keep still."

"Good for her." But Harper had to admit she was a little envious. She'd had so much fun preparing supper for her and Rusty last Friday that she found herself longing to bake again. But when would she fit that into her schedule? She'd only stopped by the café for three reasons—she felt guilty about ignoring her friends, she was dying for a chai latte, and Rusty was supposed to meet her here in five minutes. He'd called her yesterday and left a message. When she phoned him back last night, he didn't say what he wanted to talk about, but it sounded urgent. *"Too much to explain on the phone,"* he'd said, which led her to believe he had bad news about her Mercedes. Was it beyond hope? The last thing she needed was to have to buy a new car.

As she sipped her drink, she tried not to worry about her dream car and instead took notice of the fall decorations around the café. "Good grief. I forgot about the candy."

"What?" Anita asked.

"I was going to donate a few bags of candy for the Maple Falls Fall Parade." She had also planned to talk to Hayden about it first, like Rusty had told her to, and she hadn't done that either. She'd never been so scatterbrained in her life.

"That's great," Anita said. "We can use the extra."

"It would be great, if I'd actually picked up

the candy." She grabbed her purse and found her checkbook. "Here," she said after she filled it out and handed it to Anita. "Can you see that Hayden gets that?"

"Sure." Anita glanced at the amount. "Wow, that's very generous. Real estate must be doing very well for you right now."

Harper almost laughed at the irony. She shouldn't have donated that much considering her finances, but she never skimped on a worthy cause. She hung her purse back over her chair, ignoring her friend's comment.

"FYI, we're still meeting on Tuesday nights," Anita said. "We miss you, Harper."

"I miss y'all too. How's the name search going?"

"Nowhere." Anita sighed. "Every time someone suggests one, somebody else doesn't like it."

"Latte Ladies is still available."

Anita laughed. "No, thank you."

"Then what about just the Lattes?" Harper suggested. "Olivia drinks tea, but I really don't think we should go with the Earl Greys."

"Believe it or not, she actually suggested that two weeks ago, more out of desperation than anything else." Anita tapped her slender fingers against the wood tabletop. "I like the Lattes. I'm surprised no one else thought of it before. We'll put it to a vote at the next meeting. Oh, we're also putting together the candy bags for the parade.

It shouldn't take us long if you're free to join us."

She paused, ready to tell Anita that she had to work late every night until she got back on track. But she missed her friends, and the only way she'd have time to see them was if she made time. Work could wait for one night. "Count me in."

"Awesome. I know Riley and Olivia will be glad to see you too." Anita glanced over Harper's shoulder. "Hmm. That's a surprise."

"What?"

"Rusty just walked through the door. He usually goes to the diner once or twice a week, but I don't see him much here."

Harper turned around. With his wild hair molded against his head like he'd been wearing a cap all day, his bushy beard hiding his mouth, and dressed in a red-and-blue-checked shirt and baggy jeans, he looked like a lumberjack instead of a mechanic. The soles of his old work boots thudded on the café's bamboo floor as he approached.

"Hi, Rusty," Anita said as she got up from the table. "You can sit anywhere you'd like while I get you a menu."

"He's here to meet me." Harper smiled at Rusty and gestured for him to sit down.

"Oh." Anita looked confused. "Uh, what would you like to drink?"

"Water's good."

"You can't order just water in a café," Harper said. "There's over two dozen varieties of drinks here."

"Three dozen, but who's counting," Anita added with a smile.

"All right." Rusty looked at Harper's overly large white coffee cup. "I'll have what she's havin', then."

"Chai latte? Got it." Anita hurried off to fill his order.

Rusty leaned over and whispered to Harper, "What's a chai latte?"

"A spicy-sweet tea with milk."

"Oh. Well, I'm game to try just about anythin'. Except skydivin'. That's never gonna happen."

Her phone rang, and she was surprised by the name on the screen. *Don?* What was with her parents calling her out of the blue lately? She let it go to voice mail and slipped her cell into her purse, giving Rusty her undivided attention. "Speaking of skydiving, that's on my ever-expanding bucket list."

"Huh. Didn't figure you for a daredevil. What else is on there?"

"Let's see. A front seat at the Milan fashion show, standing underneath a waterfall in Hawaii, and . . ." She was about to say another one of the frivolous activities she had on a list she'd started when she was sixteen. Instead, she said,

"And of course opening my Maple Falls office."

"Hopefully that will happen sooner than later," he said.

She smiled at his encouraging words, even though he was dead wrong. Not while she was bleeding clients, and when she might have to dig deep into her savings to purchase a new vehicle. A *used* new vehicle. No way she could afford one off the showroom floor. "Okay. Give me the bad news."

"Bad news?" He sounded bewildered.

"One chai latte," Anita said as she appeared next to Rusty and set the mug in front of him. "Would you like a pastry or some biscotti to go with that?"

He shook his head. "The latte is fine, thanks."

"All right." Anita turned to Harper and gave her a questioning look. "I guess I'll leave you two *alone.*"

Seeing that her friend might get the wrong idea, Harper quickly said, "Rusty was just telling me that my car is DOA."

"Oh," Anita said, understanding dawning. "That's too bad. I know you love that car."

Rusty held up his hand, looking slightly confused. "I can fix the Merc. The part is coming in tomorrow or the next day. Once I install it, she should be good to go."

"Oh, thank goodness." Harper slumped with relief in her chair.

"Anita," one of the customers across the café called out.

"Be right there." She gave Harper and Rusty a little wave, then went to attend to the customer.

"You okay?" Rusty said to Harper, leaning forward slightly.

"More than okay." She sat up and touched the handle of the latte mug. "I was so sure you were going to tell me my car was kaput."

"Naw. It'll be fine once I get the part in. I'm sorry if I gave you the idea that there was somethin' really wrong with her."

"It's not your fault." She took a sip of the latte and set down her mug. "The way things have been going lately . . . I guess I just assumed you wanted to talk in person to give me the bad news."

"Actually," he said, "I might have some good news for ya." Picking up his mug, he took a drink and made a face. "This tastes kinda weird."

"But good, right?"

He took another sip. "Fair to middlin'. I'll finish it."

"So what did you want to tell me?" She could use something else positive right now. The good news about her Mercedes would only go so far.

"I need to buy a new house."

Harper stilled. That was the last thing she'd expected him to say. "Are you serious?"

"Yep." He pulled out several folded sheets

of paper from the back pocket of his jeans and handed them to her. "I did some lookin' around on the internet after I left you a message yesterday," he said.

But she barely heard his words. Rusty wanted to buy a house. Unbelievable. She'd been working her dialing fingers to the bone making cold calls to find new clients, only to come up empty. Then there were the late nights she'd spent on the computer, studying the market, familiarizing herself with every single property in a fifty-mile radius so that when someone did call her—and no one had—she'd be ready. And here was Rusty, dropping a potential sale in her lap. She tempered the giddiness that threatened to take over and shifted into business mode.

"You want to buy a house," she repeated, making sure she'd heard him right.

He nodded. "It's a long story."

She listened as he explained that his sister was possibly moving to Colorado, and if that happened, Senior was likely moving back to Maple Falls. "Which means he's moving back in with me," he finished.

"Are you okay with that?"

"Of course. I've missed him while he's been in Little Rock, even though livin' with Amber was the best thing for him."

Harper hesitated to ask her next question, but knowing the answer would help her find the right property for him and his grandfather. "Senior can't live alone?"

Rusty shook his head. "He's got macular degeneration."

"What's that?"

"He's losing his sight. The central vision part of it. He hasn't been able to drive in over a year."

"I bet he's not happy about that."

"Definitely not." Rusty glanced into his mug before looking at her again. "There's no cure, and eventually he won't be able to live on his own. He'll still have some peripheral vision, but . . ."

Her heart went out to him and Senior. She'd thought she understood how much Rusty cared for his grandfather when he told her about his grandparents over supper last Friday. But it was clear Senior was extra special to him and Amber. "Does he know about the move?"

Rusty chuckled. "Amber tried keepin' it from him, but he's got a way of findin' out about stuff. Can't put anythin' past him. I figured he'd want to stay in our old house, but he's okay with sellin' it. Probably helped that there's now a big hole in our living-room floor."

Her brow shot up. "What?"

The tops of his cheeks turned red. "I accidentally put it there last week when I was walking to the kitchen. The place wasn't in the best of shape when I was growin' up, and it's just gotten worse as time went on. Senior can fix a car, but when it comes to house repairs, he can barely change a light bulb. G'ma was the one who did the upkeep. It's needin' an overhaul, but I've been puttin' it off. I never thought it was so bad that the wood was rottin' under the carpet in the livin' room, though. Guess I take after Senior when it comes to home maintenance." He glanced at her. "Pretty bad, huh?"

"Believe it or not, I've heard worse. I've seen worse too. You can't imagine the shape some houses are in nowadays. Especially the old ones in Maple Falls."

"I don't have much of an excuse, though, other than puttin' off somethin' I don't wanna do. But now that Senior's ready to move on, I'll get someone to fix it up for sale."

Harper noticed Rusty wasn't looking at her now. After years of working with clients, both eager and reluctant, she could tell when someone was struggling with making such a huge life change. "What about you?"

His head lifted. "What about me?"

"Are you ready to move on?"

He paused. Took a drink of the chai. Then said, "Nothin' wrong with having a bigger house. Some land would be nice too." His gaze met hers. "And if I can help out a friend? Even better."

She held up her hands, shaking her head. "I don't want you to buy a house just to help me."

"I'm not. Senior and I are getting the best end of the deal."

Relieved, she said, "I'll make sure that happens. What's your budget?"

"I reckon I got around five hundred thousand I can spend."

Harper coughed. "What?"

"Wait. Sorry, that number ain't right." He stared at the papers in front of him as if he was mentally recalculating his funds.

"More like mid-100k range?" she said, although she had no idea how much a mechanic made. "Or around 200k?"

"Naw. More like seven fifty. But a million is as high as I can go. Not that I need something that expensive."

Her jaw dropped. "One . . . million?"

He hid a grin at what she knew must be her shocked expression. "I ain't got a lot of personal expenses, and the shop pays for itself. Last big-ticket thing I bought was my truck, and I paid cash for that."

"Um, okay, then." She gave her head a shake. A million dollars. Even if she sold him a property for seven fifty she'd get a fantastic commission. And sometimes that was all it took to shake a sales slump.

"Think you can find me something for less than that?" he asked.

"You bet I can." She smiled, but it was brief. It

still didn't sit right with her that he'd pointed out how this would help her. She was all about her clients, and Rusty would be no different. "You've got enough money to fix up your own house," she said.

"I know. But Senior wants to sell." He paused again. "*I* want to sell," he said firmly.

"It will be a big change."

He shrugged. "That's okay. Change is a good thing sometimes."

She agreed. But she still had to be sure. "As long as you're doing this for you and Senior and not for me," she said. "I wish I hadn't told you about my business woes."

"I'm glad you did."

When she met his gaze, she could see he was telling the truth. "Thank you," she said. "And thanks for trusting me to find your new home."

"New home." He scratched his chin, his eyes lighting up. "I think I can get used to that."

She picked up the pages he'd handed to her earlier and skimmed them, full of optimism and renewed enthusiasm. "This first house is a possibility," she said. "Although it's priced too high. I can negotiate that down to something more reasonable."

"I can afford the price."

"Oh, I know." She looked at him. "But I don't want you paying more than the property is worth."

"Even though you're considerin' the same thing with #6?"

"That's different," she insisted. "I don't *want* to pay that much for #6, but if I have to, I will. I'm confident the building will continue to appreciate. But you don't have to pay the listing price if this ends up being the home you want."

He nodded. "Gotcha."

She glanced at the second page. The listing was for an idyllic twenty-five-acre plot of land on Miles Road that had just hit the market. "Are you interested in building?" she asked, pointing to the picture of the property.

"I'm not opposed to it." She put the listing between them, and as he leaned forward, she caught the scent of fresh soap and laundry detergent. No fancy cologne for this guy. "That's my favorite," he said. "It's got a fishin' hole and everythin'."

His enthusiasm for something as simple as a pond had her laughing . . . until she saw who held the listing. *Oh no.*

"Whatcha think?" Rusty said, looking at her.

Harper scrambled for a response. "It's . . . nice." But the person who represented the property wasn't. Brielle Weaver. A sour knot formed in the pit of her stomach.

"I didn't see a price on it," he continued, then took another sip of his latte. "Reckon that means it's expensive."

He reckoned right. But if he wanted the property, she would do everything she could to get it for him. "I'll make a call," she said, dread swirling around the knot as she took her cell phone out of her purse and dialed Brielle's number. It went straight to voice mail. She wasn't sure whether she was relieved or disappointed. "Hey, Brielle, it's Harper Wilson. I've got a client interested in one of your properties. Call me asap." She ended the call and set her phone on the table. "As soon as she gets back to me, we'll set up an appointment."

"Sounds good." He looked at the large white mug in front of him. "You're right. This ain't half bad once you get used to it. Not that I'm gonna give up my coffee anytime soon. But for a treat, this works."

"I'd never steer you wrong," she said with a confident nod, shoving Brielle out of her mind. She could handle her, especially if it meant Rusty and Senior getting the property they wanted.

"I know you won't." He grinned.

She felt a little tug of . . . something . . . again. Even through the heavy beard, his grin was engaging. He was such a kind and gentle man, and she would do right by him—even if it meant dealing with her nemesis.

"I don't know how any of this house-huntin' stuff works," he said.

"Then you're in luck, because I do." She

grinned. "I just had a cancellation this afternoon, so if you want, we can look at the properties you picked out. If you're free, that is."

"Sure. Percy and Senior are holding down the garage today. That's why I was able to meet with you now."

"Senior's working on the cars?"

"He can see well enough to do a few things, like change oil. That's somethin' he could do blindfolded, truth be told. I won't let him, though. He's put out with me about that, even though he'll be happy jawin' with any customers that call. I usually close the shop around noon or one anyway, and Percy won't mind taking him home, or wherever he wants to go." He shook his head. "He's got a busier social life than I do."

Me too. And she would get back to that social life as soon as she made some sales, Rusty being the first one. She met his gaze. "Ready to find your dream home?"

"Yep," he said. "I'm ready."

Chapter 7

Rusty's enthusiasm for house hunting dimmed by the time evening arrived. Harper had shown him two of the houses he'd printed out for her, but neither one of them would work for him and Senior. One was brand-new construction in a sprawling neighborhood where the houses sat too close together. He didn't want to live right on top of his neighbors. The other one had a basement and a wraparound deck on the back, and neither had been shown in the pictures on the listing. The stairs would eventually cause a problem for Senior.

Then there was the Miles Road property. The Realtor hadn't returned Harper's call, and when they drove by it, they'd seen a sign on barbed-wire fencing that said No Trespassing. But even that limited drive-by had firmed up Rusty's interest. Miles Road was a short, unpaved road only a mile from the main road that led into Maple Falls. The leaves on the hickory trees were turning golden yellow amid sturdy green pines and a few bright-red maples. When they got out of his truck to take a closer look, all he could hear was the cool breeze rustling the leafy branches and the faint sound of birds chirping. Otherwise, it was quiet. Peaceful. A man could think out here. Maybe even entertain a dream or two.

"Rusty?"

He turned to Harper, unable to keep from smiling. Today she wore a cherry-red turtleneck, navy-blue pants, and a white leather jacket. He could see why she gravitated toward the color red—she was unbelievably beautiful wearing it. Even her lipstick matched her sweater. A lock of blond hair blew across her forehead, and she brushed it back behind her ear, revealing a tiny diamond stud on her perfect earlobe. *Yeah . . . a man could dream . . .*

"What do you think?" she asked.

"Gorgeous," he murmured.

She turned to face the fence. "It really is. I had no idea this place existed. It's not that far off the beaten path, but it's still private. I can see why you like this place."

He blinked, her words bringing him back from whatever trance he'd fallen into while staring at her. "Uh, yeah. I really like it."

She put her hands into her jacket pockets and turned to him. "We can't see any more than this today, but as soon as Brielle calls, I'll set up a showing."

"Thanks."

After that, she showed him one more house, but he didn't care for it.

"It's going to be dark soon," she said as they

climbed into the truck. "Did you want to look at anything else?"

He shook his head. "Naw, I'm done for the day. Sorry I'm being so picky."

"You should be picky," she said, turning to him. The sun was setting behind her, the autumn sky streaked with blues and pinks in between swirls of flat clouds. "This is a major purchase that you have to live with for many years. Sometimes even a lifetime, like your grandfather has."

"You can call him Senior. Everyone else does." He leaned back against the seat. "I reckon I'm a little overwhelmed," he admitted. More than a little, actually. He couldn't picture himself living anywhere else but in Senior and G'ma's house. Not even the Miles Road land. But out of what he'd seen today, at least he could gin up a little excitement over having his own fishing hole.

"We can go to my office, and I can show you some listings online if you'd like. Maybe narrow things down more."

Her phone buzzed in her purse, but she ignored it. Rusty was learning that when something had Harper's complete focus, she didn't get distracted from it. Right now he was her center of attention, and he had to admit it felt kinda nice. But he was tired of house hunting.

"We can do that another day," he said.

"All right." She fidgeted with the edge of her seatbelt.

Was she disappointed? "Sorry if I'm lettin' you down."

"Letting me down?" She chuckled, returning to her usual lighthearted manner. "This is all part of the process. A process that can take . . . months." She said the last word almost in a whisper before brightening again. "In the meantime I'll be on the hunt for the perfect place for you and Senior. New listings pop up all the time. But I'm not giving up on the Miles Road property."

"Thanks, Harper. I appreciate it. But don't work too hard on my account."

"That's my job. To be here for you."

He knew she was talking about professionally, but it was still nice to hear. "Hopefully that one real-estate lady will call you back. What did you say her name was?"

For a split second a cloud passed over Harper's face. Then her expression cleared again. "Brielle Weaver. I'll let you know when she does, and if I come across anything else I think you'll like."

"Great." Now it was time for him to take her back to the Sunshine Café where she had left Lois. Then they'd say goodbye or "See you later" or any number of niceties people said when they parted ways. Yet for some reason he didn't want to go just yet. Senior had texted him earlier and said he was having supper with the Prices and then playing cards afterward. They would drop him off at the house later tonight. *"Don't w ait u p,"* he'd texted, keeping his running record of at least one typo per text intact. That would leave Rusty in an empty house until then.

"Would you, uh, like to get a bite to eat?" he asked as he pulled into a spot near the café. Although both the diner and the café were closed for the day, along with the other businesses on Main Street, there were still restaurants open around Maple Falls. "We could go to the Orange Bluebird. I owe you a meal anyway." He made sure to add that last part, more for himself than her. He didn't like an outstanding debt, even something as small as supper—although Harper making supper for him hadn't been small. Not in his mind. But he couldn't admit, even to himself, that he didn't want to spend yet another night at home alone.

"You don't owe me anything," she said, then glanced at Lois, her right foot swaying partway out of his vehicle.

"That's okay," he blurted, a little embarrassed he'd assumed she'd want to share another meal together. "I'm sure you've got other plans. I've used up a lot of your time as is."

Harper tucked her foot back inside and closed the truck door. When she looked at him, she was smiling. "I'd love to have dinner with you."

His heartbeat tripled. And now the dry mouth and sweaty hands started up again. Nuts. What was wrong with him?

She clicked her seatbelt. "Can I make a different restaurant suggestion, though?"

"Sure," he croaked, sounding like a beat-up old bullfrog. He cleared his throat. "Where do you want to go?"

"Do you like pizza?"

"Sure do."

"I know the perfect place, then."

She gave him directions to Deep-Dish Delights, a pizzeria a few miles outside of Maple Falls, and they were on their way. He hid a grin, hoping she didn't see it. His thick beard was finally good for something.

When he pulled into the pizzeria parking lot, he said, "I ain't heard of this place before. I thought I knew all the pizza places in a thirty-mile radius."

"It's new. They opened five weeks ago, and everything here is delicious. I don't eat pizza much because of the calories. But occasionally I indulge."

He hurried out of the truck to open the door for her, even though she already had it partway open. "Thanks," she said, a surprised expression on her face.

"I've been trying to do that all afternoon," he said. "But you kept gettin' out of the truck too fast."

"Oh."

He stuffed his hands into his pockets, double-guessing his instinct to explain himself. He and Harper obviously weren't on a date, but considering his track record with women, he never knew whether he'd offended them or not. "If you don't want me to open your door, I don't have to."

"I don't mind," she said, her voice soft.

He glanced at her. She was so easygoing, something else he wouldn't have guessed about her. He was finding out all kinds of new things about Harper Wilson. Things he liked.

Trying to get his bearings, his gaze darted around the parking lot. "Lot's full," he said, doing his best imitation of Captain Obvious.

"They've got plenty of seating. And plenty of pizza." She headed for the door.

He followed, and she was right. The size of the restaurant was deceiving from the outside, but inside there were several empty tables. She walked over to one in the middle, and before she could sit down, he pulled out her chair for her.

"Thanks again," she said, settling into the chair.

He sat opposite her. "You're welcome."

She crossed her arms and put her elbows on the table. Leaning forward, she said, "So who taught you to be such a southern gentleman?"

He grinned. "That would be G'ma, although Senior always backed her up. Not everybody wants to have doors opened and chairs pulled out, though. The last girl I went out with . . ." He fiddled with the edge of the vinyl white-and-red-checked tablecloth. "Never mind."

"She didn't like it."

Rusty met her eyes. Candlelight from the red jar in the middle of the table caused glowing shadows to flicker across her pretty face. Was there ever a time when she wasn't beautiful? He doubted it. "About six months ago—maybe nine, I reckon, now that I think about it—I went out with the daughter of one of my out-of-town customers. The lady was so nice and *so* sure her lovely daughter and I would hit it off. And she definitely was lovely. I can give her that."

"But you didn't hit it off," Harper said.

"Nope. Not even a little. I opened the truck door for her, and she gave me a look like I had scrambled eggs for brains. When we got to the Orange Bluebird, I pulled out her chair."

"What did she say?"

He tried to imitate her high-pitched voice. " 'I'm only going out with you because my mother said she would stop bugging me if I did.' " Then she grabbed the chair and yanked it out of my hand. After we ate, she asked me if I could drop her off at a friend's house. When I took her there, she said, 'Sorry. You're nice, but you're not my type.' Turned out that friend was a guy."

"How did you know?"

"I waited for her to go inside. A dude opened

the door, and she kissed him smack dab on the lips. Guess he was her type."

Harper's mouth twisted. "What a—"

Rusty held up his hand. "The upside is it was only one date, the Orange Bluebird ain't expensive, and I'm pretty sure I dodged a bullet with that one."

She nodded. "You sure did. I can't believe you're so calm about it, though. I'd be furious."

"Sure, I was mad. But like I said, that was a while ago. I got over it."

The waitress came up and asked for their drink order. They both ordered iced tea, and then Harper turned to Rusty. "Do you like pineapple on your pizza? They have a great Hawaiian one here."

"Can't say I've had it before. Let's give it a try."

Harper ordered the pizza. As the waitress walked away, she said to Rusty, "You haven't had chai, and you haven't had Hawaiian pizza. Or minestrone. I mean this in the nicest way, Rusty . . . but have you been living under a rock?"

He shrugged, taking no offense. "Senior and G'ma liked simple, easy food. I do, too, since I cook for myself most of the time."

She leaned forward again. "Then I guess I'll have to introduce you to some more new things."

Chapter 8

Uh-oh. Harper wanted to take back that last sentence. She didn't need Rusty to get the wrong idea. She wasn't flirting with him . . . was she? She knew more than one guy who had taken her friendliness as flirtation. More like lots of guys, and she normally tried to dial it back when she was with men. But being around Rusty had made her forget about keeping up her guard.

"That sounds mighty nice, Harper."

She sat back, relieved she didn't have to make things awkward by apologizing or rationalizing her statement. This man was so pure, she almost wondered if he was pretending to be. She'd known her fair share of disingenuous people, not only in the business world but personally. Jack came to mind, and she shoved him off the cliff of her thoughts. She didn't want to think about him right now. Or ever.

The waitress set their drinks in front of them. "The pizza will be out soon," she said. "Can I get you anything else?" When they both shook their heads no, she walked away.

Rusty swiped his bangs out of his face and took a swig of tea. The pizzeria was far from a romantic restaurant, but the red candlelight was a nice touch. Most of his face was obscured by his hair and beard, but she saw his eyes clearly. Warm, gentle eyes.

She gripped the cold glass. She shouldn't be paying attention to his eyes or anything else about him. They needed to talk real estate. Despite her reassurance that being particular about buying a house was a good thing, she was still surprised at how persnickety he was being, considering how laid back he was about everything else. That made her wonder again if he was truly ready to move or if he was trying to accommodate his grandfather . . . and her.

Her phone buzzed again in her purse. There was a time when her phone buzzing off the hook hadn't bothered her. Now she was getting tired of it, especially when she was starting to relax, since moments like these had been few and far between lately. She grabbed the cell out of her bag. "I'll turn this off," she said, poised to shut down the phone.

"Go ahead and answer it," he said. "I don't mind."

"They'll leave a message." She glanced at the screen. "It's Madge."

"Then you really should answer it."

Reluctantly, she slid her thumb over the bottom of the screen. "Hi," she said quickly. "I'm with a . . . client right now." She glanced at Rusty, who gave her a smile.

"But it's after five," her mother said without returning Harper's greeting.

"You know my job doesn't have regular hours," she said, turning slightly away from Rusty.

Madge scoffed. "You're just like your father."

Harper frowned. What was that supposed to mean?

"You haven't returned any of my calls, Harper," Madge continued, her voice sounding more robotic than usual. But her next words were sharply edged. "Do I need to contact your office and make an appointment to talk to you?"

Harper pressed her lips together, not appreciating the passive-aggressiveness. "No," she said in a measured tone. "I'd already planned to call you tonight when I got off work—"

"Please do." *Click.*

Harper grimaced. Although she and her mother had been at odds more than ever lately, Madge had never hung up on her.

"Why don't we get that pizza to go?" Rusty said.

She put her cell back in her purse, still stinging from her mother's rebuke. "No. I'm still working. She can wait until I get home."

"You sure?"

"Positive. Now, what were we—" *Oh no.* Her stomach turned inside out as she spied a couple at a table for two on the other side of the restaurant.

"What?" Rusty said, his brow furrowing.

Unbelievable. Of all the places she would end up seeing Brielle and . . . wait. She did a double take at the blond, curly-headed man seated across from her. That wasn't Jack. Where was Jack? Was Brielle cheating on him?

Good.

"Harper, the pizza's here."

She blinked and looked at Rusty, then at the pizza in the center of the table. She hadn't noticed the waitress had come by, much less put a piping-hot Hawaiian in front of them. Now she was torn. She needed to talk to Brielle about the Miles Road property, but she'd hoped it would be over the phone. Not in person. And who was that guy she was with? When he leaned forward and threaded his hand with hers, she almost fell out of her seat. If she was cheating on Jack, she wasn't being discreet about it.

"Is something wrong?" Rusty turned around and looked behind him at Brielle and her mystery man.

Harper touched Rusty's arm, not wanting to draw their attention. "No, everything is—"

As if she had super spidey sense—and Harper wasn't sure she didn't—Brielle turned and met Harper's gaze. After a flash of recognition, she smirked.

"—fine." She fell back in her seat as Brielle stood. Of course she was coming over to their table. *Be professional.* Harper pasted a smile on

130

her face and, without a choice, waved Brielle over.

Rusty faced Harper. "Is she a friend of yours?"

Absolutely not. "Um, not exactly—"

"Harper!" Brielle appeared at their table, her dinner companion in tow. Now that she saw him up close, he looked young. Forget dinner companion. More like boy toy.

"I haven't seen you since I moved back to Hot Springs," Brielle continued, then put her arm around the man's slim waist. "How have you been?"

"Oh, busy as always. Lots of sales. A whole bunch of sales." Unreal. She was babbling, and she never babbled.

"The market's heating up, that's for sure. I've closed six deals this week alone." Brielle turned to her date and smiled. "We're celebrating tonight."

"Does Jack know?" Harper blurted, then bit the end of her tongue. She flipped her hair over her shoulder, hoping to seem cavalier when she was anything but.

"Oh, I guess you didn't hear." Brielle leveled her gaze at Harper. "We broke up six months ago. I thought you knew, considering he moved back to Hot Springs last year."

Now her stomach was flipping out. That explained why Jack had been so persistent in contacting her. Did he really think she'd go out with him again after he dumped her for Brielle? They'd even moved to Bentonville together, and he'd worked at her brokerage firm. But what did Harper care if they broke up? She wished she never had to deal with either one of them again.

"Oh, I'm being rude, aren't I?" Brielle turned to her dinner companion. "Mason, this is Harper and . . ."

"Rusty Jenkins," he supplied. He held out his hand to Mason, who shook it. "Nice to meet you."

"And this is Brielle," Harper said, realizing she'd ignored Rusty the entire time. Then she looked at Brielle again. "The real estate agent I called earlier today. Twice."

"About the property on Miles Road?" Rusty asked.

Brielle paused, then smiled. "Oh yes. That's right. I get so many messages and voice mails that I can't get to them all right away. I was going to return your call in the morning."

Riiiight. Sure she was going to call on a Sunday morning . . . Harper frowned. She was one to talk. She'd missed plenty of Sunday services at church lately. "That will be fine," Harper said quickly. Not only did she want Brielle to go back to her table—or disappear entirely—she didn't like the leering look Mason was giving her. If Brielle could get out of herself for a hot minute, she wouldn't appreciate her date admiring some-one else.

Brielle turned to Rusty. "You're interested in the Miles Road property?"

"Yep," he said. "It's a fine-lookin' plot of land. Not too far from my job."

Harper could practically see the dollar signs lighting up in Brielle's eyes. "And what do you do?" Brielle asked.

"I'm a mechanic."

"Oh." She glanced at Harper, then back at Rusty. "Well, Harper and I can discuss the particulars sometime tomorrow." She turned to Mason again. "We should be getting back to our table."

"Sure thing, babe." He nodded to Rusty, then turned to Harper. "Nice to meet you," he said, his gaze lingering on her. *More like leering.*

By the sudden fury crossing Brielle's face, she was now paying attention. But she was all smiles when she said goodbye to Rusty. "If the Miles Road property *doesn't* work out, I'm sure I can find you something else," she said, ignoring Harper completely before walking away.

Rusty turned to Harper, his bushy red brows knitted together. "That was, uh, something."

Harper seethed inside. The property was expensive, but Rusty could afford it. Instead of relishing watching Brielle deflate like a leaky party balloon when she heard Rusty's occupation, she was angry. How could she be so insulting to him? "I'm sorry about that," she said, her teeth clenched.

He met her gaze, storm clouds in his eyes. "You're sorry?" he said, sounding almost as mad as she felt. "It's not your fault that jerk couldn't keep his eyes off you."

Wait, he'd noticed that? And he was upset about it? "It's okay," she said, brushing off Mason's gross behavior.

"No, it ain't okay. He disrespected both of you."

Harper tensed. Was Rusty jealous? Jack sure was whenever another man noticed her and had reacted as if it were her fault. *"You're a babe,"* he'd said. *"And you're my babe, got it?"*

Ugh. So much for being "his." It didn't take him long to move on to Brielle.

"Hey," Rusty said. "You okay?"

She looked at him, searching his expression. But all she saw was frank concern, along with a trace of anger. Not a smidge of jealousy, though. That was refreshing. "I'm fine," she said, wanting to put the whole exchange behind her, at least for the rest of their meal. "Let's dig in to this pizza."

He glanced at the untouched pie. "Pretty sure it's cold by now. Want me to ask the waitress to warm it up?"

She eagerly reached for a slice. "Are you kidding? I love cold pizza."

"Me too."

As they ate the pizza—which was delicious

and enjoyed by Rusty—she fought to ignore Brielle and her creepy date, and her curiosity about why Brielle and Jack had broken up, then tried to figure out why she was wasting mental energy on either of them. *Focus on Rusty. He's your priority.* Up until Brielle showed up, it had been easy to do. But like she had so many times before, Brielle always ruined things.

When there were two pieces of pizza left, she asked for a box and the check. A few minutes later, the waitress put the slip of paper on the table. Rusty reached for it.

"This is on me," she said, grabbing the check before he could take it.

"But you made supper last time."

"I know, but tonight is a business dinner." She took a credit card out of her wallet and placed the check and card back on the table.

He shook his head. "All right, but next time I'm payin'."

A short while later, he pulled into the café parking lot. "Thanks for the pizza," he said, turning to her. "But I'm serious. Next time the meal is on me."

"All right, all right." She chuckled, finally feeling free of Brielle's presence, both physical and mental. "I won't argue with you."

"I should have your Merc done in a couple of days, Lord willin'. I can bring it to you and pick up Lois. How's she been holdin' up for you? Any problems?"

"Not a single one."

"Good ol' dependable Lois. Had her for over a decade, and she's never let me or anyone else down."

"Unlike my Mercedes." Harper sighed. "I wonder if I should trade her in on something more sensible—and reliable."

Rusty shook his head. "You don't have to do that just yet. She ain't got me beat. Haven't met a car that has, actually."

His tone wasn't bragging, just filled with the confidence of someone who knew he was good at his job. She'd had that confidence, too, up until recently. "I'll give you a call tomorrow once I hear from Brielle."

"Sounds good. Oh, wait." He scrambled out of the truck and to the passenger side. Then he opened the door. This time he held out his hand to help her out of the truck.

A warm sensation flowed through her as she slipped her hand into his. His palm was tough, calloused, and strong. She didn't need help getting out of the truck, but now that she knew he liked helping, she allowed him to. "Thank you," she said. Her foot hit the ground, and he let go of her hand.

He stepped back, and she slung her purse over her shoulder. Tonight had been nice. In fact, the whole time she'd spent with him was great, despite Brielle's interruption, and it was her fault she'd let the woman get to her. Again.

"See you later," he said.

His manners, combined with his buttery southern drawl, made her think that if he'd been wearing a cowboy hat, he would have tipped it at her. "I'll be in touch," she said and walked to her car. As she got inside, she glanced over her shoulder and saw him backing out of the parking space. She sighed.

Wait. Why was she sighing? Not over Rusty, that was for sure. She was tired, overworked, and unnerved by Brielle. Oh, and she had to call her mother now. All those things would make anyone let out a heavy-laden sigh.

But that wasn't the way she'd sighed. And the more she thought about Rusty, the more the warm feeling she'd experienced touching his hand spread to the rest of her.

She drove home, still thinking about Rusty—or more accurately, thinking about how he'd made her feel. As soon as she walked inside the house, her phone rang.

Couldn't she have a few moments to savor whatever this was she was savoring? Of course not. Grabbing her cell, she barely looked at the screen as she answered it, knowing it had to be Madge again. "Hello?" she snapped.

"Harper? Are you, like, okay?"

"Oh, sorry, Cammi." She cringed, regretting that she'd snapped at the head of the ALS gala volunteer committee. "I, uh, thought you were someone else."

"I know it's weird for me to call you in the evening. Can you talk for a minute?"

"Sure." She slipped off her shoes and walked over to the living room. She really didn't want to deal with Cammi right now, but she didn't want to be rude and put her off. "What's up?"

"Well, I don't mean to sound, you know, mean. But we've noticed you've missed the last three planning meetings for the ALS gala."

Harper cringed again. The gala had slipped her mind. "I know, and I'm sorry. I promise I'll be there for the next one. I've been so busy."

"Tell me about it. Like, I can barely keep my head above water right now. You wouldn't believe how crazy my schedule has been. Brooksy and I haven't had any time alone lately."

Harper rolled her eyes, picturing Cammi running her fingers through a lock of her straight brown hair as she complained about being busy as if she had an actual job. Her husband, Brooks, was a partner in his dad's firm in Hot Springs and made an obnoxious amount of money.

Cammi kept talking. "But we have our yearly trip to Aspen next month, so we'll get our, you know, alone time."

Harper put her feet up on the coffee table. "Are you staying at his parents' condo?"

"No. We bought one last year when we were there. Like I said to Brooksy, we might as well have our own. It's right next door to that actor who's in all those, like, superhero movies."

That narrowed it down to more than a dozen. "That's awesome, Cammi. I'm sure you and Brooksy, er, Brooks, will enjoy your time there."

"We always do. Anyway, I need to talk to you about, you know, the bachelor auction."

She sat up. "We're doing one this year?"

"Uh, yeah? We decided on it, like, meeting before last. Since then, we found all the bachelors. But one of them dropped out. Could you find a replacement?"

"Um . . ." When was she going to find time to do that?

"All of us on the committee figured you'd want to pitch in somehow."

Harper didn't miss the edge in Cammi's breezy tone. And Cammi was right, she hadn't been as involved in the ALS gala as she'd been in the past. "Sure. I'm happy to find someone."

"Awesome!" Cammi said. "Can you let us know, like, asap when you find him? We want to advertise who's in the auction."

"Of course. I'll get right on that."

"Thanks, Harper. I knew we could count on

you. I told everyone else that whoever you found would be, like, super hot."

"No pressure, then," she muttered.

"See ya next meeting." Cammi hung up.

Harper stared at her phone. Great, not only did she have to find a single guy, but he had to be *super hot*. She glanced through her phone contacts. There was Dylan, her med student friend who had bartended her business cocktail party last year. She grinned, remembering how she had planned to set Anita up with him, only to see that she and Tanner were totally into each other but acting like they weren't. Dylan was good looking and unattached, but he was also in his last year of residency, and she didn't want to interrupt that.

Then she thought of Kingston, who would definitely meet Cammi's standards. She found his number and called him even though there was a fifty-fifty chance of him picking up. He might be the only person who was busier than she was.

"Hey, Harper," he said when he answered.

"Oh good, I caught you. I have a favor to ask. Remember that ALS gala we went to a couple years ago?" she asked, then explained the bachelor auction. "Could I interest you in going up for bidding?"

"Normally, yes, especially for a good cause."

"Perfect. I can give you the details—"

"But I have to say no this time."

"What? Why?"

"I'm going to a pediatric conference that's been on my calendar for a year. I can't miss this one. It only meets every four years."

Well, that was disappointing, but she understood. "No problem, then. Do you have anybody in mind that I could ask? They need to be single," she added, leaving off the word *hot*. Who was hot and who was not was a matter of personal perception. Besides, the important thing was that the bachelors were nice and trustworthy.

"Not off the top of my head," he said. "But if someone comes to mind, I'll let you know."

"Thanks. I guess the hunt is still on."

"Good luck," he said, then hung up.

She looked back through her contacts again. Most of the names she didn't recognize right away since they were former clients. She really needed to clean up her list. Then she saw Rusty's name . . . and paused.

Rusty. Hmm. She tapped her phone against her chin. He was single. He was nice and trustworthy. Was he hot? Eh. Maybe not right now. *But could he be?*

She sat up and called his number. After two rings he answered. "Hi, Harper. Long time no hear."

She grinned at the corny joke. "Hey, I know we just saw each other, but an opportunity has come up."

"Oh? Did you talk to Brielle already?"

"Um, no. This is something completely different. How would you like to be auctioned off for charity?"

Silence. "Uh, what?"

"There's an ALS gala in two weeks." She gave him the same spiel she'd given Kingston. "I think you'd be perfect."

"I don't know," he said, speaking even slower than he normally did. "That gala sounds mighty fancy. I don't fit in with fancy so well."

She began to tell him it wasn't that fancy, but that would be a lie. The event was black tie, and while the bachelors didn't have to wear tuxedos, they at least had to wear suits. Did he even own a suit? Or a tie? She suspected he didn't have either.

Then she had another idea. "If you agree to being in the auction, I'll make sure you fit in."

"How?"

"You'll have to trust me."

Another long silence. "All right," he said. "I trust you, so I'll do it."

Harper sat back on the couch, smiling so much her mouth almost hurt. This was going to be great. Not only had she fulfilled her obligation to the planning committee in record time, but she'd also have a chance to do something she loved—giving makeovers. She'd already made over Riley for her first date with Hayden, and Anita when she helped cater her party. Now she would make Rusty look so good every woman in the room would bid on him . . . with the exception of her. No time and no money. And the idea of bidding on Rusty was absurd. She didn't date her clients, not even for charity.

"Harper? You still there?"

"Yes."

"I hope I'm doin' the right thing."

She smiled again. "You are, Rusty. I promise, you are."

Madge sat on her couch and stared at her phone, willing Harper to call her. It had been three hours since she'd talked to her, and she should have known better than to expect her to follow through. She got the message loud and clear: she was no longer part of her daughter's life.

She looked around the pristine living room at the cold white-and-gray décor. Don was a minimalist, and therefore Madge had been, too, with the exception of their vacation house on Lake Hamilton. Don had been so busy with work—and *other* things, she now knew—that he hadn't been available to give his input on the interior design. She didn't go wild with color, but she'd made sure that home was cozy and inviting, with a mix of textures, warm colors, and plenty of natural materials like wood and granite. After the house was finished, she'd always felt more at home there than here. But Don's work always took precedence before any leisure, and she hadn't wanted to spend weekends alone at what was supposed to be a family getaway.

Her heart squeezed in her chest, but she ignored the pain and reached for her phone. Just as she was about to set the device to Do Not Disturb, her landline rang. She jumped, the ring unfamiliar to her. Years ago Don had insisted on keeping the landline in case of emergency, and she rarely received calls from that number. She should ignore it, figuring the call was spam. But for some reason she answered. Out of boredom, or loneliness? Probably both.

"Hello?" she said.

"Is this Madge Wilson?"

She paused at the slick-sounding male voice speaking in her ear. Likely an insurance or warranty salesman, even though it was past nine on a Saturday night. Those cold callers didn't respect boundaries.

"If it is, I'm looking for Harper," he said, the words coming out in a rush.

She stilled. "Who is this?"

"My name is Jack Bell. I'm a . . . friend of Harper's."

Madge didn't recognize his name right away. Then again, other than Riley, Anita, and Olivia, she didn't know Harper's friends. Wait. Jack Bell . . . "Did you and Harper used to date?"

"Yes," he said, sounding relieved. "She, um, told you about me, then?"

"Once," Madge said, realizing that she hadn't heard Harper mention him after that initial time. Was that two years ago? Three? She couldn't remember. Not only had Harper mentioned Jack that day, but Don had called Madge right before lunch and said he'd be gone for an extra five days after being gone for two weeks already. She'd been so angry with him for not coming home she was surprised she remembered anything Harper had said.

"I've been trying to reach her, but she's not returning my calls."

"How did you find me?" she said.

"Harper talked about you when we were dating. Madge isn't all that common a name." He paused. "You're listed in the white pages on the internet."

She sat up straight. "If my daughter isn't returning your calls, I'm sure there's good reason. And I don't appreciate you looking up my information and calling me late on a Saturday night."

"I'm sorry," he said, his tone urgent. "I wouldn't do this if it wasn't important. Very important. I tried calling her office, but I didn't get through. I don't want to show up there unannounced. She'd probably throw me out. She'd have good reason to."

Madge frowned. What had gone on between these two? Her protective instincts kicked in.

"Don't call this number again." She unplugged the phone, then grabbed her cell and quickly dialed Harper's number. It went straight to voice mail. No surprise there. "Harper, call me as soon as you get this message." She clicked off the phone. Then her finger hovered over the screen. Should she call Don? She shook her head and shut down the cell in case Jack had somehow found this number too. She was used to handling things alone. As soon as she spoke with Harper, she'd tell her about Jack. But Don didn't need to know. He didn't *deserve* to know.

She stared at the phone again, second-guessing herself. But it didn't last long. She tossed her cell on the acrylic table. Don had never been interested in being a husband, or a parent, before. It was too late for him to start now.

Chapter 9

"Well, lookee there, if it ain't the bachelor of the year!"

Rusty rolled his eyes at Senior, then poured himself a bowl of cornflakes. He'd known he would regret telling his grandfather about agreeing to the ALS bachelor auction, and sure enough, he did. When Senior had arrived home Saturday night, it was past eleven, and he'd been so tired he'd gone straight to bed. On Sunday they had gone to church, and Rusty was a little disappointed not to see Harper there. She always sat on the opposite side of the sanctuary with her friends and their spouses. Funny how everyone at church had their unofficial official seats. Even Senior sat in the same spot he always had, in the back next to Jasper, while Rusty sat in his usual spot on the left side, sixth pew back next to Percy and Hank.

On the way home, Senior had asked about the house hunting. Rusty had filled him in, then let it slip about Harper's request. Big mistake.

"For the last time, it's just an auction. No 'bachelor of the year' stuff." He added skim milk to the bowl, said a quick prayer of thanks for his breakfast, then proceeded to eat.

Senior filled a mug with *Rusty's Garage* printed

on the side with black coffee, then sat down opposite Rusty. "I'm just joshin' ya, Rusty. No need to get so bent out of shape."

"I'm not bent— Oh, forget it." He shoveled a huge spoonful of the flakes into his mouth.

His grandfather picked up the mug and took a sip. "Good coffee. You always did make the best."

"Thanks," Rusty said, his voice muffled. He swallowed the cereal. "Are you coming to the shop today?"

"Of course. Can't wait to jaw with my friends, you know."

"Do you mind workin' the desk? I've got a part comin' in, and as soon as it arrives I need it."

"Sure. What's it for?"

"A Mercedes." He kept his head down and quickly finished the rest of his breakfast.

Senior frowned. "We don't work on foreign cars."

He slurped down the remaining milk, then popped up from his seat. "This is an exception."

"An exception?"

Rusty set the bowl in the sink and wiped off his mouth with the kitchen towel lying on the counter. "If you're gonna go to work with me, you better get ready."

Senior gestured to his red *Rusty's Garage* shirt and jeans. "Ready whenever you are, boss."

They were both quiet on the short ride to the

garage. The auction was still on Rusty's mind. He should have told Harper no. He had zero business or interest in being on stage or whatever and having women bid on him. He'd only said yes for two reasons: he was always happy to help out a charity, and Harper had sounded desperate. Still, he should have refused.

"Does this fancy ball need any more bachelors?" Senior asked as they turned into the garage lot.

"It's not a ball. It's a gala."

"What's the difference?"

Rusty shrugged. "No idea." He glanced at his grandfather. "Do you know someone who can take my place?"

"No. But maybe they could auction off an older gentleman. You know, to liven things up."

Rusty pulled into the space by the garage, put the truck in Park, then turned to his grandfather. "Are you talkin' about Jasper?"

"Jasper?" Senior laughed. "If I volunteered him for something like that, I'd be drivin' our fifty-year friendship right into the ditch." He straightened in his seat and tugged on the collar of his work shirt. "I was referrin' to myself."

Now it was Rusty's turn to laugh. "Good one, Senior."

His grandfather cast him a side eye. "I'm serious. I'm ready to mingle."

Rusty's laughter disappeared. "You are?"

"Yep."

"But what about G'ma?"

Senior's eyes grew soft. "I still love her, Rusty. And miss her. She's always right here." With two fingers he tapped his heart. "But she wouldn't want me to be alone. Truth be told, I don't want to be alone either. I'm not talkin' about finding true love at a bachelor's auction. That's just foolish talk. But I wouldn't mind spending an evenin' with a female companion every once in a while."

Rusty wasn't sure how he felt about this. He'd never thought about Senior wanting companionship with a woman. But he also understood it because that was something he wanted too. "Do you really want to do this?"

"Yep."

"Good, you can take my place."

"Oh no, that's not goin' to happen." Senior folded his hands over his chest, his forearms resting on his slightly rounded belly. "A Jenkins man is a man of his word. Your yes means yes, and you're not backin' out."

"Fine," Rusty said, blowing out a frustrated breath. "It was worth a shot. All right, I'll see what I can do."

"That'll be dandy, son." Senior opened the truck door. "Just dandy. Whatever happens, it's gonna be a lark."

Rusty stayed back, still stunned that his

grandfather wanted to participate in the auction. Then he shook his head and chuckled. Of course Senior would be game for this. He'd have a lot of attention on him, something he never shied away from. Not to mention he already had a good attitude and was geared up for the event to be fun. Rusty wished he had his confidence.

The morning went by at a brisk pace. The part for the Merc showed up an hour after the garage opened, and it didn't take long for Rusty to get the car up and running. Around eleven he called Harper. When she didn't answer, he sent her a text.

> Your car is ready. Let me know when I can bring it over.

An hour later, while he worked under the hood of Pastor Jared's Dodge Neon, his cell rang. After wiping his greasy hands on an old rag, he reached into his pants pocket and pulled out the phone. "Hey, Harper," he answered after seeing her name pop up on the screen.

"Hi, Rusty. My car is running now?"

"Took it for a test drive, and she runs fine. Hopefully this is the last fix she'll need for a long time."

"I hope so too. I'm at the office, so you can drop the car off whenever you can. Also, I found two more houses for you to look at. I have some time around noon today if you're free."

Rusty thought for a moment. They had one car up on the rack and an oil change waiting in the parking lot. Percy and Hank could take care of those while he was gone for an hour or two. "Sure. I'll be there around twelve."

"See you then."

He went to the office, where Senior sat talking to Granger Hendricks, the Maple Falls police chief. He waited for his grandfather to take a breath, then said, "I've got an appointment at noon. Could you take care of the oil change for me?"

Senior's eyes lit up. "Sure can." He turned to Granger. "Hate to cut this short, but I got work to do."

Granger nodded, his usually stern expression showing a hint of a smile. Whenever the man was around the mayor, Granger jumped at his command. But to everyone's surprise the sheriff had quietly gone along with the fall parade idea, even offering his and his deputies' services during the afternoon. "You better hop to it, then." Granger gave Rusty a nod and walked out of the office.

Rusty finished up Pastor Jared's car, washed up in the bathroom, wished he had brought a brush with him to smooth down his hair, gave up on taming it, then drove the Mercedes to Harper's office. When he walked inside, he immediately felt out of place. The décor in her office was similar to her home. Lots of white and lots of opportunities to literally leave his mark on something. A glass and chrome desk was situated in the center of the room near the back wall, the chair behind it empty. He stood and waited for the receptionist to come to the front.

A few minutes later Harper appeared. "Hey, Rusty," she said, her heels clicking against the gray wood-planked floor. She grinned. "I'm so excited to get my car back."

"I'm sure you are." He dangled the keys in front of her.

She took them, then gave him the key to Lois. "Mind if we take my car?"

"Nope. I expected you'd want to." Which was why he'd put a clean towel down on the passenger seat so he wouldn't get it dirty. As they walked outside to the Merc, he said, "There's a bill in the glove box for the part. I do have to charge you for that."

"What about labor?"

"Don't worry 'bout that. Workin' on that car is like takin' a mechanics class." He opened the driver-side door for her, then got into the car on the passenger side. She started the Merc, and it purred like a contented kitten. "Ah," she said, leaning back against the white leather seat. "Perfect."

"She sounds good, doesn't she?" Rusty couldn't help but smile. She really did love this car, and he was glad he'd made her happy. It felt good. No, better than good. *Satisfying.* "Have you thought of a name for her yet?"

"I haven't had a chance to think about that. After I went back home Saturday night, I fell asleep on my couch. I didn't realize I was that tired. Then yesterday I had an old client call me. He wasn't looking for a house, but he referred one of his friends, so I spent the whole day taking her around Hot Springs."

"How did that go?"

Harper looked at him, and he thought he saw a flash of weariness in her eyes. Then she went back to her usual bright self. "Not great. She's thinking about one of them, though, so that's good."

"We don't have to go lookin' at houses today," he said, not wanting to put her out after such a busy weekend.

"Yes, we do." She put the car in gear. "I never heard from Brielle," she said. "I did leave two more messages for her, though."

He scratched his chin through his beard. "She did say she was busy."

Harper glanced at him again as she put the car back into Park. She turned and looked at him. "I need to tell you something about her," she said. "Just know I don't ever talk about other agents with my clients. Not personally, anyway. But I want to be up-front with you."

He'd noticed the tension between the women the other night, but he'd chalked that up to Mason and his wayward eyes. "Okay."

"I'm not sure she's going to call me back."

That surprised him. "Why not?"

Harper sighed. "Because you're a mechanic, and that property is expensive."

"So?"

"She thinks you can't afford it."

He sat back against the seat. "I reckon that's not so smart of her."

"It's definitely not." She opened her mouth, then closed it. Then opened it again. Closed it a second time. Then she finally spoke. "I'll keep after her. I'll go to her office if I have to."

Harper didn't look too excited about the prospect, though. He thought about telling her never mind, but he knew she would protest. He wanted the property, and she wanted the sale. She didn't seem like the kind of person to back down from a snobby agent anyway.

She punched some coordinates into the GPS, and they were off. "We should be there in fifteen minutes or so," she said. "This house is about four miles outside of town. Four thousand square feet, so there's a lot of room. Four bedrooms, three baths, an office, two fireplaces, an outdoor kitchen, and a swimming pool. No stairs. It just came on the market and is new construction. I think you'll like it, and it's well below your price range."

"That sounds like a lot of house." Two fireplaces? A swimming pool?

"It is, but you said you needed more room. This has plenty."

"All right." She was the expert.

"You don't sound so sure."

He'd have to do a better job hiding his cards. "I guess I didn't think about buying something so big and . . ."

"Extra?"

"Yeah."

She grinned. "If you think that's extra, I should take you to see some of the houses in your upper price range. There are some that are ten thousand square feet and more."

"That's enough to fit two families."

"People like to have their space."

He didn't know what it was like to have that much space. Growing up in his house, his family barely had to yell in order to be heard throughout. Even when he thought about building on the Miles Road property, he was thinking about something on a smaller scale.

"If you don't want to see it, I can cross it off the list," Harper said.

"No, don't do that." He rubbed his chin again. "I'd like to see it."

"Are you sure?"

"Yes." She'd found the house. The least he could do was not dismiss it before he saw it. "Let's go for it."

She laughed and turned on the radio. Soft rock played through the speakers, and neither of them felt the need to talk.

He looked out the window at the passing landscape for a moment, then thought of Senior and his eagerness to be a part of the auction. Oh boy. Well, the sooner he told Harper, the sooner she could tell him thanks but no thanks. She was turning down a short street with a cul-de-sac when he said, "Um, about that gala . . ."

"You're not backing out, are you?" She pulled into a driveway.

"Can I?" he asked, a ray of hope on the horizon.

She shook her head. "Nope."

Nuts. "It was worth a shot," he mumbled, then added, "I found someone else who's interested in bein' a bachelor."

Harper put the car in Park and shut off the engine. "We can always use more. Who is it?"

"My grandfather."

Harper's mouth dropped open. "Senior?" she said, not sure she'd heard Rusty correctly. "He wants to be auctioned off?"

"Yep." Rusty raised his hand. Grease was embedded under the nails. "I promise. It was his idea."

Now this was an interesting development. "That would sure shake things up. In a good way," she added, smiling. "The gala committee will love it. I'll let them know we'll have an extra bachelor. I like his gumption."

"He's always had plenty of that." Rusty stared down at his worn work jeans. "Wish he'd passed a little bit on to me."

"You have gumption too." A strong breeze blew against the car. This was a newly developed neighborhood, and the builders had cut down most of the trees, so there was little shielding against the autumn wind. "Not everyone owns their own business."

"I'm not talkin' about business," he said, an atypical bite to his tone. He opened the car door.

"Hey." She put her hand on his bare arm. How he wasn't cold on a day like today she had no idea, but his skin felt warm. "Are you okay?"

He looked at her and nodded. "Just a little nervous about the auction, that's all."

"It's two weeks away."

"I know." He rubbed his palms over his pants legs.

His anxiety threw her for a little loop. He was always so confident. Even when he told her at the pizzeria about that horrible date he'd had, he'd shrugged off the woman's rudeness like it was no big deal. Clearly the auction was, though. "You don't have a thing to worry about. You'll have plenty of women throwing their money at you. Not in a creepy way, though," she added quickly. "Just wanted to make that clear."

Rusty sat back in the seat and shut the door. "I need to level with you, Harper. I don't think I can go through with the gala."

"Rusty—"

"It's nice that you think women will want to go out with me. That's not been my experience, though."

Her heart squeezed. It couldn't be easy for him to talk about this. She was well aware of men and their egos. As a businessperson she'd dealt with enough of them, even though there were more female real-estate agents than male in the area. Not to mention there were several female ones whose egos rivaled the men. Like Brielle. "Remember what I said the other night?" she asked, kicking her nemesis out of her mind before she grew angry again about Brielle blowing her off this morning. "For you to trust me?"

He nodded.

"I meant that." Right now wasn't the time to bring up the makeover, and they still had another house to look at after this one. And there wasn't much to make over, anyway. A shave, haircut, and new outfit was all he'd need. She thought about offering the same service to Senior, but unless he showed up wearing a barrel and suspenders, he'd be fine. The crowd was going to love both of them. "I never let anyone down," she said. "Seriously. Just ask my family and friends."

Finally he smiled. "All right. You know what you're doin', so I'll let this drop."

"That's what I want to hear."

Unsurprisingly, the first house they toured wasn't what Rusty wanted, and neither was the second one. By the time they arrived back at her office, he had to go back to work. "Don't feel bad about today," he told her. "It's just hard for anything else to live up to Miles Road."

"And we'll get to see that one, I promise. I'll talk to you soon."

"Thanks, Harper." He got out of her Mercedes and walked over to Lois, where he turned and waved, then unlocked the driver-side door and got in. Harper smiled as she watched him drive away. He was so genuine, and it couldn't have been easy for him to admit his lack of confidence about the auction. Maybe he would find a girlfriend at the gala, one who was deserving of him.

Her smile faded as a pang of . . . something sprung up in her heart at the thought of him with another woman. Envy? No, that couldn't be it. She wanted him to be happy, the same as she wanted for her other friends. But she'd never felt like this when Riley and Anita had started dating their husbands.

She shook her head. What was she doing, sitting in her car wasting time? She got out of her Mercedes and walked through the back entrance of her office. When she went to Sharon's desk to check for voice mails, she froze. Madge was sitting in one of the chairs in the waiting room. Oh no. She'd forgotten to lock her office door. And had completely forgotten to call her mom . . . again. Her mother's last message had said it was an emergency, and just as she was about to phone her back, she'd gotten a call from yet another client who'd decided not to renew his listing with her, and that had sent her brain off track . . . again. "Mom," she said, rushing to her. "I'm so sorry I didn't call you—"

"I waited to make an appointment with your receptionist, but it appears she's not here."

As her mother stood, her expression remained impassive, her eyes cold. Harper braced herself for one of the calm yet acidic guilt trips Madge was famous for. *I definitely deserve it this time.*

"She's off today," Harper said. *And the rest of the week.* Harper had had to cut her hours, and she was teetering on the edge of having to let her go. But Madge didn't need to know about that. "I really am sorry I didn't call."

"I understand. You've been busy with work." Madge tucked her hair behind her ear.

Wow. Faint acknowledgment, but Harper would take it. She still remembered the day her mother

161

had expressed her disapproval about Harper opening her own business only three years into being a real-estate agent. "That's too soon," she'd said. "You should wait until you have more experience."

Madge's lack of support had poked a hole in Harper's enthusiasm, but she hadn't let that stop her. But what if her mother had been right? Should she have waited longer before going out on her own? She was so tired and starting to feel the *D* word—discouraged. Then again, she'd been extremely successful until this past June, enough that she'd been ready to buy #6 until the slump happened.

Temporary slump, remember?

"Too busy to have time for you own mother, obviously," Madge said.

And there went the good feelings. "I have time now." She didn't, but she couldn't send her mother away. "Why don't we go into my office—"

"No need. I stopped by to let you know that Jack called me the other night."

"Jack Bell?" Harper tensed.

"He called the landline after he found my number on the internet." Her mother's hardened facade slipped slightly. "Are you in trouble, Harper?"

"No, of course not." She tried not to grind her teeth together. How dare Jack contact her family?

"I'll talk to him," she said. Not like she had a choice now. "He won't bother you again."

Madge didn't respond, as if she was waiting for Harper to give a more complete explanation. And she was tempted to. But this was her problem, not her mother's. She had to deal with Jack herself.

Madge glanced at the floor, then returned her gaze to Harper, her eyes icy cold again. "Your father and I are getting a divorce."

Harper's knees almost buckled, and she had to lean on Sharon's desk for support. No segue from Jack? Just *Oh, by the way, we're getting divorced?* "You're . . . you're *what?*" she said, her problems with Jack flying out of her brain.

"Getting divorced."

"*That's* what you wanted to talk to me about? Over the phone?"

"I had planned to discuss the topic over coffee, but you wouldn't call me back."

Harper's throat started to close. "Don't you think that we should have a discussion like that in private?"

"You've been *very* busy."

"I would have made time for this." Harper went to the front door and flipped over the sign, locked the door, then faced Madge again. "Why?"

"Couples grow apart." Her mother brushed the side of her hand over her gray wool jacket.

"I thought you two were rekindling things. That's why you went on all those trips."

"There's nothing to rekindle, Harper. It's over. You need to accept that. I'm also putting the house on the market."

"I can't sell the house I grew up in!"

"Don't worry about that," Madge said, her tone so detached they might as well be discussing how much two and two equaled. "I'll use another agent. Do you have any recommendations?"

A knock sounded on the glass front door. Harper jumped, then turned around to see her father standing outside, trying to open the door. He'd never even been to her office before.

They've both gone crazy.

"What is he doing here?" Madge said, backing away until the desk stopped her.

"Maddie, please." Don's voice sounded muffled through the thick glass. "I need to talk to you."

Madge held up her hand. "Don't let him in. I don't want to talk to him."

"Please . . ." He looked at Harper and held up his hands. "Open the door, Harper. I'll explain everything."

Her gaze darted between her desperate father and her furious mother. Suddenly she was transported to her childhood, reliving all the tugs-of-war between her parents at warp speed. Don's apologies for coming home late again from an out-of-town trip, Madge's passive-aggressive response, always using Harper as a shield: *You missed your daughter's science fair/ballet recital/*

*homecoming/prom . . . high school gradua-
tion.*" Tears stung her eyes. She was well into
adulthood, but being sandwiched between her
mother and father made her feel like that child all
over again.

"Harper, open the door." Don's voice turned
razor sharp.

"Don't you dare," Madge snapped.

Her mother's order brought Harper back to
reality. "This is ridiculous." She unlocked the
door and threw it open.

Don blew by her and went straight to Madge.
"You hung up on me last week, and now you
won't answer my calls anymore."

Madge lifted her chin. "That's my prerogative."

He spread out his arms, his face full of frus-
tration. "Why are you being so unreasonable?"

"Me?" Madge pressed her hand to her chest.
"You're the one who's *following* me."

"Because you refuse to talk!"

For a moment Harper thought her mother was
going to explode, something she'd never done
before.

But Madge straightened her shoulders. "All
further discussion will be through my attorney
tomorrow morning. Nine a.m. sharp." She
breezed past him and walked out the door without
giving Harper a second glance.

Don ran his fingers through his still thick hair
that had turned gray a few years ago. "She's

impossible," he muttered, starting to pace. "And stubborn. And nonsensical."

"Dad," Harper said.

He stopped pacing and shot a look at her. "What?"

"Is this why you called me the other day? To tell me . . ." She swallowed the lump at the base of her throat. "You and Mom are divorcing?"

"I called to ask you to talk some sense into her."

She almost laughed at that. She'd never been able to talk her mother into, or out of, anything. Madge wanted her daughter to go to private school? Harper went to private school. She wanted her daughter to have straight As? Harper had straight As. She wanted her daughter to be successful? Harper was always working on that too. She didn't want to disappoint either one of them. How ironic. Her mother was constantly disappointed, and her father was still in his own world.

Don went to her. "You've got to help me, Harper. I don't want a divorce. I love your mother. She's the best thing that's ever happened to me."

"Then why is she angry with you?"

Don's handsome face buckled. "That's between the two of us."

Harper crossed her arms over her chest. "But you want me to get into the middle of this."

"I don't want you to. I have no choice."

The phone on Sharon's desk started to ring. Harper's temples throbbed. "Dad, I—"

"Can't even help your old man?"

The ringing sound of the phone echoed in the small office as Harper composed herself. She was being manipulated . . . again. Both of her parents were masters at it. Unfortunately, she wasn't immune, not after getting hit with the news of their split. "I'll see what I can do," she said quietly.

"You're the best." Her father leaned over and kissed her on the cheek before dashing out of the office.

Harper let the phone go to voice mail and plopped down in one of the plush, faded-rose-colored chairs in the waiting room that she'd paid more than a pretty penny for. She rubbed her forehead. *Divorce.* The shock was starting to wear off. If her mother had told her this two years ago, she wouldn't have been surprised. But lately she'd thought they were reconnecting. Maybe that had been the plan. If it was, it had evidently fallen through. How could Harper be so out of touch that she had no idea they were still at odds? Her mother had pointed out Harper's busyness, but it wasn't like her parents had been available either.

Be strong. I have to be strong.

How many times during her childhood years

had she told herself those words? And they were always true. She couldn't fall apart when her parents were disintegrating. And in the past, whenever they were angry with each other, they always made up. Surely they would this time too. Maybe she was a little less sure than usual, considering they actually had lawyers involved, but that didn't mean they weren't going to reconcile. Either way, she didn't want to be part of their drama. Like her dad said, this was between him and her mother. She didn't like going back on her word, but she refused to stand in the middle of their fight this time.

Composing herself, Harper stood and walked down the short hallway to her office. She had enough things to do without worrying about her parents' relationship. They were adults. They'd figure it out.

They always do.

Chapter 10

The next morning, Madge sat in the parking lot of her lawyer's office building, the three-story architectural design straight out of the early seventies. Her heart hammered in her chest. She hadn't expected Don to chase her down yesterday. How did he know she was at Harper's office? Not that it wasn't a good guess. Other than home, there weren't too many places she went to lately.

For a split second she considered talking to him. But she had to remain firm. He knew her weaknesses and how to exploit them. He'd been doing it for thirty years.

She flipped down the car's visor, took the tube of nude-pink lipstick out of her purse, and touched up her lips, noticing the wrinkles around her mouth. Perhaps she would have a face-lift once the divorce was final. If her lawyer was successful, she'd have enough in alimony to lift her face, breasts, buttocks, and all her other sagging body parts. What was a new life without a new body?

But the idea of surgery didn't stem her anxiety. Besides, she was terrified of needles.

Madge picked up her purse and exited her car, then headed for Ms. Clair Pressman's office.

She'd only talked to the woman over the phone, and she liked what she'd heard—cold but polite, calculated but realistic: *"I'll make sure you get what you deserve, Mrs. Wilson. That's a promise."* Madge didn't doubt a single word.

Her hand touched the handle on one of the dark-brown double doors.

"Maddie! Madge!"

She froze, refusing to turn around. She should have known he would continue to make this difficult. *He's not worried about losing you. He doesn't want to lose his money or his dignity.* She had to remember that. Ignoring him, she opened the door and hurried to the elevator. When it opened, she rushed inside and pushed the third-floor button.

A hand pressed against the closing doors, pulling them apart. Don jumped in, then hit the Stop button.

"You can't just stop the elevator," she said, unable to hide her shock. "I'm sure there's a law against that."

"I can and I did."

She turned to him, expecting to see his smug, still handsome face sneering down at her. What she saw was the complete opposite. His short-cut hair was disheveled, his expensive clothing wrinkled, his gray-blue eyes bleary. She'd been too shocked and angry with him yesterday to notice those details. Then again, he'd been living in a hotel room since she kicked him out. She reached to release the Stop button, but he jumped in front of her, blocking it.

"Move," she said, refusing to meet his gaze.

"Not until we talk."

She crossed her arms. "Then I guess we're stuck here."

"I guess we are."

Her arms dropped. "You can't hold me or this elevator hostage."

His eyes pleaded with her. "Then talk to me. Not with our lawyers. Just you and me."

"I . . . I can't." Feeling her resolve slipping, she turned her back on him.

Don let out a long sigh. "How did we get here, Madge?"

She stiffened. "Why don't you ask Veronica?"

"That was a mistake. I admit it."

"What was the mistake, exactly? When you and she first got together or when you went back to her last year?"

"I didn't go back to her."

"And I'm supposed to believe you," she huffed.

He hung his head. "I'm so sorry, Madge. Sorry and ashamed. I never should have had the affair."

"Is that supposed to make me feel better? Because it doesn't."

His voice was low as he moved to stand behind her. "Veronica's not the problem. Only a symptom."

When his hands touched her shoulders, she closed her eyes. He was right. She knew that deep down. But she hadn't gone out and had an on-and-off affair for seven years. Of course, having a dalliance was easier for him. There were plenty of pretty flight attendants around, something that had always bothered her about his job. She had worried for years that he would cheat and had expressed that concern to him twice during their marriage. Both times he'd denied he'd cheated on her. *"I love only you,"* he'd said during one of the times they were in a good place. *"I want only you."*

"Stop it," she said, coming back to the present and shrugging his hands off her shoulders. She whirled to face him, fury rushing through her like a flooding river. "If you don't leave me alone, I'll get a restraining order."

His face went white. "You'd call the police on me?"

"Yes." Her chin lifted high. "I would."

His gaze held hers again, his eyes filled with confusion and exasperation. "So you're not willing to work on our relationship?"

"There is no relationship anymore. I don't think there ever was. Not a real one." *Not a loving one.*

"Mad . . . Madge," he said, his shoulders drooping. "I'm only asking for a chance to make things right. I was going to tell you about

Veronica when the time was right. I didn't want that secret between us anymore."

"And yet I had to find out for myself. We've been almost inseparable for the past two years, and you never said a single word about her. Not before we went on that cruise last year, or that trip to the Smoky Mountains the year before. Or when we traveled to Maine, New York City, Los Angeles . . ." She stopped, realizing something. He'd showered her with trips since his retirement, places she'd always wanted to go but never could because of her devotion to Harper. He'd told her he was making up for being away all that time during their marriage. Now she knew the truth—he was assuaging his guilt. All those romantic overtures, those nights together when she thought they were reconnecting . . . falling back in love . . . It had all been a ruse to make him feel better. Even confessing his sins was about his guilt. He didn't care how it made her feel.

She turned to the elevator doors and started pounding on them. "Help! Help me!"

"Madge, stop—"

"Somebody help me!"

"All right!" He clicked the button, and the elevator started moving. "You win," he said, slumping against the back of the elevator. "You'll get your divorce. Happy now?"

Her chest heaved as she fought for the air his

words had sucked out of the enclosed space. "Yes," she breathed. "I am."

Don smoothed the top of his hair, then straightened his clothes. By the time the elevator door opened, he was nearly as put together as he typically was. The only thing missing was his pilot's uniform.

How handsome he always looked in it.

Without a word he stormed out into the hallway.

She paused, trying to get her bearings. As the elevator door started to close, she jumped out. *"Happy now?"* His words pounded in her head.

Swallowing her emotions was so second nature to her that she didn't even think about it as she walked into Ms. Pressman's waiting room. It was empty. Where was Don? Had he disappeared down the stairs, reneging on their meeting again? That would be so like him. Only thinking about himself.

"Are you Mrs. Wilson?" the receptionist asked, getting up from her chair.

"Yes. I have an appointment with—"

"Right this way." The thin woman gave her a worried look behind red glasses that had a chain hanging from both sides, then headed through a doorway.

As she followed, Madge fought for her equanimity. How dare Don pull this stunt right before their meeting with the lawyers? It was all a ruse to keep her off balance, she was sure of that.

If she was upset, she might agree to an unfair settlement to get him out her life. Tempting, but it wouldn't work.

I'm going to make him pay.

She entered a large conference room, and a smartly dressed woman with straight auburn hair cut into a sharp, chin-length bob walked over to her, extending her pale, thin hand. "Hi, Mrs. Wilson. Clair Pressman. Glad to finally meet you in person."

As Madge shook her hand, she spied Don pacing back and forth near the large window. So he was here after all. Another gentleman sat at the table scribbling something on his yellow legal pad. He glanced at Don, frowned, and scribbled something again.

"Would you like anything to drink before we start?" Ms. Pressman asked. "And please, call me Clair."

"No, thank you." Madge touched her naked earlobe, just realizing that she had forgotten to put on her earrings. She was never without earrings. "I want to get this over with."

"Have a seat." Clair motioned to a comfortable-looking short-backed leather chair. "Mr. Wilson, we're ready to begin."

Madge sat down and placed her purse in her lap as Clair sat down beside her. Don continued to pace. What was he up to now?

"Mr. Wilson." The man sitting across from

Clair got up from the table. "I need you to sit down now, please."

Don halted. Spun on one heel. "She can have everything."

"What?" Clair, Madge, and Don's attorney all said at the same time.

"This is my fault." He walked to the table but didn't pull out the chair. "I cheated on my wife. Now I can see there's no turning back. So Madge can have whatever she wants. The lake house, our house, the cars, my pension." He waved his hand. "It's all hers."

"Mr. Wilson," the lawyer said, hurrying to his side. "Let's not be hasty—"

"Call me when you've drawn up the paperwork, Barry." He kept his gaze on Madge as he spoke. "I'll sign whatever you put in front of me." Then he walked out of the room.

Barry turned to Madge and Clair and held out his palms. "I'll go talk to him—"

"Ah, ah, ah." Clair held up her index finger, the short nail colored in sheer beige polish. "You heard what Mr. Wilson said. He wants to give my client everything."

Madge blinked, the full impact of what Don said hitting her. If he gave her everything, what would he have left? "But—"

"Mrs. Wilson," Clair said, putting her hand lightly but firmly on Madge's forearm. "I'll do the negotiating. That's what you pay me for."

The bald spot on the top of Barry's head turned bright red, along with his ears. "I can assure you my client isn't going to give Mrs. Wilson *everything,* regardless of what he said today." He picked up his legal pad off the table, then his briefcase from the floor. "I'll be in touch."

Once Barry was gone, Clair's lips curled into a grin. "That was easy," she said, her voice almost purring. "He admitted to cheating, and he's not going to contest the divorce. He also said he's willing to give you everything. Even if he changes his mind, we can use that against him."

A sour feeling churned in Madge's stomach. "I—I don't understand," she whispered. She knew how important money was to Don. It was why he'd insisted on working so many hours. That and using the time to have the affair. But even thinking of him sleeping with another woman didn't cut through the confusion. This wasn't like Don. He didn't give up easily, and he never gave in completely.

"I've seen this before, Mrs. Wilson." Clair turned in her chair, the cool, satisfied expression still on her face. "He's pretending to be generous to soften you up. Then, when it comes to hashing out the fine details, he'll turn on you. Don't fall for it."

Madge stared at the handle of her purse. She had no idea what to think. This was the last thing she expected Don to do. And although she needed to keep Clair's words in the forefront of her mind, she remembered the defeat in his eyes when he left the elevator. *"Happy now?"*

"Don't worry, Mrs. Wilson." Clair rose from her chair. "I'll handle this, and we'll keep in touch. This is the first meeting in the process, but I think it went very well."

Numb, Madge stood and walked out of the office, then left the building. Don's Lexus wasn't in the parking lot. Crisp brown leaves whirled around her ankles as she made her way to her car and got in. She should be relieved Don had admitted the affair and that he wasn't going to contest anything. Actually, she should be happy.

But she wasn't. Not even close.

"I'm sorry I'm late!" Harper rushed through the back door of Knots and Tangles to see Riley, Olivia, and Anita already seated for their weekly girlfriend meeting. "I had to stop by home after work, and I lost track of time."

"You lost track of your shoes too." Riley gestured to Harper's feet.

She looked down and saw one red high-heeled pump on her right foot and a purple one on her left. Good grief, how had she missed wearing two different shoes? Granted, they were the same type of shoe, and she'd bought three pairs in different colors, the third one canary yellow. Oh well, no one else would see her mistake except her friends.

"I brought y'all a treat," she said, putting the plastic cupcake carrier she held on the coffee table next to a half-filled bowl of pretzel twists and a container of cheese dip. She pulled off the cover, revealing a dozen carrot-cake cupcakes smothered with cream-cheese frosting.

"Those look amazing." Anita leaned forward. "Where did you get them?"

"I made them." Harper removed her red-and-silver scarf and stuffed it into the pocket of her coat, then slipped it off her shoulders. She draped it over the back of one of the comfy chairs, sat down, and placed her phone on her lap.

"You *baked?*" Olivia's eyebrows lifted.

"I didn't know you knew how to turn on an oven." Riley grinned.

Harper rolled her eyes. "Very funny. I used to bake all the time before I got so busy with my business."

After yesterday's bombshell from her parents, she'd closed her office for the rest of the day, gone home, and baked up a storm. In addition to the cupcakes, she'd made a loaf of yeast bread, two dozen chocolate-chip cookies, and a scrumptious chess pie. She'd also downed a whole pot of coffee last night, and because of that she was operating on two hours of sleep. She half expected one or both parents to call her, but neither one did. Hopefully no news was good news.

Today she had planned to call Jack but instead spent the day doing paperwork she'd put off for too long. Actually that was an excuse. She'd need all her emotional resources to talk to him, and they were in short supply at the moment. Besides, if Jack attempted to contact her mother again, Madge would definitely put him in his place.

"Y'all don't be shy," she said, her smile so wide it stretched her cheeks. "Help yourself."

Anita leaned against the back of the couch. "I already filled up on snacks." She gestured to the food on the table that also included a small fruit tray and pumpkin-shaped cookies that looked so good they had to be from the café. Riley and Olivia nodded their agreement.

"Then take some home with you. I've already had my fair share." Three to be exact, and she didn't need to eat any more of them—not when she'd also had a large piece of the chess pie. That combined with the caffeine from the coffee had given her a killer case of indigestion that also contributed to her lack of sleep.

"Thanks, Harper. Hayden will devour these." Riley smiled.

"So will Tanner," Anita added.

Olivia looked at the cupcakes. "I'll take one before I leave."

"Thank you." She'd figure out what to do with the rest of them later. "Again, I'm sorry I'm late. I'm here, though. Does that count?"

"Of course it does," Anita said, her brow furrowing. "You look a little tired, though."

"Baking wore me out," Harper said, waving her hand. "I'm not used to being so domestic."

Riley cracked a smile as she crossed her legs, revealing the purple, orange, and black hand-knitted socks she was wearing with her ever-present Birkenstock sandals.

Cute. "What did I miss?" Harper asked.

"We bagged all the candy for the parade," Olivia said. "And we were just about to vote on our name."

"For the thousandth time," Anita mumbled.

Olivia scoffed. "It hasn't been that many."

"Close to it," Riley said dryly.

"What are the choices?" Harper was eager to see if any iteration of the words *Ladies* and *Latte* were involved.

"The Lattes," Olivia said, smiling at Harper. "The BBBs."

"What does that stand for?"

"Bosom Buddies Besties." Riley chuckled. "We're running out of ideas, as you can see."

Olivia nodded. "And number three is—"

Harper's phone rang, and she glanced at the screen. Ugh. Of course she'd get this call right now. She grabbed the phone off the chair. "I'm sorry, y'all, I have to get this. I'll just be a second."

"It's getting close to nine," Olivia pointed out.

"I promise I'll be quick. It's not like you don't know my vote already." She hurried to the front of the store. Since Knots and Tangles was already closed, the only light available came from the few lampposts outside on Main Street. Reluctantly she answered the phone. "Thanks for returning my call, Brielle." *Two days later.*

"I hope I'm not calling too late."

Brielle's fake singsong voice didn't fool Harper. She took a deep breath. If she was going to snag a showing for Rusty, she had to play the game. "Of course not. I'm *glad* to hear from you. When can my client see the Miles Road property?"

"Unfortunately, it's under contract."

Harper stilled. "When did that happen?"

"Sunday afternoon."

Unbelievable. Not only had Brielle ignored her messages on Sunday, but she'd waited another two days to let her know the property wasn't available.

"I'm *so* sorry I didn't call you earlier, but real estate is hot right now. I've set a new sales record this month. You know how it is, don't you?"

Not lately. She also detected the sarcastic tone in Brielle's voice, as if she delighted in rubbing her success in Harper's face. *No doubt she does.*

Harper rubbed her temple. "Thanks for letting

me know," she said, somehow managing a normal tone.

"Of course. Don't worry, I'm sure you'll find something suitable for your client. You are at the top of your game, aren't you?"

What was that supposed to mean? Ugh, she didn't have the time or energy to decipher Brielle right now. "Bye," she said quickly, then hung up and pinched the bridge of her nose. She hated to disappoint Rusty, but there was no way around it other than to find him another property, and that was becoming a daunting task. She did a quick MLS scan on her phone and didn't see a single thing she could show him that met his parameters. Rats. It would be nice to give him the bad news along with some possible alternatives, but she couldn't even do that.

"We voted without you."

Harper spun around to see Olivia behind her. "I'm sorry," she said. "The call took longer than I thought. What's our name?"

"The CCs."

"What does that stand for?"

Olivia smiled. "The Chick Clique."

"That's a terrible name," she said.

"I came up with it," Olivia said, looking a little offended.

Yikes. "Oh. I'm sorry. I'm still not a fan, though."

"Neither is Riley. She chose the Lattes."

"And what's wrong with that?"

"I drink tea."

Olivia could be stubborn and a bit OCD, but right now she was being both times ten. Like she'd been at Anita's wedding. "Are you okay?" she asked.

"I'm fine," Olivia said, her tone softer. "I think I'm just tired, like you. We've been working overtime at the library getting ready for the parade and our holiday programs."

The library was on the other side of Main Street. "Is the parade going by the library?"

"No, but we're going to serve hot cider and give away bookmarks after the parade is over. It's such a short walk from Main Street that we wanted to take advantage of so many people coming to town. That hasn't happened since I was a teenager." Her gaze softened. "If you're set on the Lattes, I'll rescind my vote. I think Anita likes it too. She was voting in solidarity with me."

Harper smiled. "I can get used to the CCs. It's kind of cute anyway. The BBs and the CCs."

"That's what I thought," Olivia said. She yawned. "I have to go back to the library and finish up a few things. I'm glad things are going well for you, Harper." She gave her a hug, then walked out the front door of the store.

Harper glanced at her mismatched shoes. She didn't like deceiving her friends or keeping secrets. But she also didn't see the sense in telling them about her job woes or her parents' problems, not when she was sure things would work out soon in both areas. Business would pick up, and her mom and dad had gone through many hills and valleys in their relationship. This was just another one. She'd probably get a text in the next few days from her mother that she and Don were headed to Greece or somewhere else fun and exotic.

She went to the back of the store and helped Anita and Riley clean up. "What do you think about the CCs?" Riley asked.

"It's okay. I like how it goes with the BBs, though."

"Much better than the BBs and the LLs."

"LLs?"

"Latte Ladies, remember?"

"Right." Harper nodded. "Well, one thing we are is a clique."

"And chicks, even though I hate being called that," Anita said. "But you're right—the CCs is perfect."

"I'm so glad that's decided." Riley put a clip on a bag of pretzels and set it into the now empty bowl.

"What's the plan for Saturday?" Harper asked.

Anita slipped on her tan peacoat. "All the businesses are passing out candy and doing a small version of a sidewalk sale. I'm serving coffee and the pumpkin cookies in front of the café while Tanner is passing out cups of water and lemonade and selling hot dogs."

"The BBs are doing something in front of the store," Riley said. "Mimi's being tight lipped about it, so who knows what they're up to? Hayden's running the parade, so I'm working at the hardware store with Jasper. Hayden's parents will be working inside."

"I thought they retired when they sold the store to Hayden," Harper said.

"They did, but his dad pops in and does some work every once in a while. I think he misses it, even though he's happy being retired."

"Do any of you need help?" Harper asked.

Anita shook her head and grabbed her purse, then picked up her cupcakes. "I don't think so."

"We figured you would be working," Riley added. "I'm going to lock the door up front and head over to Price's. Hayden's waiting for me. The back door is already locked. You just have to close it. See y'all later."

After Riley left, Harper picked up the remaining cupcakes and slung her purse over her shoulder. A weird feeling came over her. The feeling of being left out.

She and Anita walked to their cars. Before she got into the Mercedes, Harper asked, "Are you sure no one needs anything? I could help pour coffee or put the hot dogs in their buns."

"Tanner's got plenty of help. He hired Jackie and Jesse Mathis to work the catering business, so they'll be there with their cousin Jimmy to man the hot dogs. Mom and Paisley are helping me with the café. Maybe one of the other businesses could use some help."

"I'll check." Harper was disappointed none of her friends needed her on Saturday. But she wasn't surprised. It was her own fault for not being available for so long. Maybe she should set up a table or booth for her own business. She made a mental note to call Hayden and ask him if it was too late to put something together.

She told Anita goodbye and opened the car door, then put the cupcake carrier on the passenger seat of her car. But when she sat in the driver's seat, she didn't start the engine. It was almost nine thirty. Was it too late to talk to Rusty? She glanced at the cupcakes. Taking those home with her would be a calorie-costing mistake, especially in her current mood. She could stop by and give Rusty the news about the Miles Road property and also the six temptations sitting next to her. That might soften the blow a little bit, although she doubted it. She was a good baker, but not that good.

Decision made, she drove out of the parking lot and headed to his house.

Chapter 11

When Harper pulled into Rusty's driveway, his truck was gone. The disappointment she felt earlier deepened as she glanced at the cupcakes. Oh well, she could leave them on the front porch. They would be safe in the carrier from any critters and pests. She started to pull a piece of scrap paper and a pen out of her purse when she saw the front porch light turn on and an old man walking out of the house, his hand hovering above his eyes, shielding them. Oh good, Senior was home. She could give the cupcakes to him.

Harper shut off her headlights, grabbed the container, and got out of the car. "Hi, Mr. Jenkins," she said, walking up to the concrete slab in front of the door. "My name is Harper. I'm . . ." She almost said "friend," and that would be true. But this was a business call. "I'm Rusty's real-estate agent."

Senior broke out into a grin and dropped his arm to his side. "Well, I'll be. I've seen you at church over the years, haven't I?"

"Yes." Although she hadn't been going much lately, and she used to attend all the time. *I have got to get my life together.* She glanced at his red sweatshirt that said *Woo to the Pig* on it.

"I went to Fayetteville," she said, referring to her alma mater, whose mascot was the Razor-back.

"Go, Hogs." Senior made a fist pump and gave her a wide smile, his teeth so perfect she was sure he took them out at night. But his smile was also warm and engaging, like his grandson's. "What can I help you with, Miss Harper?"

Oh, he was going to be an excellent bachelor. He had the same southern drawl as Rusty, and he was a cute old man to boot. Cammi had been thrilled when she called and told her she'd found two men for the bachelor auction. She'd just neglected to tell Cammi how old they were, and Cammi didn't ask, only told her to give Sunny Bigelow, the woman who was putting together the program, their information. No one liked to pass the buck more than Cammi.

"I came by to drop off some cupcakes." She held up the container.

He scratched the top of his bald head. "Kind of late to be deliverin' baked goods."

He was right about that. "I was at Knots and Tangles with the CCs and—"

"It's okay, you don't have to explain yourself. I'm just yankin' your chain a tad. Rusty ain't here right now. He's at the shop. You can take the cupcakes there."

"Oh, I don't want to bother him while he's workin'."

Senior beamed. "I don't think he'd mind one little bit. Go on. Tell him Senior sent ya."

She laughed. "I will. Nice to meet you, Mr. Jenkins."

"Nice to meet you too. Don't be a stranger, now."

Senior kept the light on and stood on the stoop until she had driven away. Rusty didn't get his manners just from his G'ma, she could see.

A few minutes later she turned into the garage parking lot and pulled into the space next to Rusty's truck. The lights were off in the main garage, but the ones in the smaller garage in the back were on. She couldn't help but smile, already feeling more relaxed as she carried the cupcakes to the open bay in the garage.

The GTO was raised off the ground a few feet, and Harper saw jean-clad legs and work-boot-covered feet poking out from underneath. Classic rock played on the radio in the background. She set the cupcake container on a table covered with tools and turned as he scooted out from under the car, a flat rolling cart underneath his back.

"Uh, hi," he said, moving to a seated position. He grabbed a cloth off the floor and wiped his hands, surprise in his eyes.

"Hi." She went over and crouched in front of him and smiled. "Senior sent me."

He grinned. "He did, huh. Now how did you two end up talkin' tonight?"

"I stopped by with cupcakes." She got up and went to the container, then held out her hands as if she were showing merchandise on a game show. "Carrot cake, to be exact."

"I did say I wanted to try your bakin'." He jumped up from the cart and walked over to her as he shoved the rag into his back pocket. "And I do like carrot cake."

"Hope you like cream-cheese frosting, because I went a little overboard." She took off the lid and picked up one of the cakes. When she started to give it to him, he held up his greasy hands.

"Need to go wash up first."

"I got it." She unwrapped the cupcake and put it up to his mouth.

He hesitated before he took a bite. "Mmm," he said, then swallowed. He ate the rest of the cupcake in a second bite and licked his lips. "That was delicious. You sure are a good baker."

She smiled, then noticed he had a bit of frosting at the corner of his mouth where his beard grew. Without thinking, she brushed it away with her finger, feeling the soft hair of his beard against her skin.

His eyes widened and he took a step back from her.

Her cheeks burned hot. "Uh, what are you working on?" she asked, walking as nonchalantly as she could to the GTO. She wanted to face-palm herself for such a dumb question. Obviously he was working on his car. But she had to shift her attention somewhere. Her innocent gesture of wiping off the frosting had turned awkward.

"The oil pan is leaking, so I'm trying to diagnose the problem. I'm hoping to get this done tonight. Today we had several folks make appointments to bring their cars in, and with the parade coming up and the . . ."

"Auction," she supplied.

"Yeah. That. And then there's trying to look at houses too. I reckoned I wouldn't get to work on her for a while."

"I won't keep you, then." She could tell him another time about Miles Road, when she had some other properties to show him. "Enjoy the cupcakes."

"Thanks." When she turned to leave, he said, "Harper?"

"Yes?"

"Are you okay?"

She opened her mouth to tell him yes, everything was fine. Perfect. Just dandy, as Erma McAllister would say. But she couldn't lie, not to him. Her bottom lip started to tremble as she tried to control her emotions. She failed. "No," she whispered. "I'm not."

Rusty went to her, unsure what to do. Harper's hands were shaking, and he saw her mouth quivering, although he tried not to pay attention to that part of her face. But it was the defeat in her eyes that shot straight to his heart. And in that moment, he wanted to put his arms around her, to stroke her soft hair, to tell her that whatever was wrong, no matter what it was, he would fix it.

Thank God he caught himself, and not just because he was filthy and she looked picture perfect even though it was the end of the day. He pulled over an old desk chair that rivaled Senior's advanced age and motioned for her to sit down. Then he quickly grabbed a few clean paper towels and set them on the seat, just in case.

"Thanks," she said, her voice sounding thick. She didn't look at him, so he wasn't sure if she was crying or not. Either way, he was concerned. "What happened?" he asked, crouching in front of her.

"I've been letting everyone down lately," she said. "Including myself."

Now that he was so close to her, he saw the weariness in her eyes. Heard it in her voice too. "You're plum tired, that's what it is," he said. "You need a break."

"I'll be okay." She sat up straight, steady once again.

"When was the last time you took a day off?"

She paused. "It's been a while."

"If you can't remember, it's been too long," he said. Then an idea came to him. "What are you doin' tomorrow?"

"Working," she said, her shoulders slumping again. "What else?"

He made a buzzer sound. "Wrong answer. You're goin' fishin'."

"Fishing? I've never been fishing before."

"Then I guess it's my turn to show you some new things."

"Oh, Rusty."

The soft way she said his voice sent a shiver down his spine. *Whoa, there.* Now—actually, never—wasn't the time for him to catch feelings. It was the time to catch a fish or two, though. "I'll pick you up in the morning. Around eight." Usually he fished at dawn, but he'd make an exception.

She shook her head. "I don't have the time, and you sure don't have the time. You've got all those cars coming in, and the parade coming up—"

"I can make the time. You can too." He stood. "Go on home, Harper. I'll see you in the morning."

"But—"

"No buts."

She looked up at him, then nodded. "All right. I'll go." She got up from the chair, and he walked her to her Merc. Before she got inside, she said, "What's the dress code for fishing?"

Rusty laughed. Of course she'd ask that question. The fish didn't care, and neither did he.

"What you had on that night we had minestrone at your house will be fine. Except the flip-flops. Tennis shoes would be better."

"So you want me to wear sweats and my glasses?"

"Yes, ma'am." He smiled at her smirk. *Much better.* "I'll pick you up in the morning."

She paused, then nodded. "All right. See you then."

As she drove away, he blew out a breath. He'd figure out a way to juggle his schedule tomorrow. His focus was on Harper now. She needed to learn to relax . . . and he aimed to show her how.

"And it can all be yours for the low, low price of fifty-nine ninety-nine."

Madge dipped the serving-sized spoon into the half gallon of peanut-butter brickle-surprise ice cream she'd bought earlier that day. This was what she was reduced to—watching infomercials and pigging out on ice cream on a Tuesday night. Even at her worst moments, she'd never resorted to such cliché behavior. But after one taste she was helpless to stop eating her feelings.

She took out a big scoop and shoved it past her lips. The cold ice cream and tiny chunks of candy filled her mouth with blissful sweetness. She would regret this later, but right now Yarnell's was the only comfort she had.

"Order now, before it's too late," the overly

excited announcer pleaded. "You don't want to miss—"

Click. She might not have had enough ice cream, but she was tired of the TV. She glanced down at her flannel nightgown and red socks—the same thing she'd put on last night when she went to bed. After the meeting with the lawyers this morning, she'd waited for Harper to call and check on her. Or—and this was more farfetched but could possibly happen—for Don to show up and beg her again to change her mind, or at least explain his reckless decision. Nothing. Not a single peep out of either one.

She shoved another spoonful of ice cream in her mouth.

When she was on her third huge bite, the doorbell rang. She froze, the ice cream half melted in her mouth. That had to be Don. No one else would stop by unannounced after 9:00 p.m. She didn't want to see him, not like this. Maybe if she didn't move, he'd think she wasn't home and he'd go away.

The doorbell rang again. Then a third time. No, he wasn't going away.

Madge hurried to the kitchen and shoved the ice cream into the freezer, the spoon still sticking out of the container. She grabbed the kitchen towel from the hook and wiped her mouth with it, then tried to smooth down her hair. Her soon-to-be ex had seen her looking worse than this, but not often. Even during her relaxed moments she tried to look her best.

As the doorbell rang a fourth time, she slowed her pace and calmly walked to answer it. She might look like a wreck on the outside, but she could still maintain her composure.

But when she opened the door a crack and peeked out, Don wasn't there.

She slammed the door and leaned against it. She'd forgotten she'd told Erma about the attorney meeting, and obviously Erma had then said something to the Bosom Buddies. Her friends were the last people she wanted to deal with right now.

"We can stand out here all night, Madge." Erma's strong voice sounded from the opposite side of the door.

"Yep," Myrtle added. "All night."

"So you might as well open up," Peg said.

"Because we're not leaving until you do." Gwen's tone brooked zero argument.

"Please, Madge," Viola said. "It's chilly out here."

"I brought pie!" Bea piped up.

To her shock, Madge almost laughed. Of course Bea had brought pie. The woman was never without food, especially during stressful times. Until now Madge had never understood why.

Knowing that all the women would keep their word—and they wouldn't starve outside, thanks to Bea—she reluctantly opened the door. "What are you doing here?"

"Being a friend." Erma plowed past her. "You can thank us later."

One by one the BBs walked through the door. "I hope you like chocolate cream," Bea said as she bustled by, carrying a clear Tupperware pie holder.

Madge's stomach churned as the ice cream she'd inhaled started rebelling. She closed the door and put her hands on her hips. "I don't know what Erma told you," she said. "But I'm fine."

Erma spun around. "Oh, we can all see that you're perfectly peachy," she said, rolling her eyes. "And for your information, I didn't say nothin' to no one."

"We've missed you." Viola put her hand on Madge's forearm. "You haven't been to Knots and Tangles in forever."

"Or church," Peg said, her brow furrowed with concern. "You used to never miss."

"We had to check on you ourselves," Gwen said. "I know it's late, but we wanted to make sure you were home."

"So I couldn't escape?" Madge said half-heartedly.

"Exactly," they all said in unison.

She froze, some of the icy loneliness thawing at the edges of her heart. She looked at these friends, women who had taken her into their circle and kept her there, even though she hadn't always fit in. Even though she had spent so much time pushing them away. They were faithful. Loyal. Two things she desperately needed in her life. "I don't deserve friends like you," she said, her voice thickening.

"Yes, you do." Erma walked over to her and put her arm around her shoulders. "Now let us help you through"—she smushed her lips together—"uh, whatever you're going through."

While she appreciated her friend's discretion, it was time to be honest with everyone. "It's okay, Erma. You don't have to keep my secret anymore." She looked at each woman in the room. The only person missing was Rosa, and Madge was grateful for that. Rosa Castillo was a decent sort, but she didn't know her well enough to talk about something so personal. "Don and I are getting a divorce," she said, not bothering to put on a brave front. She waited for everyone's shocked reactions.

"Oh," Gwen said.

"Hmm," Peg added.

"That's a shame," Viola said.

"Um, yeah. What she said." Myrtle looked at the white porcelain bowl on the small credenza in the foyer. "This is nice. Where did you get it?"

"You're not surprised?" Madge asked, bewildered by their reactions.

"A little," Bea said, setting the pie on the

199

dining-room table in the open concept kitchen. She frowned. "Then again, no."

Erma nodded. "We've suspected there was a problem for a while now. But we didn't want to pry."

Madge crossed her arms. "But my marriage was a topic of conversation between all of you, wasn't it?"

"Only because we didn't know what to do." Peg held out her hands. "What good are friends if you can't rely on them when you need to?"

Dropping her arms, Madge fought the lump forming in her throat. Not all that long ago she had been a part of a similar conversation with Erma's granddaughter, Riley. Madge and the rest of the BBs, in addition to Harper, Anita, and Olivia, had rallied around Riley in a similar way after she discovered a long-buried family secret. Riley had burst into tears, also something Madge was close to doing. But the young woman had let her friends help. Madge needed to do the same.

She gave them all a shaky smile. "Anyone want coffee? It's a long story."

"You sit down," Erma said. "We'll make the coffee."

Bea nodded. "And I'll cut the pie."

Madge swallowed, overcome by their kindness and loyalty. "Thank you. Thank you all." She wasn't alone after all.

Chapter 12

Harper leaned back in the cloth camping chair, the autumn sun warming her face, one of Rusty's fishing poles laying in the grass beside her. She closed her eyes, feeling the tension drain from her body. *Bliss.*

Thank goodness she hadn't given in to her earlier impulse to call Rusty and cancel their fishing trip. On the way home from the garage last night, she'd realized she hadn't told him about the Miles Road property being off the market. That put her into work mode again, and she went straight to her home office and stayed up past midnight searching for comparable properties for him to look at . . . and finding none. Since she couldn't make listings appear out of thin air, she shifted her attention to business strategy. There was still a smidge of hope she could purchase #6, but only if a suitable property for Rusty became available in the near future or she suddenly had a boom of new clients. Both scenarios required a miracle.

When she woke up this morning, though, Rusty, not business, was on her mind. She marveled at how he'd quickly ascertained she was upset, something only her closest friends could do. She had known them for years, though. Rusty had figured her out in record time. If she canceled their trip, he might be concerned, and she didn't want that. Besides, he'd taken the day off on her behalf, and she had given her word that she would show up. Bailing on him was not a good look. She also looked forward to having a little time off, even if fishing was involved.

A light breeze rustled the colorful leaves on the elm and oak trees surrounding the pond. The sun's rays glistened off the gently rippling water as she stretched out her legs and glanced at the black leggings and tennis shoes she'd chosen to wear. She crossed her ankles and stuck her hands into the front pocket of her red Razorback sweatshirt. She'd even decided against putting on a full face of makeup, although she couldn't resist a little mascara and lip gloss. No need to get too crazy.

She'd expected him to take her to one of the nearby lakes—Catherine, Hamilton, or even Ouachita, although that lake was farther away. Instead, they were at a large pond fifteen minutes outside Maple Falls, on a rustic road she hadn't known existed.

What she also hadn't expected was for him to insist they leave their cell phones at home. "I can't do that," she'd said, gaping at him like he'd left his brain at the garage.

"Sure you can. The world won't crash and burn if you miss a phone call or two."

"My career might," she mumbled, but he was already walking to his truck. She sighed, then went back into the house and left the phone on the kitchen counter. When she got in the truck, she said, "Before we go, I need to tell you something."

He raised one eyebrow before shifting the truck into Drive. "Is it work related?"

"Yes—"

"We'll talk about it later." He looked at her, his expression stern. "Whatever it is, it can wait."

Now that she was fully relaxed—something she hadn't thought possible lately—she was relieved not to talk about work. She didn't even miss her cell phone. There was plenty of time to tell him about Miles Road. All she wanted was to enjoy her day off and not think about her parents or her business.

"Hey, Harper."

She lolled her head to the side and opened her eyes. "Yes?"

"The fish are in the water, not on the grass." He slowly turned the little handle on his fishing reel. That was the first thing he'd taught her when they arrived—the parts of the pole, then how to attach fake worms to a hook. She suspected the rubber bait was for her benefit.

"You need to put your pole in the pond if you're going to catch anything," he added.

"Oh, let's leave them alone to do their fishy things," she said.

He chuckled, then reeled in the rest of his line before setting his pole on the ground and sitting next to her. "Sorry the fish ain't bitin' today," he said. "This is usually a dependable fishin' hole."

"I'm perfectly happy just sitting here." She closed her eyes and sighed. "I wasn't excited about touching a slimy fish anyway."

"They're more scaly than slimy."

"And that's any better?"

He grinned, shaking his head. "Guess not."

They both sat in comfortable silence for a while. After a few minutes, she opened one eye and glanced at him. He didn't have his eyes closed, but he was leaning back in his chair, his hands clasped behind his head, touching the back of his *Rusty's Garage* ball cap and looking as serene as she felt. "You were right," she said.

" 'Bout what?"

"Taking time off. I've been so consumed with work and . . . other things that I didn't realize how much I needed to just . . ."

He unclasped his hands and rested his palms on his thighs. "Just what?"

"Be." She opened her eyes and looked at him. "Just be."

He smiled and nodded. "There's somethin' about spendin' time in nature that soothes the soul."

Harper gazed at the pond, mesmerized by the shimmering water. Two brown leaves fluttered to the surface, then floated away.

Rusty opened the small red cooler on the ground between their chairs. "Ready for a sandwich now? It's almost noon."

"Yes." She sat up as he handed her a sandwich in a plastic baggie.

"Hope you like ham and mustard." He took another sandwich out of the cooler. "That's all I had at the house."

"Sounds delicious." He'd come prepared, including packing their lunch.

"Chips?" He held out a snack-sized bag.

"Of course."

As they ate their lunch and finished off the bottles of water he'd brought, neither of them said much. But the silence wasn't awkward. He was so easy to be around. Calming too. She didn't have to pretend that everything was fine when they were together. She didn't realize how much of her life had been a facade over the past few months, trying to fool everyone that everything was okay. She'd been fooling herself most of all.

When they were finished eating, he said, "Guess there's no reason to stick around if we ain't gonna catch anythin'. I know another fishin' hole we can go to. Maybe we'll have better luck there."

She was about to agree, then thought of something. "I have a different idea," she said.

"What's that?"

"I'm going to give you a makeover."

His eyebrow raised. "A what?"

"Makeover. Haircut, shave, a new outfit." She leaned forward. "It will boost your confidence for the auction."

He touched his shaggy beard. "I do look like a wreck, don't I?"

She looked at him. Actually, he didn't. He looked like Rusty, and he was as far from a wreck as possible. "No," she said. "You don't. But this is a formal event."

"And I need to fit in as much as possible." He started rubbing his palms on his jeans.

"It's okay." She put her hand over his to stop his nervous movement. "Trust me, remember?"

He glanced at her hand on his, then nodded.

When she started to pull her hand away, she was aware of a light tingling sensation on her palm. His hands were much larger than hers, and she felt a callus on top of one knuckle. The mark of a man who worked hard with his hands.

"All right," he said. "Let's get this over with."

She removed her hand. "You're going to knock the ladies right off their feet when I'm done with you."

"Yeah, right." He got up from the chair.

She watched as he picked up the cooler, surprised at his negative reaction. Did he really not know what a great guy he was? Any woman at the auction would be lucky to have a date with him. He just needed a little encouragement.

"You can drop me at my place, and I'll come pick you up in an hour or so," she said, rising from the chair.

He frowned. "We're not going now?"

"I need a shower, makeup, and different clothes." She gestured at her sweats, then pushed up her glasses. "I can't go anywhere looking like this."

"Why not?"

"Because . . . because I never have." Not until today. She tugged on one of the wayward strands of hair that had fallen from her messy bun.

He moved closer to her. "Harper, you look fine."

"Fine isn't good enough."

His head tilted to the side, and he didn't say anything for a long moment. Then he nodded. "All right. I'll take you home."

Relief flooded through her. She hadn't realized how tense she'd been while he was so quiet. If they were going somewhere other than a fishing hole, she needed to look put together. What if they ran into one of her clients or another agent? That was a valid concern.

But deep down it was also an excuse. She'd always loved fashion, but was she hiding behind it too? The expensive designer clothes, the high heels that more often than not made her feet hurt, the makeup and hair that always had to be perfect.

"Harper?"

She turned to see he'd already picked up the poles and folded the camping chairs. Quickly she slid the chairs into their covers and hoisted them over her shoulders. When they got into his truck, he turned on the radio, and they headed to her house. She barely heard the music, still thinking about her inability to let the world see her without the extra trappings.

When he pulled into her driveway, she set aside her thoughts. This afternoon was about Rusty, not her. "Thanks," she said, opening the door. "I'll pick you up around two thirty. Does that sound okay?"

"Sure."

He still didn't sound too enthused, but she would change that. By the end of today, he would look like a new man—and hopefully have some added confidence too.

It was closer to three thirty when Harper turned into Rusty's driveway. The moment she'd walked in her own front door, she'd checked her phone, despite her promise not to. Good thing she did, because she had three voice mails from potential clients—one she'd cold-called three weeks ago and had given up ever hearing from, one who was planning to move from California to Hot Springs, and another one who wanted to list their house. By the time she'd scheduled everyone, it was already almost two thirty. She showered, dressed, and put on her makeup as fast as she could, then called Rusty to tell him she was on her way to his house. Surprisingly, it went to voice mail.

As she got out of her Mercedes, she couldn't stop from visually evaluating the exterior of his home now that she saw it in the daylight. *Wow.* Considering how well he kept up Rusty's Garage, she was shocked at the state of the property. Thick bushes covered up almost three quarters of the picture window. The red brick was chipped in some places, and the sidewalk from the driveway to the front stoop was cracked. The screen door hung crookedly, and the roof needed repair. His house didn't look like a dump, but it was definitely neglected.

She stepped around another large crack in the cement driveway, walked to the front door, and rang the doorbell. Silence. Okay, the bell was broken. Add that to the list of repairs. She opened the screen door and knocked on the solid wood door, then peeked into one of the three thin, rectangular windows set at an angle but couldn't see anything inside. Then the door opened.

"Hello, there, Miss Harper," Senior said, giving her a charming smile. "Rusty told me you were comin' over. He's upstairs gettin' a shower. Gave me instructions to keep you company until he finished sprucin' himself up, so come on in. I've got some fresh sweet tea ready for ya."

"Thank you." She followed him inside. Why was Rusty just now taking a shower?

Her mind shifted to the house again. Minus the hole in the floor, the living room didn't look to be in horrendous shape—on the surface, anyway. It definitely needed a lot of updating.

"Mind your step," he said, pointing to a dark-green carpet that had been pulled back to reveal an opening at least a foot in diameter. "Rusty had a little mishap the other day."

"I heard." She stepped over the hole and followed Senior into a kitchen that looked straight out of the fifties, right down to the muddy brown linoleum and ice-green walls. A small table was situated in the middle of the dining space, and a plain glass pitcher with amber liquid and floating ice cubes sat in the center. Three glasses with roosters etched on the sides stood next to the pitcher, along with a glass plate filled with Oreos. Double-stuffed, she noticed. Three small glass plates decorated with the same roosters sat next to the Oreos.

"Have a seat." Senior pulled out one of the chairs from the table. "Would you like some tea?"

"Yes, please." She smiled and sat down, setting her handbag on the linoleum floor.

He poured a glass and set it down in front of her, then picked up the plate. "Can I interest you in an Oreo?"

"I'd love one."

"Don't be shy. You can have more than one."

"All right, I'll take two." She put both Oreos on her plate as he sat down.

"Funny how we haven't exchanged pleasantries before," Senior said, sitting down next to her. "I thought I knew everyone in Maple Falls."

"I didn't grow up here." She explained how she'd gone to private schools her whole childhood and didn't start getting engaged with the community until after getting her real-estate license. "My parents don't technically live in Maple Falls, but my mother made some friends here several years ago." Harper wondered if the BBs knew about the divorce. Surely Madge wouldn't have told any of them before telling her own daughter.

He took a sip of his tea. "Rusty tells me you're helpin' him find a new place. As you can see, this one needs a little sprucin' up."

"It's cute, though. I love the vintage vibe."

Senior smiled, a faraway look in his eyes. "We couldn't bring ourselves to update it," he said. "I built this house in seventy-one, right after Judy and I got married. She decorated it herself." He touched the glass of tea in front of him. "Shortly after we moved in, she found these at an estate sale. Haven't used them since she passed. Until today."

Harper's heart squeezed. "I can tell you loved her very much."

211

"I did." Senior cleared his throat. "She was the best wife a man could have, and a wonderful mother and grandmother." A shadow passed over his face. "Our son Junior was a free spirit, and we learned the hard way he was going to do his own thing. But gettin' the chance to raise Rusty and Amber . . . Well, that was a blessin' indeed." He looked at Harper. "Family. Gotta love them, but they sure can be messy."

"Yes, they can." She took a sip of the tea, pushing the quick thought about her troubled parents to the side. "Delicious. Did you make this?"

"Naw. Lipton did." He grinned and snuck an Oreo off the plate as Rusty walked into the kitchen.

"Hey, Harper," he said, his damp hair slicked back from his forehead.

"Hi," she said. "I'm sorry I'm late. It, uh, took longer for me to get ready than I thought." No need to admit she'd done a little work on her day off.

"It's all right. Runnin' a little behind myself." He glanced at his grandfather. "Oreos, Senior? Really?"

"You said to fix her a snack."

"I meant the coffee cake I picked up on the way home." Rusty turned to Harper, and the top of his cheeks that weren't covered in red hair turned rosy. "Sorry about that."

"I'm not. I love Oreos." She twisted one apart and licked the cream filling.

Rusty's eyes widened, then he turned away. "Uh . . ."

"Uh, what, Rusty?" Senior asked, leaning back in his chair and grinning.

"Have you seen my shoes?" His gaze dashed around the kitchen as if he was going to find them in the sink, refrigerator, or stove.

Harper bit into the cookie and glanced down at his bare feet. They looked nice, with neatly trimmed nails.

"Which ones?" Senior asked.

"Sneakers."

Senior shook his head. "How should I know where your shoes are?"

Rusty rolled his eyes. "Then why didn't you say that in the first place? I'll be right back, Harper."

After he left the room, Senior chuckled. "My boy's sweet on you, Miss Harper."

Harper shook her head. To her surprise, her face heated. She focused on the half-eaten Oreo. "I don't think so."

"You're just sayin' that 'cause you're used to guys payin' attention to ya, a pretty girl like yourself. Reckon it can be hard to tell when the interest is real or not."

She started to deny his words, but they hit close to the truth.

"My Judy was a stunner," he said, then tapped

one finger against the table. "And don't think for a minute I didn't notice how she grabbed the fellas' attention in her younger days. She grabbed mine right off the bat."

"Did that make you jealous?" She remembered Jack's reactions when men noticed her. "When they paid attention to her like that?"

"Naw. Judy never gave me no reason not to trust her, and she was the only woman for me. I wasn't about to let that bitter weed infest our marriage."

"That's so sweet," she said. She thought about her parents again. What had caused their marriage to go off the rails? She knew her mother had been unhappy, even though she tried to hide it—and she hid it well because her father never seemed to notice. Was that why Madge wanted a divorce? She was tired of being ignored? But that didn't explain the past two years, when Don had been overly attentive.

Not your business, remember?

"Okay, I'm ready." Rusty entered the kitchen, white sneakers on his feet, baggy jeans and a black-and-white plaid shirt covering the rest of him. A thick hank of bangs had dried enough to fall over half of his forehead, as if he'd shoved them to the side before walking into the kitchen. The ends were well past his eyes.

"Where were the shoes?" Senior asked.

"Next to my bed," Rusty muttered. "Guess I forgot I put them there."

214

Senior winked at Harper. "What did I tell ya?"

Harper didn't think forgetting where a pair of shoes was indicated anything. She waved him off with a smile. "Thanks for the tea and cookies, Mr. Jenkins."

Senior rose from the table and took her hand, then kissed the top in an overly dramatic gesture. "Please," he said. "Call me Russell."

"Give me a break." Rusty shook his head, but there was a hint of a smile on his face. "She'll call you Senior like everyone else does."

His grandfather chortled and let go of her hand. "You two have a nice outing, ya hear?"

She couldn't help but grin back. "We will." *I hope.* Contrary to his placid demeanor this morning, Rusty seemed on edge. And what Russell, er, Senior chalked up to being sweet on her had to be his grandson's apprehension about the auction. Nothing else.

As they walked out of the house, Rusty said, "Don't pay him no mind."

"Why not? He's adorable. The women are going to love him at the gala."

"I'm sure they will." He turned to her, the wind whipping his long hair. "Are we taking my truck or the Merc?"

"My car," she said.

"I'll grab my coat." He walked over to his vehicle and grabbed a gray zipped hoodie with a frayed hem, then went to the passenger side of her car.

"That's your coat?"

"Yep." He slipped it on, and she noticed the white hood ties hung unevenly. Then he opened the car door and got inside.

She shook her head and sat behind the wheel. She had her work cut out for her.

Chapter 13

I don't know about this, Harper." Rusty sat down in the chair at Artie's Barbershop and looked at his reflection in the mirror.

"You said you trusted me."

"I didn't know that meant shaving all my hair off."

She stood on one side of him, Artie on the other. Rusty was his last customer of the day, and other than the three of them, the shop was empty. Good thing, too, because Rusty reckoned he and Harper were about to get into their first argument.

"Artie's not going to shave off your hair," Harper said, looking at Rusty's reflection in the mirror. Then she glanced at Artie. "You're not, right? Just a low taper with a side comb-over."

"A low what with a what?" Rusty asked.

"I'm cuttin' your hair," Artie said. "That's all you need to know."

Harper sat down in the empty barber chair next to him and thumbed through a hairstyle magazine while Artie went to work. Clumps of hair dropped to the floor as he ran his razor over Rusty's head. "When was the last time you had a haircut?" Artie asked. "I haven't seen you here in a long time."

"Can't remember. Been meanin' to get one, though."

Artie moved the razor away from Rusty and leaned forward. "You're not the first guy who was dragged here by his girlfriend," he said in a low voice.

"She's not—"

But Artie was already back at work. Rusty glanced at Harper, but she was still reading the magazine. Fortunately she hadn't heard what Artie said. His nerves were already jangled enough, and he didn't need a know-it-all barber making things worse.

The day had started out so well, despite not catching anything. Harper had been resistant to his no-work-no-cell rule, but once she started to relax, he couldn't remember when he'd had a better time fishing. Truth was the fish *had* been biting, but he'd been so distracted by her he'd let them get away. Seeing the small smile on her gorgeous face as she enjoyed the sunshine was better than catching a sunfish or three any day.

Then she mentioned the makeover—and his insecurities reared up. It was nice of her to say that the women at the auction would want to bid on him, but he knew better. Some would for sure because they wanted to support the ALS charity. But there was no way a bidding war would happen, not over him. That wasn't realistic.

Still, he'd reluctantly agreed to the makeover, mostly so he could spend more time with Harper. Then she'd surprised him by wanting to go back home and change when she didn't need to. She already looked great. No, more than great. She was beautiful.

Then he'd seen something in her eyes he was more than a little familiar with. *Self-doubt*—a term he'd never expected to associate with Harper Wilson. But all he'd come up with in reply was, "You look fine." *Fine.* Talk about underwhelming.

On the way to her house, he'd hemmed and hawed about giving her a more appropriate compliment, but the moment had passed, and he didn't want to make things awkward between them. He was already feeling enough awkwardness for both of them.

After he dropped her off, his apprehension returned. Should he invite her inside when she came over or just meet her in the driveway as she pulled up? If he did decide to invite her in, did he have time to clean up the house? Should he offer her a drink? A snack? He'd whipped into the grocery-store parking lot and picked up the coffee cake and powdered iced tea, then hurried back home. He was overthinking things, but he couldn't help it. He ran inside, barely glancing at Senior, who was sitting in his old recliner in the living room, and took a shower. Forty-five minutes and three clothing changes later, he was ready for Harper's arrival.

Two-thirty came and went. When three rolled around, he started to pace. Was she standing him up? Why would she, when giving him a makeover was her idea? And it wasn't like this was a date, anyway. He was the one who was making more of the situation than he should. He'd eventually talked himself back to the real world, but he'd also sweated through his shirt. After shower number two, he saw that she'd called and apologized for being late. Then he'd felt like an idiot. All that fretting for nothing.

"There you go." Artie brushed the hair off Rusty's neck. "A brand-new you."

He stared in the mirror. The hair on the sides was cut close to his scalp, the bangs and crown were left longer. He kind of liked the style. Even better, his head felt lighter and cooler. Harper knew what she was doing—this was a fine haircut.

"If you use some of this pomade," Artie said, pointing to a flat can on the counter in front of the mirror, "you can slick the top to either side or to the back." He turned the barber chair toward Harper. "What do you think, young lady?"

She glanced up from the magazine, then took a long look, her eyes widening. She smiled. "Perfect."

Her approval helped him relax. If she liked his haircut, he was good to go.

"Now, time to get rid of that beard," Artie said.

"All of it?" Rusty asked.

"Every scraggly bit."

His hand flew to his chin. "Long beards are in style," he said.

"Neat beards are," Harper said, lifting one eyebrow. "Not the 'I got lost in the mountains for ten years' look."

"That bad, huh?"

Both Harper and Artie nodded. Rusty settled back in his chair. Nothing left to do but give in.

It didn't take long for Artie to work his barber magic on Rusty's beard, and soon he was clean-shaven. "Your skin's a little dry, which is normal when you shave off a beard as long as yours. Use some lotion for a few days, and it will be fine."

Rusty nodded as Artie turned him in the chair to face Harper again. "How does it look?" Rusty asked.

Harper's mouth dropped open. "I . . . I . . ."

"Uh-oh." He frowned. She'd had a better reaction to his haircut. He'd actually thought the shave was the bigger improvement. Her expression said otherwise. "Guess I should have left the beard," he muttered.

She got up and dropped the magazine in the chair. She looked at his face, one side first, then the other. "Wow."

"A good wow, or a—"

"Good." She took a step back. "*Very* good."

An unexpected thrill raced down his spine. For a split second he enjoyed the feeling, then came back to his senses. He didn't need to turn to mush over a simple compliment.

"Another satisfied couple." Artie draped the black cape over the small counter in front of the mirror.

"You mean 'customer,'" Rusty quickly corrected.

Harper turned away. "We're not a couple, Artie."

"Oh. My mistake." He chuckled. "Not the first time I've made that one either."

Rusty stood and fished his wallet out of his back pocket, glad his emotions were set back to rights. Maybe he shouldn't be so hard on himself. Who wouldn't appreciate a beautiful woman's compliment? Appreciation, that's all he'd felt. Nothing more than that.

"Hey, I'm paying for this," Harper said.

"Why would you do that?"

"It was my idea."

He shook his head. "I needed a haircut anyway. You just got me off my duff to get one."

She crossed her arms over her chest. "But you're doing me a favor by being in the auction."

"That's not a favor. I'm glad to help out a good cause."

"I'm still paying."

He put his hands on his hips. "No, you're not."

"Are you sure you two aren't a couple?"

They both looked at Artie, who had started laughing. "I don't care who pays," he continued. "It's past closing time, so make a decision already."

Rusty quickly opened his wallet and handed him a credit card before Harper could get her purse. "Add a 30 percent tip to that," he said. "You earned it."

"Thanks." Artie headed to the cash register at the front of the shop.

"Hmmph," Harper said.

Rusty turned around. "Hmmph," he repeated, then smiled.

Harper's eyes met his, their color changing from light blue to almost cobalt. Another shiver went through him.

"Here's your receipt." Artie tapped Rusty on the shoulder. "Next time don't wait so long."

"I won't." He took the slip of paper and crammed it into his pocket.

"Y'all have a good night."

"You too," Harper said, and they left the barber shop.

The cool fall air rushed against Rusty's short, cropped hair and naked face. "Now that feels nice," he said as they went to her car.

Harper walked to the driver's side. Before they left she'd told him not to bother opening her doors since they would be getting in and out of the car a lot. That had piqued his interest. Getting a haircut and beard shave had never crossed his mind, though.

"Gotta admit, I'm glad to finally get this taken care of. Kinda feel like a new man now."

"You're going to be a new man, all right."

He arched a brow. "What do you mean by that?"

She didn't say anything. Only smiled.

When they got into the car, he ran his hand over the back of his head, needing the distraction. "This is gonna take some gettin' used to," he said as she pulled out of the space.

"If you like the haircut, you're really going to like what comes next."

He knew better than to ask her what that was. She would just say, "We'll see." Or "Trust me." She seemed to enjoy reeling him in, and he wasn't minding that one bit. All he could do was wait until she showed him what she had in store next.

When Harper first embarked on operation Fix Up Rusty, she'd thought it would be easy. A shave and haircut, a brand-new outfit to wear to the gala, then they'd grab a bite to eat before she dropped him off at his house. Afterward she'd go home, try to resist doing any more work for the day, and end her night with a cup of chamomile tea and a rerun of *Matlock*, one of her favorite old shows.

But Rusty had to go and ruin everything.

She currently sat in a chair in the men's section of Dillard's at the Hot Springs Mall, waiting for him to try on another suit. This was his fifth one, and she didn't think she could take seeing him come out of the dressing room one more time, gala or not. As it was, she needed a fan and a glass of water. Or a cold shower. Actually all three, because Rusty Jenkins, Maple Falls's resident mechanic and good ol' southern boy, cleaned up good. She hadn't expected him to be the spitting image of the actor from that time-travel show set in Scotland. She'd only watched one episode, and she couldn't remember the actor's name, but she did remember how he looked in a kilt. *Hmm, how would Rusty look in a kilt?*

Real good.

"How about this one?"

Steeling herself, she lifted her gaze as he walked toward her. Oh my. He looked handsome. No, not handsome. Hot. Super hot, in fact. He'd tried on blue, black, and two different-colored gray suits. They'd all fit him to perfection. Who knew he was hiding *that* body under those baggy clothes he wore all the time?

Yes. This is the one.

She stood and walked to him, even though she should probably keep her distance. But she couldn't resist seeing him up close. The light-tan suit fit as if it were cut specifically for him. The pants tapered at the ankle and weren't too short or long, and the jacket hung on his shoulders without being tight around the arms or waist. The ice-blue dress shirt was the perfect accent color. All he needed was a tie to complete the outfit.

"Do I look okay?" he asked, wearing the same uncertain expression that had appeared when they walked into the store.

"Um . . . turn around." Telling herself that she was only checking to see if the suit fit as well in the back as it did in the front and that she wasn't taking advantage of the view—even though she totally was—she nodded when he again faced her. "Yes," she said, trying to sound as if she were talking to Kingston or Dylan or her brother, if she had one. By some miracle she managed to pull it off. "This will do."

"Finally. I'm pert near done with tryin' stuff on. Can I take off this monkey suit now?"

"Wait, you need a tie. Hand me the jacket." When he slipped it off and gave it to her, she said, "I'll be right back."

"Okay."

He was being a good sport about this, considering he wasn't used to wearing a suit or trying on one in front of someone else other than his G'ma, and that had been more years ago than he could remember. He'd explained all that when they were searching for the shirt, then asked, "How do you know what to pick out?"

"Fashion is my passion," she'd said, picking up a crisply folded pale-yellow shirt from the stack on display.

"I thought real estate was." He looked down as she held the shirt against his torso.

"I'm a woman of many interests." Yuck. The yellow definitely didn't work with his coloring.

"I'm starting to realize that."

The department was almost empty save for one saleswoman helping a couple who were looking at dress shirts in the big-and-tall section. Harper found the ties and picked out a chocolate-colored one with thread-thin diagonal gold stripes. She held it against the jacket—*Perfect*—then hurried back to Rusty, who was tugging at his open shirt collar.

"Put this back on," she said, holding the jacket out to him.

"Yes, ma'am." But he was smiling as he took it from her.

Whoa. Her knees wavered. She'd suspected he had a nice smile hiding under that beard, but whew, where was a cold-water fountain when she needed one?

After he put on the jacket again, she showed him the tie.

He eyed it dubiously. "Okay, but I don't know what to do with it."

"You can't tie a tie?"

"Never needed to. G'ma tied one for me a few

times when I was little. Senior showed me how to once, but I forgot."

"You didn't wear a tie to prom?"

He shrugged. "I didn't go to prom. Did you?"

"Yes."

"Let me guess: you were the prom queen."

She winced. "Yeah, I was." She remembered how thrilled Madge had been when Harper came home from school the week before and told her she'd been chosen. She also remembered the fun they'd had shopping for a dress, shoes, and jewelry. Then they'd both gotten their nails done. That had been more fun than the prom itself. She'd gone with the star basketball player, and he'd gotten too handsy on the way home from the dance, and when she put the kibosh on anything ever happening between them, he'd dropped her off at home in a huff, mad that he hadn't gotten what he wanted.

"I can show you how to tie this," Harper said, shoving aside the unpleasant memory. She moved closer to him until they were only a few inches apart. Wow, he smelled sublime. If "appealingly unpretentious" had a scent, it would be called *Rusty*. "First you, um, have to . . ."

He frowned. "Finish buttoning my shirt?"

"Right. That." Oh, this was a bad idea. She should have waited for the saleswoman to do this. Better yet, just buy the ensemble and have Senior show him how to deal with the tie. But she'd already committed to this. It was just a tie. This was just Rusty.

"Okay, I'm ready."

Just Rusty . . . just Rusty . . . There was something about a man in a suit that made her weak in the knees. And a man as good natured, gentle, and yes, as *hot* as Rusty almost took her breath away. "First you have to lift up the collar." Once he did that, she said, "Then you wrap the tie around your neck, like this." She lifted the tie and looped it around his neck, trying to hide the fact that her hands had inexplicably started trembling. "Then you form a knot." Explaining each movement as she did it, she ended up with a decent Half Windsor. She slowly pushed the knot up to the center of his collar. When she lifted her eyes, her toes curled in her flats. Then her gaze dropped to his clean-shaven chin. She ran her fingertip over his smooth skin, unable to resist touching him.

He cleared his throat and moved away from her. "I can take it from here." He pushed down the collar and turned around to face the mirror. After a quick glance he said, "Good enough," then hurried back to the dressing room.

Harper put her hand over her heart, the beat thumping out of control under her palm. *What just happened?* As her pulse slowed, her mind cleared. She'd touched him. And not just a little touch either. She'd let her finger slowly trail the side of his jaw . . . and she'd enjoyed every second.

Oh no.

Rusty burst out of the dressing room at warp speed, tugging his shirt down. Then he spun around, dashed back, and hurried out with the suit and shirt and tie slung over his forearm. "I'll pay for these," he said, not waiting for her to follow him.

She stayed put, trying to figure out what to do next. This was unfamiliar territory. Normally she had to fend off unwanted advances, not commit them. Ugh, she wanted to kick herself. Obviously she'd made him uncomfortable, or he wouldn't have been in such a hurry to leave the store. Should she apologize? Blow it off and pretend it never happened? Had she ruined one of the best days she'd had in a long time? More like forever.

Harper picked up her purse and walked to the checkout area, trying to regain her equilibrium, but she was still off-kilter by the time she reached the counter. Rusty was already signing the electronic pad to finish the purchase. He didn't acknowledge her as he thanked the saleswoman and took his suit—now hanging in a flimsy garment bag—and the bag with his shirt and tie from her. He clumsily held the suit and turned to Harper. "Anything else?"

His expression was unreadable, and her stomach sank. She was sure he needed a pair of dress socks and possibly dress shoes, but she didn't dare go there. "No. We're all done."

He nodded and headed for the exit, leaving her behind.

Rusty was grateful for the cold air that hit him when he walked out of the department store. He knew he was being a complete jerk by walking out on Harper, but it couldn't be helped. If he hadn't left, he might've done something dumb. Like pull her into his arms and kiss her.

It wasn't her fault that he wished her innocent gesture of brushing something off his chin was something different. Or that he couldn't pay attention to anything she was doing when she showed him how to tie his new necktie. How could he when all he could focus on was her mouth, which had been only inches away? He'd never considered himself a weak man, but there was something about Harper that could easily zap his resolve to remain platonic. And it wasn't just her looks, although they factored into the equation. She was the whole package—smart, savvy, generous, funny . . . He could go on and on . . . and on . . .

The door opened behind him, and he gave his head a hard shake. *Get a grip.* Inhaling a deep breath, he turned and tried to relax enough to give her a smile. If he ignored his weird behavior, hopefully she would too. "Where to next, boss?"

"Back home."

Her smile was strained, and it was his fault. He moved to stand beside her. "I'm sorry," he said. "I shouldn't have rushed off like that. I, uh . . ." Great. Now he had to explain why he'd run off, and he wasn't sure how.

"I don't blame you." She stared down at the sidewalk. "I shouldn't have, um . . ."

"Brushed something off my chin?"

Her head popped up. "Yes, that. I, uh, should have just told you about it." The tension around her eyes eased a bit. "Sometimes I'm a little too audacious for my own good."

"Now that's a word I haven't heard in a long time." Grinning, he gestured to the parking lot, glad she wasn't mad at him. "Let's get out of here."

After he hung up his suit on the small hook in her car and put the bag with the rest of his outfit in the back seat, he got into the Merc, and she started the engine. When it began to purr, he sat back, satisfied he'd finally solved the problem with her car. The next time he saw her Merc at his garage, he was sure it would be for routine maintenance.

As Harper headed back to Maple Falls, he asked, "Are you hungry? Two Oreos and some powdered tea ain't much of a snack."

"I am, a little." She glanced at him. "Did you have something in mind?"

He paused. He did, actually, but he reckoned she wouldn't be interested. But the night sky was clear, and the viewing would be perfect. She'd already seen the inside of his house anyway. Why not let her see the backyard too? "How would you like to do a little stargazin'?"

"Where?"

"There's a spot in the backyard where you can see millions of stars on a night like this one. We can grab some burgers or chicken on the way."

"Are you suggesting a picnic?"

"Yeah. I reckon I am."

Harper slowed the Merc as a stoplight turned red. She turned to him and smiled. "That sounds like fun."

After picking up some fast food, they headed to his house. "Sorry everything is in shambles," he said as he opened the front door for her. "I'll get this place together some day."

"Like I said, I've seen worse. No need to apologize."

The light in the living room was on, but Senior wasn't in sight. "Bet he turned in early. Don't forget about the hole."

She stepped over it. "It's only eight o'clock."

"He's had a busy week."

They went to the kitchen, and he set the food on the table. "I'll be right back," he said. He ran upstairs to the spare bedroom and straight to G'ma's cedar hope chest. He grabbed an old patchwork quilt her mother had made back in the forties, then another newer, smaller blanket for good measure. Tucking both under his arm, he hurried back to the kitchen in time to see Harper nibble on a french fry.

"Sorry," she said. "I'm starving, and these smell so good."

"Ain't no skin off my nose. I wish you'd told me you were so hungry, though. We can eat in here if you want."

"I'd rather eat outside."

"Me too. Just one thing." He pulled his cell phone out of his pocket and put it on the table, and she grinned, then pulled hers out of her purse and set it next to his.

He flipped on the outside light and unlocked the back door. Carrying the bag of food, they crossed the crooked flagstone patio to the center of the yard. The grass wasn't too high right now. If this was June, it would be up to their ankles, but it was just long enough that after he spread out the quilt and they sat down, it made for a soft, comfortable spot.

They dug into their supper—a double hamburger for him and chicken fingers for her, along with french fries and soft drinks. She glanced up at the sky. "You're right. This is a nice open space," she said. "I can already see lots of stars."

"You'll see more once I turn off the light. With all the surroundin' trees it can get pretty dark out here. I figured it would be easier to eat with the light on."

"Thanks." She was sitting cross-legged and facing him. Her high-heeled black boots were set to the side on the quilt. She picked up her drink and took a sip. "I didn't realize it was so peaceful back here. I've shown one house at the end of this street. Otherwise I'm not familiar with the neighborhood."

"It's quiet. Lots of older folks. Amber used to joke that we lived on Retirement Boulevard."

"She's your sister, right?"

He set the last bite of his hamburger back in the paper wrapping. "Yep. Do you have any siblings?"

"No." She leaned back on her hands. "When I was younger, I used to wish I did, but now I see that God knew what He was doing when it came to my parents. I don't think they could have dealt with another child."

"I can't see you bein' a handful."

Harper shook her head. "I wasn't." She sighed. "It's complicated."

They were nearly done eating, and he could tell she didn't want to talk about her parents. He knew more than anyone that family could be a touchy subject. "I'm gonna turn off the light," he said, getting up from the quilt.

"Sure," she said, her tone uncharacteristically somber.

He dashed to the house, opened the back door, then stuck his arm in between the door and the jamb and turned off the light. When Rusty sat back down on the quilt, he said, "The best way to watch is lying down. But close your eyes," he added. "I want you to be surprised."

She stretched out on the blanket, and he lay beside her, making sure to put a polite chunk of space between them. Things were going well right now, and he didn't want to make it weird between them again. "Ready to be dazzled?" he asked.

"Yes."

"Open your eyes."

Chapter 14

Harper was overwhelmed by what she saw. "Oh, Rusty," she said. "It's beautiful."

"Told ya." He pointed to the black-velvet sky covered with sparkling stars. "You can see the Big Dipper over yonder, plain as day. Orion looks close enough to touch, don't it?"

Orion was the only constellation she recognized due to its signature belt. She nodded. "I've never seen so many stars in my life," she whispered. Then again, other than occasionally glancing up at night, did she ever bother to really look? Or take the time just to gaze at them like she was doing now? "This definitely lives up to the hype."

"Yeah," he said softly. "It sure does."

They lay in silence for a long while as they viewed the twinkling white dots above. The air was colder than it had been earlier, and even though she still had on her jacket, she started to shiver a little. But she wasn't about to go inside, not anytime soon, no matter how cold she got.

A short time later Rusty said, "You're chilled."

It wasn't a question, and there was no reason for her to fib about it. "A little."

"Here." He picked up the other blanket and spread it out over her. "Better?"

"Much." She snuggled under the wool, the fabric softer than she anticipated. Turning her head to the side to look at him, she asked, "What about you?"

"I'm warm enough." He put his hands behind his head.

"There's plenty of room under here if you change your mind."

Oops. She probably shouldn't have said that. It was an innocent offer but could be easily taken the wrong way. When he didn't say anything for a moment, she was sure she'd made him uncomfortable again.

"Thanks," he said quietly. "But I'm good."

Relieved he didn't seem bothered, she looked up at the sky again. But another feeling niggled at her. Disappointment. Because the idea of snuggling with Rusty under the stars suddenly became extremely appealing.

"Do you know which planet is the brightest at night?"

Whew, he was changing the subject. "Venus," she said, happy to focus on anything except, um, him.

"Correct. Obviously, you paid attention in school."

"Of course I did. You're in the presence of a valedictorian."

"Really?" He turned to look at her, although there wasn't enough light to see his expression.

"Yes. Top of my class . . . of fifty-four."

"Hey," he said. "That's nothin' to sneeze at. I was a C student myself, although I did pretty good in my math and science classes."

"That doesn't surprise me." She continued to stare at the ocean of stars. "How many do you think are up there?"

"More than one hundred billion," he said without hesitation.

"You sound confident in your answer."

"I also paid attention in school. Science, remember?"

She watched the sky, feeling small and insignificant in the presence of so much starlight. After a few minutes, she said, "My parents are getting divorced."

Seemingly unfazed by the abrupt change of topic, he responded. "I'm sorry, Harper. That's tough."

"It is." She hadn't planned to tell him, but she felt a little lighter having said the words out loud. Still, she was surprised when tears formed in her eyes. Shoot. The last thing she wanted to do was cry over her mother and father's disaster of a relationship.

"Are you okay?"

"I will be." She brought the edge of the blanket up to her chin. "Their relationship hasn't been good for a long time, so it's probably for the best. But it still . . ."

After a moment he said, "It still hurts?"

She swallowed. "Yes."

"I know what you mean. My folks divorced when I was real little, and my grandparents stepped in the gap right away. They were better parents than my own would have ever been, especially Junior. But somethin's still empty in my heart. I reckon it's a little hole, if I had to put a name to it."

Harper could hear the pain in his voice. "I wish things had been different for you."

"Hey," he said softly. "My life has been fine. More than fine, actually. Like you said, family's complicated. We ain't perfect, so we can't expect everyone else to be."

"Tell that to Madge." She sighed. "I didn't care anything about being valedictorian. But I knew she did."

"What about your dad? I'm sure he was proud of you that night."

"I wouldn't know. He missed my graduation because of work." A bitter taste filled her mouth. Why were so many high school memories bugging her now? She'd graduated years ago, and she thought she'd put that behind her. Suddenly feeling too hot, she pushed the blanket down to her waist. "I don't want to talk about them anymore."

"All right," he said, his tone amiable. "Then let me show you somethin'. Look up there."

"I have been looking."

"No, I mean right there."

She narrowed her eyes, trying to figure out what he was pointing to. "What is it?"

"It's the Dog Star. Or Sirius, as the scientists call it." He pointed straight up. "It's the brightest one in the sky."

"There's lots of bright ones up there."

"It's right . . ." He took her hand and aimed both of them at the star. "There."

"Oh, I see it now." But she wasn't paying attention to Sirius. His hand felt warm and strong. *Like he is.*

He started to let go of her hand, but she stopped him. "Thanks, Rusty," she said, squeezing his fingers.

"For what?"

"For listening to me. And understanding what I'm going through. And making me take time off work. All of it." She brought their hands down together. "This is the best day I've had in a long time."

"Me too."

Suddenly the porch light came on. They both sat up as Senior stepped onto the patio. "Rusty?" he called out. "You out here?"

"Oh brother," Rusty said, yanking his hand from hers and scrambling to his feet. "Yep. I'm here."

"Anyone with you?"

He hesitated. "Just Harper. We're star gazin'."

"Right." Senior chuckled. " 'Star gazin'.' Is that what you young people call it these days?"

"Knock it off!" Rusty shouted. He looked at Harper. "In case you haven't noticed, Senior likes to tease. Feel free to tell him to shut up. He's always jumping to conclusions."

Harper stilled, shocked that he would yell at his grandfather. He'd also been quick to point out to the barber, Artie, that they weren't a couple. He *really* didn't want anyone to get the wrong idea about them. That . . . stung.

But she'd said the same thing in the barber shop, so why was she being so hypocritical? And why was she so bothered by his insistence that they were only friends? She didn't have time for a boyfriend or a date even if she wanted one— not that she'd had any success in that department. Her prom date hadn't been the first guy to try something with her, and by the time she'd met Jack she'd given up on men all together. Still, Jack had been persistent, and she'd decided to give him a chance . . . and then he dumped her.

But Jack had never made her feel the way Rusty did. Safe. At ease. Accepted as herself.

Oh no. The truth hit her like a tsunami. *I like Rusty. I really, really,* really *like him.*

She grabbed her boots and jumped to her feet. "I gotta go," she said, hurrying toward the house. Here she was, making the mistake of falling for a guy when she shouldn't be falling for anyone—especially someone who absolutely positively only wanted her friendship. How could she be so stupid?

She dashed past Senior, wishing she could kick herself because she was *literally* running away from Rusty. He had to think she was nuts. But she was too freaked out to stick around.

"Don't rush off on my account," Senior said as she blew by him.

"I forgot I have an appointment." Her stockinged feet hit the linoleum floor. "A Realtor's job never ends!" She winced at her lame excuse, grabbed her purse off the table, hopped over the hole in the living-room floor, dashed out of the house, then almost tripped on the crack in the driveway before jumping into her car. *Please start. Please start.* This would be the worst time for her Mercedes to break down again. When the car purred to life, she grabbed the steering wheel and nearly squealed out of the driveway.

When she was out of Rusty's neighborhood, she slowed down, but her thoughts continued to race. She had a problem, a big one, and his name was Rusty Jenkins.

No, that wasn't fair. He couldn't help it that he was so . . . so . . .

So wonderful.

He wasn't the one turning her life upside down. She was doing a bang-up job of that herself.

By the time she reached her own neighborhood, she was a little calmer. She would get over this. Her life was full, too full to deal with romance. Today had been an outlier, and tomorrow she would go back to working ten hours or more a day now that she had three new leads that hopefully signaled the end of her slump. The Mercedes was running smoothly, and Rusty was confident he'd fixed all the problems, so there was no need to interact with him.

Wait . . . She was still his real-estate agent. And she hadn't told him about the Miles Road property. She triple-tapped her forehead with the heel of her hand for forgetting something so important. *Time to regroup.* Okay, she would tell him that Miles Road was under contract, then she would find a house for him to buy, then she would sell his house, and *then* they wouldn't have to see each other . . .

Except for the auction. "Argh!"

She could do this. She could be professional. She was a master at it. Eventually these inexplicable feelings for him would disappear, and her life would go back to normal. Whatever that was.

She turned onto her road, suddenly exhausted. She wanted nothing more than that cup of tea and to fall into bed. *Matlock* would have to wait for another night.

But as she approached her driveway, she saw an unfamiliar car parked in front of the garage door.

When she pulled up, the door opened, triggering the automatic outdoor lights. She was about to grab her phone to dial 911 when she finally recognized the car and the man standing next to it. Her entire body froze.

Jack.

"Well," Senior said, staring at the kitchen entry-way Harper had just escaped through. "Wasn't that somethin', her running off like that?"

"Yeah." Rusty ran his hand through his hair, then stopped when he felt the short ends. He'd completely forgotten about his haircut until now. In fact, it was the last thing on his mind. Harper was the first, and the second. Third and fourth, too, because he couldn't figure out what he'd done to make her jackrabbit out of there.

"Uh-oh." Senior pointed to her cell lying on the kitchen table. "She'll probably need this soon." He turned to Rusty, his mouth open as if he wanted to say something else, then clamped it shut. His eyes nearly bugged out of his head. "Boy, if I didn't know any better, I'd believe there was a stranger in my house." He grinned and walked over to him, then reached up and tousled the top of his hair. "You look mighty fine, son. Mighty fine."

Thanks to Harper. He could still sense the soft warmth of her palm in his hand. When she said she couldn't see Sirius, he'd jumped at the chance to help her find the famous star—and what better way than to guide her hand to where it was? Lying under the stars with her hammered home what he'd spent the entire day trying to ignore: He was falling for her. Hard. And when she surprised him by not letting go of his hand, he'd experienced a few minutes of pure heaven.

Then Senior showed up and spoiled everything. Normally his grandfather's teasing didn't bother him. But the old man had broken the spell, and Rusty had jerked away before Senior caught them holding hands and embarrassed Harper.

Turned out she'd been embarrassed anyway. That had to be the reason she'd left so fast.

Senior walked over to the fridge. "I came in here to fix me a nightcap, and I saw the straw wrapper on the table," he explained, as if anticipating Rusty's question about why he'd interrupted them. "When I didn't find you in the house, I thought I'd check the backyard." He pulled out a bottle of spicy tomato juice and shut the refrigerator door. "I remembered you used to go outside on clear nights like this. Didn't figure you'd be out there with Miss Harper, though."

"Don't give me that line of bull." Rusty plopped down at the table. "You knew exactly what you were doin'."

Senior set the juice on the table, his jovial expression gone. "Hey," he said, sitting down next to him. "I was just havin' a little fun. I didn't realize things were so serious with you two."

"They're not."

"Don't be so sure about that."

Rusty didn't have the patience for Senior's attempt at encouragement. "You saw how she hightailed out of here."

"Because of her *appointment*."

Rusty could see that Senior didn't believe her excuse any more than he did. That said, she did work a lot of long hours. More likely she wanted to make sure that Senior knew there was nothing going on between them, like she had at Artie's. He'd said the same thing, too, about being strictly friends . . . but in his case he hadn't been telling the truth.

"You really like this gal, don't you?"

Rusty shoved back from the table. He remembered the first time a girl had crushed his hopes. It was at the end of his junior year, and Sabrina Hackett had been his lab partner in chemistry. He liked her so much that he let her copy his homework before class every day. After six months he'd found the courage to ask if she wanted to take a ride in the '82 Charger he'd just finished restoring. *"Maybe we could get a hamburger or something,"* he'd added, rubbing the eraser of his pencil so hard it fell off.

"That's so sweet, Rusty," she said, her expression a mix of humor and pity. *"But you're a good*

friend. I don't want to ruin that." She didn't have a problem copying his homework for the rest of the year, though. Like a moron, he let her, and they both got As in the class. After that, she never spoke to him again.

After he graduated, there were two more women he'd been interested in. Both had said basically the same thing: he was good enough to be a friend but not good enough to date. Then there was that disaster of a blind date he'd told Harper about, the one that made him look like an enormous loser.

And when it came to women, he was.

"Rusty?" Senior snapped his fingers. "Still with me?"

He shrugged. "Don't matter if I like her. I've been here before, and I know what's going to happen."

Senior crossed his arms. "And what's that, exactly?"

"She'll keep her distance so no one thinks we're together." He gave Senior a withering look. "We'll run into each other at the gala, and she'll be polite but avoid me all night. She'll probably drop me as a real-estate client and use another mechanic for her car."

"Wow," Senior said wryly. "That's a lot of fortune-tellin' you're doin' over there."

"Like I said, I've been here before."

"Have you told her how you feel?" Senior asked.

His gaze flew to him. "No."

"Why not?"

"And get shot down? Forget it."

Senior rubbed the gray stubble on his chin. "What if she don't?" He leaned forward, his expression serious for once. "What do you have to lose by tellin' her the truth?"

My dignity? "Why are you pushing this?"

"I reckon you're readin' the situation all wrong," Senior said. When Rusty scowled, he sat back in the chair. "But what do I know? I'm just an old man who was married for over fifty years."

"I'm goin' to bed," Rusty said, jumping up from the chair.

Disappointment flashed in his grandfather's eyes. "What about this?" He held up Harper's phone.

"I'll get it to her tomorrow," he said, then went upstairs, kicked off his shoes, and plopped onto his bed, still wearing all his clothes, including his gray hoodie. Falling for Harper had been too easy, and he should have known better. He couldn't be upset with her either. She hadn't led him on and had been forthright that their relationship was strictly professional, with a dash of friendliness thrown in. Besides, expecting her to have any feelings for him was ludicrous. She could have her pick of any guy. Why would she choose him?

He rolled onto his side, his conversation with Senior sticking in his mind. *Am I really seeing this wrong?* His track record with women proved he was a master in that department. But what if Senior was right? What if there was a chance—no matter how minuscule—that Harper was open to something more than friendship? Was it worth the risk to find out?

He put on his shoes and went downstairs. The light was still on, and Harper's phone was still next to his. He knew how attached she was to her cell, and waiting until morning to return it didn't sit right.

And maybe . . . just maybe . . . while he was there, he might test the waters to see if Senior was right. Because if Harper Wilson *was* interested in him . . .

He grinned. *I'd be the happiest man in the world.*

He left the house and got into his truck, then headed for her house.

Senior stuck his head out of his room and peeked at Rusty opening the front door. A few seconds later he heard his grandson's truck roaring to life. Hopefully what he'd said to Rusty tonight had stuck. When he went into the kitchen and saw the cell phone was missing, he grinned. That boy was headed to Miss Harper's.

He fixed himself his usual nighttime snack—

peanut butter spread over graham crackers with a dash of Tabasco on top. Judy had never understood how he could eat something so disgusting, but the combo worked for him. He sighed. Not a day went by without him thinking about her, and right now he wished she was here to help him help Rusty.

He turned on the tap, filled a glass with water, and sat down at the table. He'd never had a moment's trouble with his grandson. Couldn't say the same for Junior, though. That child had brought enough sorrow to him and Judy over the years, the apex being when he abandoned his children. That had turned out to be a gift, raising Amber and Rusty. But that didn't mean he still wasn't disappointed in Junior. Roxy too. How could a mother ditch her own children for a new family? He shook his head. That was unfathomable to him, but she went and did it, leaving two precious kids behind.

He and Judy had prayed over the years that their grandchildren wouldn't be too scarred from their parents' abandonment. If Amber was, she didn't show it. His granddaughter was tough, but she was also a loving and sensible wife and mother.

Rusty was a different story. The boy was soft through and through and had inherited Judy's sensitive side. He'd taken his mother's rejection hard and internalized it, according to Judy. Senior wasn't too keen on psychobabble, although those daytime medical shows were fairly entertaining. But he was starting to see that Judy was right. Rusty Jenkins III had the confidence to take apart a car engine and put it together blindfolded, but when it came to relationships, he was at a loss.

Senior shoved away his half-eaten snack. There was nothing he could do except offer encouragement and advice. Although the way Rusty had responded tonight, he might not do that again anytime soon.

He closed his eyes and said a little prayer that his gut was right about Miss Harper. He'd seen the way she looked at Rusty when he walked into the kitchen earlier tonight. She couldn't keep her eyes off him—admiring eyes, Senior noticed. He wasn't blind just yet, and the few minutes of conversation he'd had with her over Oreos and powdered tea proved that she wasn't only a pretty face. On the surface they were as opposite as salt and pepper, but often that was a good thing when it applied to couples.

Just don't break his heart, Miss Harper. It's been broken enough.

Harper parked her car on the street and jumped out as Jack walked toward her. "Don't come any closer," she said, walking to the end of her driveway and stopping there. "I'll call the police, I swear!" Then she remembered her phone. Oh no, she'd left it at Rusty's. But Jack didn't know that, thank God.

He halted, leaving several feet between them, then held up his hands. "I'm sure you're still mad at me—"

"Oh? What gave you that idea?" She crossed her arms over her chest.

"You have a right to be, and I'm sorry for what I did. But I really need to talk to you. It's important."

She hesitated. He had gone to a lot of trouble to track her down, and he'd been persistent. He'd never been violent in the past. Just a class A jerk. "I'm listening."

He looked over his shoulder at her house, then back at her. "Can we go inside? It's a long story."

Harper pinched the bridge of her nose. She didn't have the capacity to fight him right now. "Fine. But only until you've said whatever it is you need to tell me. Then you have to leave."

"I promise I will."

A few minutes later they were sitting at the table, not in the living room. She didn't want him to feel comfortable, and she didn't offer him a drink. "All right," she said. "Spill."

He tugged at the collar of his dress shirt. He was still wearing a tie and a sports jacket, as if he'd been working up until the moment he came over. That didn't surprise her. He'd always worked late—or so she'd thought when he was tardy for their dates, until near the end when he didn't show up for them at all. *Too busy cheating on me with Brielle.*

"It's good to see you again," he said.

She tapped her finger on the table. "I said spill."

He glanced away, then looked at her again. "All right. First, I'm sorry I broke up with you. I should have never done that."

"Does that include cheating with Brielle?"

His eyes widened. "I never cheated on you. Honest. She's the one who said you cheated on me."

Harper gasped. "What? I would never do something like that to you or anyone else."

"I believe you . . . now. I didn't at the time, though. She was so convincing . . ." He shook his head. "That doesn't matter right now. What matters is her latest scheme."

Panic hit her. "Which is?"

"She's out to ruin you. That's why she moved back to Hot Springs."

"I don't understand."

Jack looked at her. "Brielle has always seen you as a threat, ever since you both worked at Front Door Realty. You're younger than her, and when you joined the company, she'd been the top seller for five years straight. Then you toppled her the first year you were there."

"I worked hard to reach that goal," Harper ground out. "You know that."

"I do. So did everyone else there. But that made Brielle jealous. She'd been planning to open her own brokerage firm right before you opened yours. So she blames you for undermining her."

Harper held up her palms. "I *cannot* believe this."

"And when you and I started dating, it broke the last straw," he continued. "She'd asked me out a few times over the years, and I didn't exactly turn her down, but I put her off. She finally stopped right around the time you started at Front Door." His eyes softened. "I was knocked out the first time I saw you, Harper. You're an incredible woman. I didn't realize how much so until I lost you."

"You didn't lose me. You *dumped* me." Her insides rattled as she tried to comprehend everything he was saying. "If you thought I was cheating, you should have said something."

"I know. But I was so hurt. More than that, I was angry. No one makes a fool out of me." His eyes narrowed. Then he sighed. "Except Brielle."

Still stunned, Harper said, "I don't get it. You moved away with her. I thought you two were going to get married."

"Hardly. Even before we moved, we were on the rocks. But her plan to open an office in Bentonville together was an offer I couldn't refuse. It was an opportunity of a lifetime business-wise.

The market is red hot right now, and there's no sign of it contracting anytime soon.

"Then why did you come back?"

"When I severed our relationship, she severed our partnership. There were some legal hassles to get it done, but we both wanted out. Then I moved back here to figure out my future." He faced her. "I'm not asking to get back together—"

"Good, because that is *not* going to happen."

He averted his gaze again, nodding before he looked back at her. "When Brielle came back to Hot Springs, I knew she had to be up to something. So we talked. She thinks I came back for you. Even when I told her that she was wrong, she wasn't convinced. That's when she told me she was going to put you out of business."

"She sounds crazy." Harper pressed her lips together.

"She's insecure and bitter, and not just about you. She hates me too. And I'm to blame for that."

"Because you moved back here?"

He shook his head. "Because she loves me. But I don't love her. I tried, but I couldn't make myself feel something I didn't. I feel bad about that, because when she's not being malicious, she's fun to be around. And I admire her business acumen. She's brilliant. Unfortunately, she's putting her tactics to work against you."

"Like poaching my clients," Harper said, the pieces starting to fall into place.

Jack nodded. "She's spreading rumors too. Like—"

"I don't want to know." She got up from the chair and turned away, hugging her arms. So that's why her clients were canceling and not returning her calls. "What am I supposed to do?"

"You could play her game," Jack suggested.

"No." She turned around. "I would never do that."

"Then ride it out. You're as driven as we are. People will realize the rumors are false, and if she doesn't stop poaching, I'll report her." He stood and walked over to her. "You'll bounce back from this."

His confidence in her should have made her feel better. Instead, her guard went up. "Why are you helping me?"

He smiled. "Because I made a huge mistake. I'm trying to make up for it."

She didn't categorize dumping her for another woman as a mistake. It was an active choice. Everything he said about Brielle was starting to sink in. "I appreciate you telling me all this," she said, willing to give him a little credit.

"I'm glad I finally could."

"It's late." She glanced at the square acrylic clock on the wall above the foyer. It was only nine, but it felt much later.

"My cue to leave?" he said.

"Yes."

Without argument he moved toward the door, and she walked him outside, stopping on the front stoop. The cool night breeze hit her as she swiveled to face him. "Good night, Jack."

"Harper," he murmured, taking her hand. "I know I said I wasn't here to get back together, but . . ." He moved closer. "Are you seeing any-one?"

Rusty immediately came to mind. *I wish.* She shook her head and tried to pull away from him. "No."

Jack cupped her face as headlights appeared in her driveway. She saw a truck pulling up. Her stomach turned inside out.

Rusty.

Chapter 15

Rusty gripped the steering wheel so tight his knuckles cramped. He ignored the pain, frozen in his seat as he saw a man touching Harper's face. Even when he stopped the truck behind the black Lexus in her driveway, the guy still held her hand. So her appointment was actually a date. The punch to his chest made it hard to breathe.

Harper rushed to his truck, her date following her. Rusty wanted to throw the phone out the window and drive away, but he couldn't. He always did the right thing, even if it made him look like a fool.

She rapped on the window. He gulped and scrambled for composure before pushing a button on the truck door. The window slid down. "Hey," he said, struggling to keep his tone neutral. "Sorry. Didn't mean to interrupt."

"You're not interrupting," she said as the man appeared next to her. He was a slick-looking fella with short black hair, clean-shaven and dressed like a businessman. Similar to what Rusty looked like after she'd made him over. Obviously she had a type, and it wasn't him. Under the high-class window dressing, he was still the same Rusty—mechanic, garage-shop owner, and a bust with the ladies. The same guy who didn't have a chance with Harper Wilson.

"You left your phone," he said, handing it to her.

"Thank you. I realized that when I got home." She glanced at the guy who hovered behind her, scowling at Rusty as if he was trespassing. He sure felt like he was.

"Do you want to come inside for a drink?" she asked, smiling oddly, as if her teeth were too tight.

Seriously? She was inviting him to be a third wheel? "Naw," he muttered, swaying on the edge of losing his cool. "Just wanted to make sure you had your phone."

"But—"

He rolled up the window and shoved the truck into Reverse. Harper and the man drew back as he backed out of the driveway and sped off.

His chest burned as he went back home. He never should have listened to Senior. Or even himself. He tried to convince himself that this wasn't the same as being rejected. She could date whoever she wanted to, even after they had spent a wonderful day together. Well, it was wonderful for him. Probably just an ordinary day in the life of Harper Wilson.

But why hadn't she told him she had a date? Why lie and say it was an appointment? If they were such good friends, she should have told the truth. He wouldn't have liked it, but he could have avoided what just happened.

He hit the steering wheel with the side of his fist. He wasn't mad at her—except for her thinking he'd want to tag along on her date. That pricked his ego. No, he was angry at himself for believing he had a chance with her. Like he'd told his grandfather—he'd been here before. This time, though, it was different. This time it *hurt*.

And this time he'd learned his lesson. For good.

"Who was that?"

Harper spun around, aggravated at the possessive tone in Jack's voice. "A . . . friend," she said, walking back to the house. Had Rusty seen Jack touching her face? Holding her hand? She couldn't believe Jack had pulled that stunt. Actually, she did believe it. What she couldn't fathom was that she had fallen for it. She should have shoved him out of the house and locked the door behind him. Instead, she had chosen to be polite, and he'd taken advantage of that.

Never again.

"Harper, wait."

She stopped in front of her open door, then reluctantly turned around. "Thank you for warning me about Brielle. Please leave now."

His eyes narrowed. "Because of that guy?" He

pointed his thumb in the direction of the street as if Rusty was still there.

I wish he was.

Harper opened her mouth, ready to tell Jack no, it was because she would never get back together with him and he needed to get that through his thick head. But the words wouldn't come. "Yes. Because of Rusty."

Jack hung his head, then looked at her again. "I had my chance," he said, sounding disappointed but also resigned. "If you need some help taking care of Brielle, let me know. Purely business, I promise."

She softened her tone. "I can handle her."

"I know you can." He gave her a little wave, then got into his Lexus and drove away.

She shut the door, her cell phone in her hand. She quickly brought up Rusty's number and called it.

"Hey, this is Rusty. If this is an emergency, call . . ."

She listened as he gave out the number for his towing service, then directed the caller to leave a message. "Hi, Rusty, it's me. Thanks again for bringing over my phone." She paused, unsure what else to say. *Tell him there's nothing between you and Jack. Tell him you can't wait to see him again. Tell him how much he means to—*

Beep!

The recorder timed out. She ended the call.

Telling him what was on her heart wouldn't change anything. Not when he didn't feel the same way.

Harper drew in a breath and headed for her home office, knowing she could find refuge in work. Now that she knew what—actually, who— had tanked her sales, she needed to figure out her next move.

But as she sat down at her desk and turned on the laptop, her mind drifted back to Rusty. The relaxation she'd felt at the fishing hole. The fun they'd had doing his makeover—after they'd gotten past the discomfort she'd created by caressing his chin. She closed her eyes, remembering that moment with a mix of regret and pleasure.

Holding his hand while they gazed at the stars . . .

She opened her eyes and stared at the computer screen. The last thing she wanted to do was work. Then she realized . . . that was all she had. Her parents were wrapped up in their drama, and she didn't want to bother her friends with her professional and personal problems. Riley and Anita had their husbands, and Olivia had her educational pursuits. They didn't need her tugging them away from their lives.

Above all, she didn't want them to see the truth. She was Harper Wilson, successful business-woman, flawless fashion maven, a rising star.

She couldn't let them know her life was falling apart.

The First Annual Maple Falls Fall Parade kicked off to huge success. Rusty closed the garage for the day so Percy and Hank could enjoy the festivities. Right before the parade started, he and Senior, along with Amber and his niece and nephews, set out their camping chairs in front of Price's Hardware. The downtown area was as full as he'd ever seen it. He recognized a few people who had moved away, and he was glad to see them return for the parade.

"It's starting!" his oldest nephew, Kyle, said.

Senior got up from his chair. He arched his back, then motioned to his great-grandchildren. "C'mon, youngins. Let's get a closer look." When Amber started to get up, he shook his head. "I can handle 'em. We ain't goin' far."

She sat back in her chair, relaxing a little when she saw they were only a few feet away. Senior had the kids sit on the edge of the curb as Sheriff Hendricks's car rolled by, his lights flashing.

"This is nice," Amber said. "I'm glad to see they're bringing parades back."

"Thanks to Hayden." Rusty glanced at Hayden and Riley, who stood a few feet away behind a table set up with brochures and information about Maple Falls and the surrounding area. "He worked to get this off the ground."

"The kids are loving it. Even that big one over there." Amber laughed and pointed as Senior grinned and waved at a pair of clowns walking by.

Rusty laughed and took a sip of warm cider.

Amber stuck her hands into the pockets of her dark-orange fleece vest. "Have you found a new place yet?"

He paused. He hadn't spoken to Harper since Wednesday night. He'd silenced his phone as soon as he got home, and on Thursday morning he saw that she'd left a voice mail. He hadn't listened to it yet. Eventually he would have to, but when she came to mind—and she did, frequently—all he saw was that guy touching her face and holding her hand. "Still lookin'," he said, hoping that would satisfy his sister's curiosity.

"Austin and I made our decision," she said. "We're going to Colorado. I'm going to tell Senior this evening before we go back home."

"He already knows," Rusty said.

Amber looked at him, then shrugged. "I'm not surprised. Did you talk to him about selling that dump?"

"*I* live in that dump. And it ain't exactly a dump."

"It's totally a dump." She pushed aside a strand of red hair the same color as his and hooked it behind her ear, which was also covered in freckles. "What did he say?"

Rusty watched Bubba Lewis drive by in his '49 Ford truck. "To sell the dump."

"See? Even he thinks it's unsalvageable."

For some reason he felt compelled to defend the house. "It can be fixed up. And there's plenty of space in the backyard to build an addition. The neighborhood's real quiet too."

His sister gave him an odd look. "Since it's got lots of potential, it should be easy to sell, right?"

Seeing there was no convincing her, he relented. "Sure." The parade was almost over, with the town's one fire truck bringing up the rear. "When are you moving?"

"Austin's leaving next week to get settled into his new job and find us a place to live. As soon as he does, we'll pack up and go. So probably six weeks to two months."

"Right before Christmas?"

She sighed. "Yeah. The timing isn't great, but it can't be helped. Even if he doesn't find a house by then, we'll rent something and move. We don't want to be apart longer than that."

That meant he had two months to find a house or property to build on, if he was lucky. He was on a time crunch now, so he had to talk to Harper. Maybe that's why she'd called, to tell him she'd finally gotten in touch with Brielle. That would be good news, he supposed.

Once the parade passed them by, the boys ran to their mother. Emma, the only girl and Amber's youngest, climbed into his lap. "Lookee what I got, Unca Russy." She held up a small lollipop, one of the candies the clowns had tossed out to the kids. Emma was three years old and the spitting image of Amber. Her flaming-red hair curled from underneath a small purple beanie, and freckles sprinkled across her eyelids and cheeks. She fussed with the wrapper until he took it from her and opened it. She popped the sucker in her mouth and leaned her head against his chest.

He kissed her temple and looked at Amber, who was corralling her three boys—eight, seven, and five. Senior stood behind them to make sure they didn't run off into the street, even though it had been blocked off for the parade. He shifted his gaze to Rusty, sadness in his eyes.

I'll miss them too.

"Everyone ready for a hot dog?" Amber asked. The boys raised their hands while Emma stayed put in Rusty's lap.

"Me," Senior said, raising his hand. "I'm starvin'."

Rusty carried Emma across the street as they headed for Sunshine Diner. They spent the rest of the afternoon going up and down Main Street and visiting with people in the community. But there was one person he didn't see—Harper. No doubt she'd skipped the parade to work. He was relieved. Doggone it, he was disappointed too.

He reeled that emotion back in. The sooner he got over her, the better.

They went back to his house, and Amber loaded the kids to take them back to Little Rock. Senior looked at Rusty. "Do you mind if I go with them?" he asked, glancing at his grandchildren again. "I'd like to spend as much time as I can with them before they move away."

"Of course." Rusty hadn't said anything to him about seeing Harper, and Senior fortunately hadn't asked. "I'll pick you up next week."

"Ain't no need. Amber already said she'd give me a ride back."

"While y'all and the kids were getting cookies at the café, I ran into one of my high school friends," Amber said. "We're going to meet up the day before the auction." She poked her head into the back seat of the car. "Jace, you give your brother his pumpkin bucket back right now." She stood and glowered at Rusty and Senior. "Thanks for stuffing them with sugar today."

"You're welcome," they both said at the same time.

Amber huffed, then half smiled. "You're putting them to bed tonight, Senior."

"Gladly." He winked at Rusty.

After he helped Senior pack and everyone left for Little Rock, Rusty went back inside the house—or the dump, as Amber called it. The silence hit him hard. When she and the kids were here, the entire place was filled with noise—the kids playing, talking, yelling, and yes, occasionally crying, because siblings could be mean to each other. He'd teased Amber enough over the years, although when he was little, he was the one who ended up crying. He chuckled. Despite the chaos, love reigned. Like it had when he was growing up here.

Dang it, now he had a lump in his throat.

He walked out to the back porch and looked at the dead leaves dotting the ground. He wasn't much for yardwork—not that he hated doing it, but he was fine with his landscaping resembling a more natural state. Still, he grabbed a rake from the garage and started making huge leaf piles.

Half an hour into the task, his phone rang. He flinched. What if it was Harper? Knowing he couldn't put her off anymore, he withdrew the cell from his pocket, then saw the unfamiliar number. The same mix of relief and disappointment hit him. He shrugged it off. "Hello?"

"May I speak to Mr. Jenkins, please?"

The voice sounded vaguely familiar, but he couldn't place it. "Speakin'."

"This is Brielle Weaver. We met a while ago at Deep-Dish Delights."

Rusty kicked at a stray leaf. Why was she calling him and not Harper? "Yes," he said. "I remember." How could he forget her donkey of a date and how the man had leered at Harper?

269

"I wanted to let you know that the Miles Road property is for sale again."

He stilled. "Again?"

"It was under contract for a few days, then the buyer changed his mind. Didn't Harper tell you?"

He gripped the phone. "No, she didn't mention it."

"I tried getting in touch with her," Brielle continued. "But I haven't been able to reach her. I hope you don't mind that I'm calling you directly. If you're still interested in the property, I can set up a showing asap."

He couldn't respond. Why hadn't she told him?

"I can't say I'm surprised she didn't say anything to you," Brielle said. "Harper does have that reputation."

"What reputation?"

"I probably shouldn't say . . ." After less than a second's hesitation, she plowed ahead. "Harper and I used to work together, so I've known her for a long time. She hasn't always been—how can I put this?—aboveboard in her business dealings. Several of her clients are unhappy with how she's treated them."

"How do you know that?"

"Real estate has a grapevine like anywhere else," she said quickly. "Mr. Jenkins, if you're interested in looking at the property, I can set up a showing for you. Just let me know when you're available."

He hesitated. "Shouldn't Harper be a part of this?"

"I suppose. But do you *really* want someone representing you who isn't completely honest?"

This didn't make any sense. Everything he knew about Harper was the exact opposite of what Brielle was saying.

She didn't tell you the property was under contract. She didn't tell you she was seeing someone. When he thought about it, how well did he know Harper?

I thought she was different.

"Mr. Jenkins?" Brielle said. "Can I set up that appointment for you?"

He tried to think rationally, but the hurt he'd felt seeing Harper with another man washed over him, compounded by all the rejection he'd felt in his life. The dates that ended disastrously. His sister and his friends getting married and moving on with their personal lives, leaving him behind. The parents who didn't want him. Now Harper, who he had thought was trustworthy on a business level, hadn't bothered to tell him the Miles Road property wasn't for sale. But now it was.

"Mr. Jenkins? Are you still there?"

His jaw jerked. "Let's talk."

Chapter 16

On Monday morning Harper shoved her glasses closer to her eyes, pushed her feet into her warm, furry slippers, and got up off the couch. For the past two hours sharp wind and heavy rain had battered against her house, and according to her phone the temperature was in the forties. She tried to convince herself that was the reason she'd decided to work from home today, despite the fact that nasty weather had never kept her home before. And certainly that didn't explain why she hadn't showered or gotten dressed since she came home from the fall parade Saturday evening. Two days in a row wearing the same pj's was a record for her, and not one she was proud of.

On Friday she realized she'd forgotten to call Hayden about setting up her own booth at the parade. It was too late to do anything at that point, but she decided to go anyway and assist anyone who needed her. She had arrived just before the festivities started and checked with Riley first, who was with Hayden at the Maple Falls information tent set up at the end of Main Street.

"Peg had to cancel at the last minute," Riley said. "Mimi could use an extra hand."

"Is Madge here?" She hadn't spoken to her mother since the day she'd showed up at Harper's office.

"No. Mimi said she had other plans."

Her mother had always enjoyed volunteering, and it was strange for her to miss an event like this . . . unless she was avoiding it on purpose. *I have got to call her.*

"Wait until you find out what the BBs are doing," Riley said.

"Uh-oh." Forgetting about her mother, she asked, "What do you mean?"

Riley smirked. "You'll see."

When Harper arrived at Knots and Tangles, she was horrified by the idea the older women had cooked up: braided pigtail wigs made out of yarn. Not just any yarn, but bright neon colors that could be seen from the moon.

"Aren't you a peach for helping us out," Erma had said, handing her the worst color of the bunch, an eye-burning shade of lime green. But Harper had committed to help, so she put on the wig and went outside to greet passersby with Bea and Myrtle. Their wigs—pink and purple, respectively—weren't as hideous. *Lucky them.*

Despite the fashion faux pas, she'd enjoyed talking to customers and telling them about Knots and Tangles. The wigs were a hit, and Erma sold several kits during the day. It was nice to put work on the back burner for a little while, and she hadn't bothered to try to promote her own business, a first for her.

But there was another reason she'd decided to come to the parade. She needed to talk to Rusty and had hoped to see him at some point. During the past two days she'd been tempted to call him again and not only clear up why Jack was there but also finally tell him about Miles Road. She never should have put that off. But she held back. She wanted to have that conversation in person, especially when she clarified that Jack had only been there to warn her about Brielle. That would take some time to explain.

Finally she spied him right after the Maple Falls Fire Department had driven by. He was sitting next to a woman, and Senior was seated in front of them, talking to four young children. When she saw the woman's red hair, she guessed it had to be his sister, Amber.

"Erma, do you need me for anything else?" she'd said.

Erma put her hands on her hips, her bright-purple wig askew, making the pigtails uneven. Somehow it worked on her. "No, we can handle things from here. Thanks for your help. Did I tell you you're a peach?"

Everyone was a peach to Erma, except maybe Jasper Mathis. "Yes, but I like hearing it." She slipped off her wig and handed it to Erma.

"Oh, you keep it, dear. We have plenty here."

"Uh, thanks." As Erma went inside, Harper turned in time to see a small girl climb into Rusty's lap and snuggle against him. Even when she was dating Jack, marriage had been a distant thought, an event that might happen, but only when she reached all her business goals. Kids were *never* on her radar. She didn't consider herself the motherly type. But seeing Rusty holding his niece filled her with warm awe. They looked so comfortable together. And when he gave her temple a tiny kiss . . . Harper melted inside.

"Hi, Harper."

She spun around to see Pastor Jared standing behind her. He was around her age, but anyone could see he had an old soul. He was dressed casually in jeans, a black shirt, and a chocolate-brown jacket with an *I love Jesus* pin on the lapel.

"It's good to see you," he said, smiling. "We've missed you in church lately. Also on the softball team this past summer. We could have used you on second base again."

Although his words were delivered in a kind tone, she felt guilty anyway. "I'm sorry," she said. "Work has been crazy." *My whole life has.*

"No need to apologize. Just wanted to let you know that you're missed. See you soon." He waved to her and headed down the sidewalk toward the café.

Harper looked at the wig in her hand. She

missed attending church. Up until this past summer she'd been a faithful attendee.

She lifted her head and tried to find Rusty again, but he and his family had disappeared, and she didn't see them for the rest of the parade. When she went home, she tried to psych herself up to do some work, but she never made it past the kitchen.

A *boom* of thunder made her jump, and she rose from the couch and padded to the kitchen. She poured herself a glass of milk, then squirted at least half a bottle of chocolate syrup into it. Not bothering to get a spoon, she swirled the glass a few times and took a big gulp. Then another, and another, until the milk was gone and all that remained in the bottom was the syrup. She drank that too. For a hot minute she felt better, then her stomach lurched. *I shouldn't have done that.* Just like she shouldn't have spent all day yesterday baking. Her marble island countertop was covered with plates and platters of calorie-laden treats—chocolate-chip cookies, pumpkin-spiced muffins, apple strudel, Parker House rolls, and cherry-topped cheesecake. What was she going to do with all this food?

The doorbell rang, and she froze, then glanced at her two-day-old attire and cringed. It was one thing for her to be dressed down, another for her to abandon hygiene completely. Hopefully who-ever was at the door was just a delivery driver dropping off a package. She hadn't ordered anything lately, but sometimes they left her neighbor's packages on her doorstep by accident. Just in case, she went to check. If it was a package, she needed to bring it inside before the rain soaked through the cardboard.

But when she opened the door, her father was standing on her front stoop.

"Dad?"

"Hi." His hands were shoved into his windbreaker pockets, and his longish hair was plastered to the side of his head, even though his jacket had a hood. "Can I come in?"

"Of course." She took a step back and let him inside, noticing his almost full, shaggy gray beard that reminded her a little of Rusty's. Everything seemed to remind her of him. Whatever the case, it dawned on her that she'd never seen her father this unkempt before. The Wilson family was always well dressed. Except for today. "Is everything all right?" she asked, closing the door behind him.

He turned and faced her, his eyes bleary. "No, sweetheart. It's not."

Harper's heart melted a bit at the endearment. Don didn't dole out affectionate words too often. "Give me your jacket," she said, holding out her hand. "I'll make us some coffee. Do you want some cookies? Pumpkin bread? Cheesecake?"

"No, thanks," he said, his brow lifting at the sight of her counter. "Bake sale?"

She shook her head. "Bad day."

He nodded. "Gotcha. Been having a lot of those myself lately."

When they were settled in the living room, her dad in an armchair directly across from her, Harper said, "Is this about Mom? The divorce?"

He nodded. His coffee remained on the clear glass and metal coffee table in the middle of the room. "I've lost her, Harper," he said, staring down at his bare feet, showing he hadn't taken the time to bother with socks. "I've really lost her this time."

"This time?"

He lifted his eyes. "You know more than any-one how rocky our relationship has always been." His shoulders drooped. "I'm sorry you had to witness that."

"It's okay—"

"No. It's not." He scrubbed his hands over his cheeks. "I'm sorry about a lot of things. Like not being there for you when you were growing up."

Or ever. She kept that to herself and took a sip of the coffee, then blanched and set it on the table near his. Never again was she going to ingest that much sugar at once. "Thanks, Dad," she said, acknowledging his words. She didn't know if the apology would change anything, but he was trying. "Why are you here?"

"To apologize."

"Accepted."

"And to confess." He sighed, then sat back and threaded his fingers through his damp mop of hair. "Your mother won't talk to me, so I guess you're the lucky one who gets to hear about my sins."

Rattled, Harper held up her hand. "I don't think that's a good idea—"

"I had an affair."

Harper stilled. She should shut down this line of conversation right now, but the sorrow and remorse in his eyes stopped her.

"Her name is Veronica. She was a flight attendant I met years ago. The details aren't important. Just know that I ended it. Since then I've been trying to work things out with your mother, but she's so stubborn."

"She has to be hurt, Dad. You can't do something that horrible and expect her to be okay with it." Harper was far from okay with it, either, but her father's genuine anguish took some of the sting away.

"I didn't realize how hurt she was until now. Your mother has always kept her emotions locked up tight. She's been that way since I met her, although when she was younger she would relax more often. Now she's wound up tighter than a spring, and I can't get through to her. We're supposed to sign divorce papers on Wednesday.

I gave her everything, even though my lawyer thinks I'm insane."

"Everything?"

"My pension, both houses, the cars . . ." He shrugged. "She deserves all of it, for putting up with me. I was gone all the time. She practically raised you alone. Then I go and . . ." His eyes filled with tears. "I'm sorry. I'm so sorry for everything."

"Oh, Dad." Harper got up and knelt beside him, surprised at the compassion filling her heart. She should be furious with him for cheating on her mother. And she was angry about it. But she could also see he was genuinely repentant.

"Can you forgive me? For not being the father you needed me to be?"

Tears slipped down her face. "Yes," she said thickly. "I forgive you."

He leaned forward and hugged her tightly. She buried her face in his shirt, the few memories she had of him interacting with her coming to the fore. He hadn't been entirely MIA her whole life. There were times he had been present, like once when he'd seen her play softball when she was in elementary school, and he'd taken her and her mother out for ice cream to celebrate her batting a triple. When he'd flown in one weekend when she was a freshman in high school and surprised her and Madge with a weekend trip to Disney World, one of the items on her bucket list. She still had the stuffed Minnie Mouse he'd bought her.

He pulled away. "I don't know how to make years of neglect up to either of you. I've tried with your mother. Taken her places she always wanted to go, buying her things she always wanted. I thought we were making progress. Then she found out about the affair and filed for divorce."

Harper sat cross-legged on the floor. "Did you ever think that maybe it wasn't the things or the trips she wanted? Or I wanted? Although Disney was really cool." She wiped the tears from her face. "All we wanted was you."

"And I want to be here for you." He gave her a watery smile, then rubbed the back of his hand over his eyes. "It's too late for your mother and me. Is it too late for us?"

"No," she said, even though her guard was still up. "But I have to be honest. I don't know what our relationship should look like right now. I'm a grown woman."

"Who still wears bunny slippers?" His eyebrows arched.

"You noticed those."

"They're kind of hard to miss," he said. "I know what you mean, though. I guess we have to take it one day at a time."

She nodded, then got up from the floor and sat back on the couch. "You look awful, by the way."

"Yeah, I know. You don't look so great yourself, though."

Harper tucked her feet under her and sighed. "Touché."

"I tried calling you," he said, picking up his coffee. "When you didn't answer, I went to your office and saw it was closed. I got worried until I saw your car in the driveway. Are you on vacation?"

She shook her head. "Just didn't feel like working."

He scoffed. "I might not have been around much when you were growing up, but I know you well enough that if you don't want to work, there's something seriously wrong. I can relate."

She stared at her bunny slippers on the floor, a joke gift from Anita two years ago. Her instinct was to dismiss his comment and either show him the door or make him something to eat. She was that baffled. But this would be a good time to test his sincerity about working on their relationship, so she took a risk. "I think . . . I think I've fallen in love with someone. Or in really, really, *really* serious like. I'm not sure."

"All right." He set the coffee cup back down. "This is probably more your mother's territory—"

"Never mind," she muttered and started to get up off the couch.

"Wait a minute, you didn't let me finish." He

gestured for her to stay seated. "I want to help, if I can." When she was seated again, he said, "Why do you think you're in love? Or like?"

"No clue. I'm so confused."

"Is he the reason you're hiding out at home?"

"I'm not hiding," she started, then sighed and told him about Rusty, her car, the house hunt, the gala, the makeover, and their stargazing. Then she told him about Jack, the Miles Road property, her job tanking, her goal to buy a building and open up a second office in Maple Falls, and finally, Brielle.

"Wow," he said, his brows lifting. "You've got a lot on your plate."

"I always do." She sighed. "I'm tired, Dad. When Jack told me about Brielle's sabotage, I was upset. But I knew I could rebuild my business if I wanted to." She looked at him. "I'm not sure I want to anymore. At least not to the way it was. Then again, maybe I just need a vacation."

"Or you're reevaluating things. You get that workaholic tendency from me, by the way. I wish I'd taken a step back when I was younger and organized my priorities better. But I liked being a hotshot pilot and making money more than having a balanced life. In the end I had money, but it cost me my marriage and a relationship with my daughter." He paused, not looking at her now, seemingly lost in his thoughts. Then he turned to her again. "Where does Rusty fit into all of this?"

"I don't know. I'm not sure about anything right now."

"Well, you don't have to figure it all out today. Take some time to rest and relax. That will help clear your head. Trust me, it works."

"It's weird hearing you talk about relaxing," she said. "I don't think I've ever seen you do that."

"One of my many mistakes." He finally picked up the coffee and took a sip.

She watched him, feeling a connection between them she never had before. "Do you want me to talk to Mom?"

"Yes. But not about us."

Harper frowned. "Then what about?"

"She misses you very much. It was hard on her when you went away to college, and you've been gone ever since."

"I've been around. Just not much lately." But when she stopped to think about it, she had been more absent than present. While she'd been better at juggling her priorities in her past, spending time with Madge had been pushed farther and farther down her list over the years. Her father was right. They needed to talk. "I'll call her," she said, determined to keep that promise. No more procrastinating.

Her dad smiled. "Great. Just don't mention the

divorce. You were right about not wanting to be in the middle."

"You really are sincere," she said softly.

"Yes, I am." He set down the coffee. "Guess I'd better be going. Thanks for listening."

She got up from the couch. While she wasn't ready to trust him completely, she was glad they had both shared something so personal with each other. "What's your hurry?" she asked, pushing up her glasses. He looked on the thin side, as if he hadn't been eating lately. "I can fix us some lunch, and we have plenty of dessert."

His eyes softened. "That sounds wonderful, sweetheart."

"How about tomato soup and grilled cheese? That was always my favorite on a cold, rainy day."

"Mine too. I used to get it even when I was out of town, if I could find it." He stood with her. "I make a mean grilled cheese, if you don't mind me helping out."

Without saying anything, she gave him a hug. "You already have, Dad," she said, squeezing him tight.

Wednesday morning, Madge ran a brush through her newly shorn hair—a spiked pixie with streaks of pink threaded through the gray. She smiled. She'd always wanted a super-short hairstyle but thought she might look too boyish. Don had always complimented her on her sensible, classic haircuts. But on her recent visit to the salon, she had conferred with her stylist, and they'd decided on this hairstyle, Madge acquiescing to the pink at the last minute. When Vincent was finished with his handiwork, she'd loved it.

The time she'd spent with the BBs last week had been healing. They had stayed late, even breaking out the cards and playing Uno with two decks. It was the distraction and comfort she had needed, and she'd promised the BBs she wouldn't miss the next meeting. And she hadn't, showing up a little early and purchasing several skeins of yarn before they'd started working on the joke wigs they were making for the fall parade. The project was fun, and while it wasn't knitting, there was still the repetitive task of attaching hair to the wig base, and she'd realized how much she missed knitting and spending time at Knots and Tangles. But she'd balked at going to the parade. She wasn't up to mingling with a crowd yet. Her friends understood.

And then there was Harper. That was more complicated. Her daughter had called three times since Sunday night, but Madge didn't answer—or check the three messages she left. *Let her know what it feels like to be ignored.* She was being childish, but she couldn't help it. Despite the comfort she received from the BBs, her heart was still raw.

She glanced at her watch. She had to be at the lawyer's office in three hours and had planned some retail therapy as a distraction at the Hot Springs mall before she went. A new hairstyle required a few new outfits, and she had pored through Pinterest to find some that fit her updated look—slim jeans, oversized sweaters, deconstructed jackets. If she felt a little crazy on her next shopping trip, she might buy—*gasp*—a pair of leggings. She grabbed her purse and left the house, then realized she'd forgotten her earrings again.

She ran back inside the house to her bedroom, opened her jewelry box, and saw the three classic pairs she usually wore—gold hoops, silver hoops, and diamond studs she'd bought for herself ten years ago when Don had scheduled work on their anniversary. There were other pairs of earrings in the box, and she shuffled through them . . . and spied a pair of gold-beaded hoops, the epitome of nineties style. She had saved these? She thought she'd thrown them out years ago.

Madge picked up one of the earrings, her chest constricting. Don had bought her these on their third date, at a cheap jewelry shop in McCain Mall. She'd worn them until the gold plating had worn off, not because she loved the style but because they were from him.

Memories flooded over her so quickly she lost her breath. The tears in his eyes when he said their vows. His awestruck expression at Harper's birth. The image of him holding his tiny daughter, his eyes red rimmed as he touched her hand and she gripped his finger. They had been so happy back then. So full of hope. Where had it gone wrong?

Could we start over again?

The image shifted to a faceless woman in Don's arms. In his *bed.* She started to shake, and she threw the earrings across the room. Whatever speck of hope was left in their marriage had died when she discovered the affair.

I'm signing those divorce papers. I'm going to be free.

She settled her nerves and calmly went outside to her car. The storm over the past two days had brought in a warm front, the up-and-down temperatures part and parcel of Arkansas autumns. But the warm air didn't reach her frigid heart, and the ice wall protecting it was thicker than before. Don had betrayed her. He'd destroyed their marriage. He would have to live with that.

Chapter 17

A re you all right, Harper?"

Harper blinked, then realized she had been staring out the window at the Sunshine Diner instead of paying attention to Bailey, one of the diner's waitresses. "Oh, I'm fine," she said, trying to play off that she was anything but fine.

"Do you know what you want to order?"

"A grilled chicken salad." Over the last two weeks she'd completely gone off the rails with her eating, and she needed to get back on track. "No dressing or roll."

"Gotcha."

"Thanks."

As Bailey walked away, Harper stared at the clock on the wall. Almost 12:30 p.m. Her stomach backflipped. In half an hour, her parents would sign their divorce papers, according to her father. She was tempted to try to call her mother one more time, having made several attempts to reach her since Dad had stopped by on Monday. Over an excellent grilled cheese sandwich—he'd been spot on about his skills—and creamy tomato soup, they'd had a long conversation about the particulars of their jobs, something neither of them had discussed with each other before. Her father was more than a little obsessed with the details of the planes he had flown, but otherwise she'd enjoyed listening about his adventures as a pilot. Before he left, he'd told her how proud he was of her, and that had stuck with her since.

Not hearing from her mother had been frustrating, though it did dawn on Harper that she had been just as evasive with Madge lately. *No wonder she doesn't want to talk to me.*

Before Harper left for work this morning, she'd sent both her parents a simple text.

I love you.

A lump formed in her throat. She couldn't imagine her mom and dad not being married. But in less than an hour, they would be. Her chest was heavy with regret. Maybe she should have brought the two of them together and let them hash things out instead of leaving them alone. Or she could have made time for her mother, at the very least. She wasn't naive enough to think she could have fixed their relationship, but perhaps some mediating on her part could have helped.

She glanced out the window again, her gaze landing on #6. What was she doing here at the diner while they were going through such a painful time? What kind of daughter was she to leave her hurting parents alone? She picked up her cell and tapped out a short message.

Where are you? I want to be there for both of you.

She set her phone on the table and drummed her fingers against the Formica top, praying one or both would reply. Deep down she knew she was probably too late. She'd been too involved in her own life and problems to take her parents' issues seriously. The only thing she could do now was wait for one of them to contact her and tell her their marriage was over. Thirty years down the drain with the stroke of a pen. Unreal.

"Harper."

She glanced up to see Rusty standing near her booth. Her breath involuntarily hitched. He hadn't shaved and his chin was covered with light-red scruff. A *Rusty's Garage* ball cap covered his short hair, but he wasn't dressed for work. Instead, he wore a purple-and-black plaid shirt and blue jeans that were a little baggy, hiding his trim physique. Although she was agonizing over her parents, she couldn't help but notice that he looked amazing. But he didn't have his usual friendly expression on his handsome face. In fact, he didn't look all that happy to see her.

She was glad to see him, though. Since Sunday she'd left several messages on his voice mail, but he didn't call her back. She'd ended up going to the garage and finding out he'd taken a few days off. In a last-ditch effort, yesterday she had stopped by his house. No answer there either. "I've been trying to call you," she said, gesturing for him to sit down across from her.

He didn't move.

"I've been busy."

Too busy for me? The thought shoved its way to the front of her brain before she could stop it. She didn't expect him to drop everything when she called, but he could have at least responded that he'd gotten her voice mails.

"I ain't gonna be able to make it to the auction," he said. "I got too much work to do. Sorry."

"Hi, Rusty," Bailey said as she returned and placed a salad in front of Harper, her gaze bouncing back to him, then to her again. She frowned slightly. "Sure you don't want dressing?"

Harper shook her head. She didn't want dressing. She didn't even want the salad anymore. "I'm fine." Talk about a whopper of a lie.

Bailey turned to Rusty. "Do you want anything?"

"Yeah, but I'll put my order in at the counter." He spun on his heel and followed Bailey to the front of the diner.

Not even a goodbye. Stunned, Harper watched as Rusty stood by the cash register and talked to Bailey, the reality that he was bailing on the auction finally sinking in. But that didn't bother her nearly as much as his frosty demeanor.

She slid out of the booth and walked over to the counter. Dishes and utensils clanged in the kitchen, and the scent of sizzling hamburgers and salty fries saturated the air. Tanner was manning the grill, flipping burgers and barking orders to Frank and Mabel, his longtime employees. But she barely noticed the usual diner noise and scents as she waited for Bailey to put in Rusty's order.

"It'll be a few minutes," Bailey said as she walked out from behind the counter, her pad and pencil in hand. "We're swamped."

He nodded, and as soon as Bailey left to take a customer's order, Harper moved to stand next to him. "You're upset," she said.

He stared straight ahead at a chalkboard that listed the day's specials. "Yeah. I am."

She glanced around the diner, hoping no one was listening to their conversation, although in a town as small as Maple Falls, the chance of that was zero. Still, she asked the question anyway. "Did I do something wrong?"

He faced her. "Why didn't you tell me the Miles Road place was off the market?"

How did he find out about that? "I meant to," she said quickly. "That's what I was calling about—"

"We spent an entire day together." His brow flattened. "You could have said somethin' then."

She opened her mouth, ready to tell him that

he was the one who'd insisted she didn't talk about work. But that was a cop-out. Her being scatterbrained and off her game wasn't an excuse for being unprofessional. "I'm sorry," she said. "I forgot to mention it."

"You're my agent. How do you just *forget* something like that?"

"I . . ." Then something happened that Harper had never experienced before: she found herself at a loss for words, as if a fog had enveloped her brain. When it came to Rusty, being his real-estate agent wasn't what first came to her mind. In fact, it was dead last.

"Brielle called and told me it was back on the market," he said.

She clenched her jaw. So that's how he'd found out. She wasn't surprised the woman had tried to poach Rusty. *Disgusting.*

"Here you go." Bailey brought out a large plastic bag with Styrofoam containers inside.

He took them from her. Then he glanced at Harper before he walked away.

Bailey moved closer to her, shoving a pencil behind an ear that was pierced from the lobe to the top. Small gold hoops shone from each hole. "Everything okay?"

Harper watched Rusty leave the diner. "I don't know," she whispered. He had a right to be irritated with her, but she hadn't expected him to be this upset. Still not knowing what she should say, she followed him out the door. "Wait," she called out as he rounded the corner to the back parking lot.

He stopped, then faced her. His eyes were blank, but his Adam's apple moved up and down. "I'm busy right now, Harper."

She halted in front of him and tugged at the hem of her brown suede jacket. "I'm sorry, Rusty. I should have told you about the Miles Road property. I know I let you down. It's just that . . ."

"Just what?"

That you make me forget about my problems. That spending time with you is magical. That you're an amazing guy, and I can't stop thinking about the two of us . . . together.

She put on her real-estate smile, even though her heart was only half in it—the half that wanted to make Rusty happy. "I'm going to call Brielle and get you that showing."

"She already offered to show it to me."

"Did you take her up on it?" She fought to remain calm, almost afraid of his answer.

He paused, then shook his head, the tight tension at the corners of his mouth relaxing slightly. "Didn't set right with me doin' that. You're my agent. I want you to show me the property. I'm going to see this through till the end."

Her knees nearly buckled with relief. "Thank you, Rusty." She should have known better than to doubt his integrity. He was the most standup guy she knew.

His gaze met hers, and although she couldn't decipher his expression, she knew exactly how she was feeling—ashamed and frustrated at herself. She'd always put her clients first . . . and Rusty was more than just a client to her. How could she have been so careless?

"I gotta get this food back to Percy and Hank," he said, holding up the bag.

"Right. Food." Questions filled her mind. Was he back at work? He wasn't dressed like it. Had Senior gone home? Did Amber know when she was moving? And was he really dropping out of the auction?

"I'll call you with an appointment time," was all she said.

"I'll make sure to answer." He went to his truck and set the bag on the seat. Then he climbed in and drove away.

Harper hugged her arms as he left the parking lot, then walked back inside the diner, trying to drum up enthusiasm for showing him the Miles Road property. She slid into the booth. Now she had to deal with Brielle again. But instead of being angry, all she felt was tired.

She glanced at the clock above the serving counter. One o'clock. She quickly checked her phone to see if either of her parents had texted back. They hadn't.

Harper leaned her forehead against the heel of her hand and closed her eyes. *Divorce time.*

"Can I get you anything else?"

She glanced up at Bailey, who now looked truly concerned. Digging deep, Harper somehow managed to smile. "Just a box," she said, as if her world wasn't disintegrating. "This was too much for one meal."

Bailey glanced at the untouched salad, then nodded. "Sure thing. Be right back."

Her smile fading, Harper stared at the evenly sliced grilled chicken breast perched on a bed of fresh greens. Her parents. Rusty. Brielle. Her business. All of it blended into one tangled ball of stress. Her stomach lurched. She couldn't solve her parents' problems, but she had to do something about Brielle, she had to make things right with Rusty, and she had to get her business back on track.

She had no idea how she was going to do any of it.

Twenty minutes before she had to sign the documents ending her marriage, Madge turned into the law office parking lot and pulled into a space. After shutting off the engine, she glanced at all the shopping bags covering the back seat. When she'd arrived at the mall, she had hit one store after another, blindly grabbing tops, pants, and accessories off the racks, purchasing them without trying them on. With each dollar she spent, she'd expected the pain in her heart to diminish. It didn't. Now she was stuck with hundreds of dollars of stuff she barely remembered buying.

She touched her head to the steering wheel, continuing her fight against the tears that had threatened to fall for the past two hours. Until now she'd been able to shove the imagery of the affair aside, refusing to dwell on the specifics of what Don had done. Now she couldn't stop thinking about it.

Is she younger? Thinner? Prettier? Better?

Rage exploded inside her, and she pounded the steering wheel with the heel of her hand. *I'm the one who stayed home and took care of everything! I raised Harper and dealt with the tears when Don didn't show up for her milestones. I'm the one who was lonely . . . who slept in an empty bed when he was gone and . . . and . . .*

Sobs heaved from her chest, and she couldn't stop them. All those nights alone, longing to have her husband next to her, for his touch and support. Phone calls didn't make up for the lack of intimacy, and because she'd had a daughter to take care of, she had learned early on to toughen up. Back then she couldn't let anyone see her cry, especially Harper. Now all she could do was cry.

A knock sounded on her car window, making her jump. Don. Of course it was Don, and he was seeing her at her absolute worst.

"Open the door, Maddie."

She tried to stem the tears, and when she couldn't, she put her head on the steering wheel, ignoring his pleas. Finally he walked away. She would get it together somehow before she headed into that office and signed those papers. She just needed a minute—

The passenger door opened, and Don slid into the seat.

Madge glared at him, too weak to sit up and angry she'd forgotten he had a key to her car. "Go . . . away . . ."

"No. Not this time."

Wiping her face with her fingers, she fought for breath, refusing to look at him.

"Are you okay?" he asked softly.

"No." She scrubbed her hands on her black pants. "I'm not okay. I've *never* been okay since the moment I met you."

"Never?" He shifted in his seat. "There wasn't a single moment of our marriage that made you happy?"

She blew out a breath. If she said no, he would know she was lying. "There were far more unhappy moments."

"Yeah." He nodded, staring at his hands. "There were. I'm sorry for that, Maddie."

"Apologies aren't going to work this time, Don. I stopped believing them long ago."

"I understand. But that doesn't mean I'm not

sincere, or that I don't regret what I've done to hurt you and Harper. She misses you, by the way."

"You two have been talking about me?" Fresh pain stabbed her heart.

"We've been reconnecting. She said she tried calling you, but you won't call her back."

Madge lifted her chin. "Now she knows how it feels." She sounded petty, but she didn't care. She glanced at her watch. "We're going to be late," she said, starting to open the door.

"I just want you to know something, Maddie, before we end things. I'm in counseling—something I should have started a long time ago. I'm a deeply flawed man who has made irreparable mistakes, and I've lost almost everything because of it."

" 'Almost'?"

"Not that I deserve it, but our wonderful daughter has decided to forgive me. She doesn't trust me, and I don't blame her for that. But she's giving me a chance."

Was he trying to make her feel guilty? Or manipulate her into also giving him another chance? "I . . . I'm glad you two are working on a relationship." The words were true. He was Harper's father, and he needed to be there for his daughter. Madge didn't want their divorce to get in the way of Harper's relationship with Don.

"And I'm grateful there's a little part of you

that was able to say that. You're the best, Madge, and I took you for granted. I love you," he added, tears rolling down his cheeks. "I love you very much. My hope is that someday you can forgive me for all the ways I've hurt you, but even if you don't, I'll never stop loving you."

She couldn't move. Don was crying. Her always upbeat, nothing-was-ever-wrong husband was actually crying. He was baring his heart, something he'd never done before. He'd always breezed into town and claimed the role of the fun parent and the carefree spouse while she shouldered all the responsibility. She didn't recognize the broken man sitting next to her.

He opened the door and exited the car.

Slowly she picked up her purse from the passenger-side floorboard and headed for the building. Don walked a few paces ahead, then opened the door for her to walk inside. When they reached the elevator, he pressed the button. It immediately opened, and they both stepped inside.

Madge glanced at his profile as he pressed the button for the third floor and the doors closed. Was he really changing? Could they come back from this? Did she even want to?

Before she could change her mind, she clicked the Stop button and stepped in front of him. "I don't trust you," she said, looking up at him and meeting his eyes.

He nodded. "I know."

"I'm also mad at you."

"Oh, honey, I *know.*" He let out a bitter chuckle. "You have the right to be."

"But . . ."

Don took a step forward, closing the space between them. "But?"

"I can't believe I'm going to say this." She swallowed. "I still love you, too, fool that I am."

He fell against the steel wall as if her words had knocked the wind out of him. "You do?"

"But that doesn't mean anything." She turned her back to him.

He put his hand on her shoulders. "It means everything to me, Maddie."

She turned and gazed at him. There was a tenderness in his eyes that she'd never seen before, even during their most intimate moments. A raw emotion she had always craved from him but had never gotten—until now. "Where do we go from here?" she whispered, confused.

"That depends. Do you still want to sign the papers?"

After a long moment, she shook her head. "Not right now."

"Oh, Maddie—"

"But I reserve the right to start the proceedings again. You have a lot of making up to do, Donald Wilson. I do too."

The phone in the elevator rang. Don reached

over her and answered it. "Hello . . . Everything is okay. Just a glitch." He reached around with his other arm and hit the button to resume movement. "See, the elevator is working now . . . All right, thanks for checking." He hung up the phone, his arms still around Madge but not touching her, his eyes still filled with love that melted some of the ice around her heart. He straightened as the elevator doors opened.

"Finally," a tall, thin woman with long brown hair said. "I thought the elevator was broken again. Someone said it got stuck recently."

She and Don exchanged a look, then stepped out. "Nope, working just fine."

"Have a good day," the woman said as she stepped in.

"We'll talk later," Madge whispered. Don nodded his reply.

They walked to the receptionist's desk. "We have an appointment," Don said.

"Wilson, right?"

"Yes," Madge replied. "Sorry we're a few minutes late."

"Mr. Crenshaw and Ms. Pressman are waiting for you."

As they followed the receptionist down the hall, Don leaned over and whispered, "We're about to have two confused and disappointed lawyers on our hands in a few minutes."

She smiled, shocked that she was able to and

buoyed by the spark of hope inside her. For once, she wasn't the one disappointed.

As Rusty drove the short distance back to the garage, he fought a losing battle. For a split second during his conversation with Brielle on Saturday, he'd considered taking her up on her offer to exclude Harper. But he couldn't bring himself to do something that backhanded and had quickly ended the call by saying Harper would be in touch with her soon. She hadn't sounded too happy about that, for some reason.

It still stung that Harper had withheld that information from him. She knew how much he wanted to see that property. With Amber possibly leaving in two months or less, it was crucial he found a place soon for him and Senior. It would take time to build a house, and he had resigned himself to the fact that once he sold Senior and G'ma's house, he and his grandfather would have to move into an apartment or put a trailer on the property—if that was what he ended up buying.

He shook his head as he turned into the garage parking lot. The headache that had started two days ago was drilling into his temple now. He'd decided to take some time off and go fishing to clear his head, but the weather had nixed that, so he ended up puttering around the house. He fixed the hole in the living-room floor, repaired the leaky faucet upstairs, and scrubbed the linoleum floor in the kitchen, among other things. By the time he'd gone to bed Tuesday night, he'd been plum exhausted—but his mind was still alert.

It wasn't just the stress of house hunting and selling or that his sister was moving across the country, although both definitely played a part. No matter how hard he'd tried, he couldn't stop thinking about Harper or feeling guilty that he was avoiding her. When he'd seen her at the diner today, he couldn't dodge her anymore, and he'd intended only to tell her he was dropping out of the auction and that was it. It wasn't right to back out like that, but he definitely didn't want to go now. He'd talk to her about house hunting later.

But she'd followed him to the counter and asked if he was mad. He'd been tempted to tell her no. Good guys never got angry, right? But once he admitted he was, a sense of satisfaction washed over him. At least he'd been able to tell her the truth about that.

The satisfaction had disappeared when he saw something in her eyes while they were standing outside and she admitted she'd let him down. He couldn't put his finger on it, but whatever it was had his pulse skyrocketing. In that moment, it was almost as if she was . . . longing for something? Then it went away, she said she'd call him, and his pulse returned to normal. Weird.

He drove into the parking lot and dropped off lunch for the guys. "You stickin' around?" Percy asked.

"Are we busy?" Rusty asked.

"Naw." He wiped his hands on a shop towel and reached for the plastic bag holding two Reubens and large fries.

"I'll be back tomorrow, then."

When he arrived home, rain started to fall again, only a light sprinkle instead of the thunderstorms they'd had two days ago. He got out of the truck and headed inside, barely looking at the neatly manicured lawn he'd spent so much time cleaning up. A few more leaves had fallen on the grass, but he'd deal with them later.

He walked inside the house and sat down in Senior's recliner. He should have changed his clothes and gone back to the shop to work on the GTO, but he didn't feel like doing that right now. A brittle chuckle escaped. He'd never refused a chance to work on a car. Not until Harper.

Thrusting his hand through his short hair, he stared at the green carpet under his feet. Then he got down on his hands and knees and started ripping it out. The physical work helped him refocus his thoughts, and he worked straight through the afternoon and supper. By nightfall, he had a large pile of torn carpet and carpet padding in the middle of the living room that included not just that area but also the stairs and the hallway on the main floor.

Starving, he grabbed some graham crackers and peanut butter, nixing the hot sauce Senior liked to add, and walked out to the back deck. He dipped a cracker in the jar, scooped out a bite and ate it, then looked up at the stars. The clouds had cleared, revealing a sky teeming with twinkling lights. How many times would he see this incredible view before he had to move?

And despite everything . . . he wished Harper was here to see it with him.

"Thank you for agreeing to see me," Harper said as she sat down in the chair across from Brielle's desk Thursday morning. She'd thought about calling her directly again, but suspected she'd get ignored again. Besides, the two of them had a lot to discuss, so she made an appointment with Brielle's secretary.

She quickly glanced around the spacious office. Every single award Brielle had won was prominently placed on the walls or on a bookshelf directly behind her desk. Harper kept her awards in her office at home.

"Of course, of course." Brielle picked up a bottle of Perrier and took a sip, not bothering to offer Harper a drink. "What can I do for you?"

Oh, you've done enough. Harper crossed her legs and looked Brielle straight in the eye. "Rusty—Mr. Jenkins—told me you contacted him about the Miles Road property and said it was back on the market."

"It is," she replied without a flicker of emotion.

"You do realize I could report you for poaching my client?"

Brielle threaded her fingers on both hands into a fist and rested it on her desk. "He's *still* your client, correct?"

"Yes. But only because he's a good guy who understands loyalty."

One corner of Brielle's lips lifted. She picked up her phone and tapped on the screen. "When would you like to see the property?"

"I'll get to that in a minute." Harper leaned forward. "I want to talk about Jack first."

Brielle paused, her index finger hovering above the phone screen. "What about Jack?"

"He told me everything, Brielle. The poaching, the rumors, the lies." Harper's fingernails dug into her palms.

Brielle glanced away. "I don't know what he's talking about. I haven't spoken to Jack since I moved back here."

"You haven't?"

"Not since I kicked him out a year ago."

"Wait, I don't understand." Harper frowned. "*You* kicked him out?"

"Yes." Brielle put down her phone. "He's a class A jerk. I'm better off without him in my life."

"Then why did he tell me you were trying to kill my career?"

Brielle shrugged. "To get back at me? I don't know. Besides, you're doing well, aren't you? You've always been a top seller, and I saw that you hit the million-dollar club last year."

Harper was completely confused. Had Jack lied to her about Brielle? Or was Brielle lying to her now? She wasn't sure what to believe.

Brielle picked up her phone again. "Do you still want to schedule a showing?"

"Yes," she said, her eyes not leaving Brielle as she reached into her purse for her own phone. But Brielle was tapping on the phone as if Jack's accusations meant nothing. And if they weren't true, they didn't.

Which meant Harper's business was failing on its own, and Jack was trying to get revenge on Brielle for dumping him by making her look bad—although that seemed convoluted. But what did she know? She couldn't wrap her mind around sabotaging someone else's career or using an ex to get payback on another ex. This was making her head spin.

"What day?" Brielle said, still scrolling through her phone.

"The earlier the better." She didn't want Rusty to miss out on Miles Road a second time.

"How about this Sunday?"

"Perfect." That was after the ALS gala. She'd

be tired after working the gala all day Saturday, but working-while-tired was nothing new to her.

"You can drop by my office to get the key," Brielle said. "My weekend secretary will be here to give it to you."

Weekend secretary. Harper didn't even have one secretary anymore. "Great. I'll see her then."

Brielle pushed away from her desk and stood. "There's been a lot of interest in the property since it came back on the market," she pointed out. "I'm glad we could fit your client into the schedule." She smiled thinly. "It's good to see you again, Harper."

Harper eyed Brielle's outstretched hand. Then she stood and gave it a quick shake.

Brielle gestured to her open office door. "I hope you don't mind if I don't see you out. I've got a full schedule for the rest of the day."

"So do I, of course." Harper attempted a nonchalant laugh, but she sounded like a strangled goat.

Brielle tilted her head, her smile widening. "Of course."

Harper rushed out of the office, then stopped in front of her Mercedes and shuddered. *Ugh.* At least she didn't have to deal with her anymore now that she'd obtained a showing. She got into her car and called Rusty, excited to give him the good news.

"Hi, Harper."

Her enthusiasm dimmed a smidge. In the past when he answered her calls he sounded affable, as if he'd been smiling when he saw her name on his screen. Today he was polite. No, worse than that. Bland—and Rusty was never bland. "I've got us a showing for the Miles Road property," she said, shoving some animation into her voice.

"When?"

Yes, he was definitely bland today. She told him the time. "I'll pick you up half an hour before."

"I'll meet you there."

"Oh." Now he sounded downright distant. Was he still mad at her? He didn't seem the type to hold a grudge. "If that's what you want."

"Thanks." He hung up the phone.

She pulled down the visor mirror to check her makeup before she left the parking lot. Her makeup looked fine—she hadn't bothered with fake eyelashes today—but she was still frowning. Were things ever going to be right between her and Rusty again?

She was almost halfway to her office when a question popped into her mind—one that she should have asked Brielle. If Brielle wasn't out to steal Rusty as a client, then why had she called him and not her about Miles Road? And she hadn't denied that she had called Rusty without notifying Harper first.

She pushed it out of her mind. She'd gotten a showing for Rusty. That's what mattered. Knowing she didn't have to see Brielle or Jack again? Priceless.

Chapter 18

Friday evening, Madge knocked on Harper's front door. When had she last visited her daughter at home? Months, at least. When Harper had called her yesterday afternoon and apologized for breaking her promises to call, she'd invited Madge over for coffee after work. Madge had jumped at the chance.

After telling the lawyers they had decided not to divorce yet, she and Don had quickly left the office and gone to an Italian restaurant for supper. The conversation was superficial, and the neutral location precluded them from talking about their issues. But having a meal together was a start, and before they left, they'd decided to get together again and talk in a few days. Don hadn't pushed her to meet sooner, and she was thankful he hadn't. Maybe he was actually changing, but she wasn't ready to let down her guard.

Harper opened the door and immediately hugged her mother. "Finally we're together!"

Madge closed her eyes, relishing her daughter's hug.

Harper stepped back and looked at Madge's new style. "Oh wow. I love your hair!"

"Thank you. I needed change."

"It suits you so well."

Harper was impeccably dressed in slim plum-colored pants and a turtleneck shirt a shade lighter. Her nude chunky-heeled pumps clicked on the wood floor as Madge followed her inside.

A few minutes later, Madge was seated on the couch, a mug of black coffee in one hand and a small plate with a chocolate-chip cookie on it in the other. She set the plate down on the coffee table. "You're baking again," she said.

Harper nodded. "I really enjoy it. The only problem is finding people to eat what I bake. I've already put on a few pounds lately."

"I can't tell." Madge picked up the cookie and took a bite. Soft, chewy, and perfectly sweet. "These are delicious. If you ever decide to give up real estate, you could be a baker." It was a joke, since Madge knew her daughter would never leave her job.

But Harper didn't laugh or even crack a smile. "How's the coffee?" she asked.

"Good."

There followed a stretch of awkward silence as they both sipped their coffee and Madge finished her cookie. "I'm sorry I kept putting you off so much," Harper finally said. "I shouldn't have done that."

"And I shouldn't have gotten so angry with you. Things have been so tense between me and your father, and I lost my perspective."

"Speaking of," Harper said, gripping her cup. "How are things now?"

Madge gave her a faint smile. "We didn't sign the papers."

Harper leaned forward until she was perched on the edge of her chair. "Really? You changed your mind?"

"Yes, for now. We have years of issues to work out." She glanced at the crumbs remaining on her dessert plate, then back at her daughter. "I'm glad you and your father are working on your relationship too. I should have done more to encourage that."

"Mom, don't you think you did enough?" Harper said. "You were always there for me growing up. I wouldn't be where I am without you."

Madge reached for Harper's hand. "I was hard on you sometimes."

"And a little smothering—let's be honest."

She sighed. "I felt I had a lot to make up for because of your father's absence."

Harper nodded. "I understood that, too, once I got older." She squeezed Madge's hand and let go. "I think all three of us are starting over, in different ways."

"What do you mean?"

Harper paused, and Madge noticed that she wasn't wearing her false eyelashes today. Good. She looked much better with her natural ones.

Her daughter was such a beauty, both inside and out.

"I'm thinking about taking some time off," Harper said.

"That's a great idea. A vacation would do you a world of good."

"I don't mean a vacation. I'm talking about a month. Maybe more."

Alarm rose within her. "Is something wrong at work?"

"Yes, but I think it might be a good thing." At Madge's puzzled look she added, "I'm still figuring stuff out, though. Reevaluating, Dad calls it."

"I'm doing some of that myself."

Harper sipped on her latte. "Like going back to interior design school?"

"No, nothing that crazy. I thought about buying some leggings, though."

Harper laughed. "You should do both."

Madge shook her head. "I'm too old to go back to school."

"You are not. There are plenty of nontraditional students in colleges today. Besides, you love interior decorating, and you're good at it. The lake house looks like it belongs in a magazine."

"I did enjoy decorating that." Madge mulled the idea over. "I'll think about it," she said.

"What about the leggings?" Harper asked.

"Oh, I'm *totally* getting those." They both

laughed, and she took Harper's hand again. "I love you. And I'm proud of you, no matter what you decide to do. I know whatever it is, you'll be successful."

"Thanks, Mom," Harper said, tears in her pretty eyes. "I love you too."

"If I was younger, I'd take you straight out to the woodshed, young man."

Rusty shot a glare at Senior, who was adjusting his bow tie while he waited for an Uber to pick him up and take him to the ALS gala. He'd offered to take Senior himself, but his grandfather refused. "If you're not going, I'm not riding with you," he'd huffed.

"We don't have a woodshed," Rusty said, irritated that Senior was being so ridiculous.

"I'm surprised you didn't build one, considerin' all the repairs you've done on this house. Never seen it so spiffy before."

When Amber dropped Senior off yesterday afternoon, he'd been in awe at what Rusty had done. Rusty was a bit impressed with himself, he had to admit. Over the past week he'd given up his time on the GTO and worked on the house. He'd replaced the carpeting and subfloor with vinyl planks that looked like real wood. With the help of online video tutorials, he'd also put tile in the kitchen. Turned out he was a decent handyman when he set his mind to it. And all the sweat equity he'd put in the house had been a good, tiring distraction.

He'd been prepared to turn in early tonight, unwilling to think about Harper having a good time at the gala, maybe even with that guy he'd seen her with. Then Senior had started riding his back about dropping out of the auction.

His grandfather, dressed in a powder-blue tuxedo with a ruffled shirt and now slightly crooked bow tie, sat down on the couch next to Rusty and narrowed his gaze. "How about you go upstairs and put on those fancy clothes Harper picked out for you? I'll cancel the ride, and we can go to this shindig together. There's still some time."

Rusty shook his head. "I ain't goin'."

"Never thought I'd see the day my grandson acted the coward. Rusty, you disappoint me." When he didn't get a response, he added, "I wish you'd tell me what happened between the two of you."

Nothing. And that was the point. Although he still thought of her every single day—and plenty of times a day too—he was sure that eventually she would return to "out of sight, out of mind" status, like she had after that dance they'd had together at the Castillo wedding.

He knew his grandfather was waiting for an answer. He wasn't giving him one. He was already a disappointment; there wasn't much further down he could go.

A honk sounded from the street outside. Senior got up and adjusted his tie again. Before Rusty could tell him it was almost straight up and down now, he said, "Don't wait up." Then he walked out the door.

Rusty grabbed the TV remote and flipped through the channels, too wound up after Senior's scolding to relax. As usual, there was nothing on, so he landed on a football game. Mississippi State against Alabama. He tried to concentrate on the game, but his grandfather's voice kept sounding in his head. Shutting off the TV, he grabbed his keys and headed for the truck. He'd work on the GTO tonight. He'd neglected her over the past two weeks.

Anything to keep his mind off the auction and the fact that he'd given Harper—and by extension the gala committee—his word, then reneged on it. Not only was he disappointing his grandfather by not going, he was also disappointing himself.

Harper paced back and forth behind the makeshift stage at the community center. Cammi and the other gala volunteers were finishing up the final touches before opening the doors and letting the guests into the hall. All of the bachelors had already arrived, except for two—Senior and Rusty. Her stomach curdled. Up until this afternoon she'd kept herself busy with baking to steady her nerves until she had to get ready. She'd even made treat bags for all the volunteers with the goodies she'd made. That had been fun, and so was surprising everyone with their individual bags. What had been an attempt at distraction ended up being a joy.

Now that she had some downtime, Rusty came back to her mind. She wished he was coming tonight. She also wished she'd tried to talk him out of canceling, but that ship had sailed. Still, that didn't stop her from remembering how hot he looked in his suit, and how she'd been serious when she said he would earn a lot of bids. She tapped her chin. Maybe it was a good thing he had decided not to come. She didn't think she could watch while other women bid on him. As for her participating in the bidding, she was too broke to buy a bachelor, even if she wanted one. Not without dipping into her tiny nest egg, which she had hit hard over the past several months.

"Excuse me, ma'am."

She turned around to see a fresh-faced kid wearing a navy-blue sports jacket, white shirt, and khaki pants, his black bangs slicked to the side while the rest of his head was shaved nearly bald. "Yes?" she said, chafing at being called "ma'am." *I'm not that old.*

"I'm one of the bachelors for the auction tonight." He grinned, his teeth so white and even she suspected he'd gotten his braces off last week. "Do you know where I'm supposed to go?"

"The auction isn't starting for another forty-five minutes or so," she said, giving him her best Realtor smile. She better get used to it, because she knew she would be smiling a lot tonight, regardless of how she felt. "Do you know Cammi?"

"The short girl with the weird laugh?"

She kind of liked this guy. "That's her. She'll make an announcement ten minutes before the auction begins. You'll get your instructions then."

"Cool, thanks." He started to walk away.

"Please tell me you're out of high school," she blurted. "You have to be eighteen to be in the auction."

He grinned again. "I'm twenty." He turned and walked away.

Okay, no harm, no foul, and she didn't regret checking his age. The last thing any of the gala committee members needed was to break the law.

"There she is!"

Harper's smile was genuine as Senior walked toward her. He cut a fine, yet wildly out of style, figure in his seventies-era tuxedo, and he totally made it work. She walked over to him. "Hi, Senior."

"I'm at your service," he said, bowing slightly at the waist. "If you bid on me, that is."

She smiled again but couldn't help looking over his shoulder.

"I'm sorry, sugar, he ain't comin'. I tried talkin' sense into him, but he's bein' stubborn."

"That's okay," she said, brushing off her disappointment. She shouldn't have gotten her hopes up. "Let's fix this tie." She straightened the bow until it sat in the correct position.

"It's a shame," Senior whispered, his voice so quiet she barely heard him.

"What is?" She stepped back and checked him over.

"Oh, nothin'. Some things ain't meant to be, I guess. Now, what do you need me to do?"

"Mix. Or mingle. It's up to you."

His eyes lit up. "I can both mix *and* mingle, young lady."

She laughed. "Thank you for coming, Senior."

"I wouldn't miss somethin' this fancy for the world. I'm sure the evenin' will be very interestin'. Now, if you'll excuse me, I have some schmoozin' to do. I saw plenty of eligible-lookin' ladies coming through them doors, and I aim to plead my case." He winked at her and walked away.

She adjusted one of the off-shoulder sleeves of her shimmery eggplant, flared-skirt dress and walked from the back of the stage. She shouldn't be upset with Rusty. She'd pushed him hard to come to this and then let him down when it came to something important to him. All she could do was try to have a good—no, decent—time tonight.

She watched the crowd in front of her. Usually she'd be out there networking, trying to meet new clients and talk to existing ones. She even recognized a few among the guests. Tonight would be the perfect time to fix some of the damage done to her career and maybe find out why it had happened.

She couldn't bring herself to do either. She'd always been a social butterfly, but right now she wanted to find a cocoon somewhere and hide out tonight. She lingered around the side of the stage, hoping no one noticed her before she had to make an appearance.

It seemed like an eternity until Cammi finally took the podium, instructing everyone to take their seats at the round tables and for the bachelors to head to the back of the stage. Harper searched for Senior and caught his eye before he headed for the front. He gave her a jaunty nod and practically skipped off, waving hi to various ladies who called out his name. She was impressed. When the man schmoozed, he schmoozed.

Harper looked for an empty place to sit—not an easy thing to do since the gala was sold out. All she could find was a table near the front with three empty seats. She stopped next to an elderly woman who looked to be Senior's age. "Hi," she said. "Is anyone sitting here?"

"I was saving those for my friends. I guess they decided not to show up." The woman shrugged her small shoulders. "Chickens."

She smiled and sat down. "Harper Wilson."

"I'm Hazel. Nice to meet you."

Cammi tapped on the top of the microphone. A high-pitched squeal sounded in the room. "In a few minutes we will be starting the, you know, auction," she said, then giggled as if what she said was hysterical. "Please pick up the programs at your table for more information on tonight's eligible bachelors. On the back of each brochure is a number that you'll use for bidding. So, like, good luck!" One more giggle and she put the microphone back on the stand.

Harper didn't look at the brochure. She wasn't interested in bidding on anyone, and she sure didn't want to see Rusty's photo smiling at her. "Any of the bachelors strike your fancy?" she asked Hazel. This lady would be perfect for Senior.

"Oh yes," Hazel said, her slightly trembling voice filled with excitement. "This one right here."

Harper looked down and saw the tip of Hazel's wrinkled index finger touching the chin of the young man she'd met before the gala. She grinned. Was that guy in for a surprise. "Well, good luck, then. I hope you win."

"Me too." Hazel lowered her voice. "Tonight

has already been so much fun. I'm actually glad my friends decided not to come. They can be such old party poopers sometimes. I say you're as young as you want to be." She tapped her temple. "In here I'm twenty-five!"

Cammi returned to the mike. "Now to introduce, like, the emcee for tonight's auction. My amazing husband—Brooks. Sorry, ladies, he's taken!" Cammi flashed her wedding ring, then stepped aside as Brooks appeared from behind the curtain.

"What an odd young woman," Hazel commented.

Everyone clapped as Brooks gave the audience a huge smile that would rival the cheesiest game show host.

"All right, bidders, here are the rules for tonight's auction."

Harper tuned him out as he explained how bidding worked. A flute of bubbly champagne sat in front of her, along with a small plate of assorted canapes. She stared at a round, thin cracker laden with cream cheese, a tiny bit of smoked salmon, and a sprinkle of dill.

"Thank God I found you."

Harper jumped as Jack slipped into the seat beside her. Oh no. "What are you doing here?" she growled.

"My company is one of the gala sponsors this year." He leaned closer to her. "Brielle is here."

"What? Why?"

"You know she doesn't miss a chance to network."

That was true. "We talked, by the way," Harper said, forgetting to whisper. "She said she dumped you and kicked you out of the house."

Jack rolled his eyes. "Do you really believe that? She'd never admit I broke up with her."

"Could you two keep it down?" Hazel said, her penciled-in eyebrows forming a *V* above her eyes. "I'm trying to hear the instructions."

"Sorry," Harper said.

"Why don't we go outside and talk," Jack said, whispering again.

She wasn't getting into the middle of Jack and Brielle's personal mess. Shaking her head, she leaned away from him and stared at the stage as the first bachelor came out and the audience started bidding.

Jack muttered a curse under his breath and rubbed the back of his neck. "She's coming this way."

Harper turned around to see Brielle heading straight for them. For crying out loud. This was turning into a circus. Or a nightmare.

"Hello," Brielle said to Harper as she sat down at the table. Then she turned to Jack and scowled.

The crowd broke into applause, and Brooks motioned for the first winning bidder to come up onto the stage and meet her bachelor. Harper glanced around and saw the smiling and laughing faces of the attendees. Everyone seemed to be enjoying tonight—except for her.

"Hey," a man's voice rang out from the back of the room. "Where are the bachelorettes?"

"They'll be at next year's gala," Brooks said smoothly, then said the date. "Mark your calendars, single gents!"

"Harper," Jack said, his mouth inches from her ear. "I need to talk to you."

"Now, ladies, you're going to love our next bachelor." Brooks held up his notes. "A man of *experience,* this bachelor enjoys playing cards, fishing, and strolls under the moonlight, as long as he's home by nine. Introducing Russell Jenkins Sr.!"

Senior sauntered out, his hands in the pockets of his pants, as casual and pleased as could be. Even Harper smiled when he pointed and winked at several women in the audience. Immediately, brochure numbers flew up, and Senior basked in his glory.

"Oh, why not." Hazel lifted her brochure. "He's a cutie."

Jack nudged Harper's side. "Harper—"

"I'm watching the auction."

"Don't tell me you're planning to bid on one of these guys."

She looked at him. "What if I am? That's my business, not yours."

"Your business used to be mine, remember." He reached for her hand under the table.

Yuck. Yanking her hand out of his, she scooted closer to Hazel, not missing the glare Brielle was shooting her.

The bidding went on longer than expected, and the winner wasn't her seatmate but an older woman who looked age appropriate for Rusty's grandfather. When she reached the stage, Senior said, "Hello, darlin'," and they walked off together. If Harper wasn't so tense from being seated next to a guy who wouldn't get the message and a woman who couldn't stop launching visual daggers at her, she would have sighed, it was so adorable.

Jack rose from the table and left. Harper slumped back in her seat.

"I don't like him," Hazel muttered, pointing an arthritic finger over her shoulder in Jack's direction. "He seems like a slimy character."

"Trust me, he is."

Brielle leaned over the table. "You're not going to get him back."

Harper tried to count to ten, only making it to five. "I don't *want* him back. He's all yours."

The next bachelor was the young man she'd met backstage, and as soon as Brooks stopped talking, Hazel went into action and Harper ignored Brielle. After a few bids, Hazel won. "Oh, wonderful!" she said, clasping her hands together. She turned to Harper and whispered, "My granddaughter will be so surprised."

"You're fixing them up?"

Hazel nodded. "I'll be their chaperone, of course."

"Of course." Wow, Harper had certainly read that situation all wrong. Hopefully Hazel's granddaughter didn't mind her playing matchmaker.

Brielle pulled out her phone, apparently losing interest in both Harper and the auction. The young man came over to Hazel, looking more than a little uncertain. He introduced himself as Beckett, and once Hazel explained that he would be going out with her granddaughter, he appeared visibly relieved. When Hazel showed him a picture of her, he broke out into a grin. He gave Hazel his number and said he would catch up with her after the auction.

For the rest of the auction, Harper and Hazel chatted as the bachelors were brought out one by one. Brooks was an excellent emcee, Jack hadn't returned, and Brielle was still scrolling through her cell. For the next half hour, Harper actually enjoyed herself.

Finally Brooks moved to stand at the center front of the stage. "That's all for our auction tonight, ladies and gents. Unfortunately one of our bachelors had to cancel. Thank you for your generosity, and a big thanks to our bachelors for helping the fight to find a cure for ALS."

Everyone started to clap—until Cammi ran onto the stage and whispered to her husband. He nodded and started speaking into the mike again. "Ladies and gents, the fun is not over yet. We have one more bachelor who's just arrived."

Harper frowned, hearing the murmurs of confusion and excitement in the crowd. Even Brielle was paying attention.

"Ooh," Hazel said. "I wonder what handsome man is showing up next?"

"Our final, *final* bachelor is about to come out," Brooks said. "Is everyone ready to meet him?"

"Yes!" the audience said in loud unison.

Harper had to hand it to Brooks. He knew how to get a crowd going. He had even her wondering who the mystery bachelor was.

"Ladies and gents, here he is!"

The curtains opened, and Harper's jaw dropped. "Rusty?"

Chapter 19

If Rusty had been anxious before, he was plum terrified right now. He hadn't even opened the truck door earlier before he marched back into the house and put on the clothes Harper had picked out for him. No matter how much he'd tried to talk himself out of going, he hadn't been able to follow through in the end. He didn't want to let down the ALS charity. Or Senior. Truth be told, he didn't want to let down Harper either. He'd given her his word, and he would keep it.

Now he wanted to run and hide. Bad enough his dress shoes were squeezing his feet, but he was also breaking out in flop sweat as he walked onto the stage. All eyes were on him, the people applauding like they were at a football game and not some high-falutin' charity event. But he was aware that the emcee had hyped up the crowd right before he'd come out. That was the reason everyone was excited, not because a working-class joe with too-tight shoes and a sweaty forehead was standing in front of them.

He tried not to look at the crowd too much, but he couldn't help it. Maybe focusing on only the front tables would help his pulse settle, he decided—until he saw Harper. His heart jumped to his throat. Despite her open-mouthed surprise, she looked gorgeous. Even more beautiful than she'd been at Anita's wedding, if that was possible. He couldn't tear his eyes away.

Then she lifted her head, and their gazes met. His heartbeat thudded in his chest, so strong he was sure everyone in the place could hear it despite the crowd noise. The emotion in her stunning blue eyes took his breath away . . . and somewhere deep inside his heart a flicker of hope ignited.

A man slid into the seat next to her. The same one he'd seen her with before. The guy leaned close to Harper and whispered something in her ear. The hope disappeared.

"Opening bid is one hundred dollars," the emcee blared. "Who will bid one hundred—"

Numbered papers flew up in the air. Rusty frowned. He tugged at his collar, then caught Harper shaking her head. He stopped and saw her gesturing for him to move to the left. He did, then she tilted her head to the right. Oh, she wanted him to walk around. That was better than just standing there.

"We're at nine hundred dollars, folks!"

He halted and gaped at the emcee. *Nine hundred dollars?* He turned to look at Harper, then saw Senior, who had appeared out of nowhere, sitting right behind her and grinning like an absolute fool.

"Nine hundred going once . . ."

Rusty scanned the crowd. Who was fool enough to spend that much money on a date with him?

"One thousand!"

He recognized that voice. He looked at Harper, who had a strained smile on her face as she held up her brochure. The guy sitting next to her was also looking at him, his perfect face scrunched into a scowl.

She's bidding on me. What does that mean?

"Two thousand."

Rusty turned to see Brielle holding up her number. But she wasn't looking at him. She was smirking at Harper.

The hum of the crowd dimmed as his gaze darted from Brielle to Harper's surprised expression. Then Harper frowned and lifted her own number again. "Twenty-five hundred!"

"Three thousand!"

"Thirty-five hundred," Harper countered.

Rusty didn't know what to do. Everyone else had put their numbers down and were watching the two women fight . . . over him.

"Five. Thousand. Dollars." Brielle sat back in her chair, giving Harper a haughty look.

"Ladies and gents," the emcee said. "We have a record bid right here. Told you we saved the best for last."

Harper didn't move, but Rusty could tell she was mulling things over. His heart hammered in his chest. Five thousand dollars was an insane amount. She wouldn't possibly bid any more than that . . .

She grabbed a glass of champagne and gulped it down. "Ten thousand," Harper said, this time looking at him.

The crowd gasped.

"Ten thousand dollars, going once."

Still smirking, Brielle shook her head and set down her number.

"Twice."

"Are you crazy?" the guy sitting next to Harper exclaimed.

Rusty's eyes locked with Harper's. The hope ignited again. Was this for real? She was actually spending all this money for a date with him? Shucks, he'd go out with her for *free*.

"Sold for ten thousand dollars!"

The man rolled his eyes and crossed his arms over his chest as the color drained from Harper's face. She looked at Brielle, who sat calmly sipping her champagne and scrolling through her phone.

Dread orbited his gut as the truth plowed into him. They weren't fighting for a chance to go out with him. They were fighting each other.

"Harper, come meet your bachelor!"

The emcee's unrelenting cheer grated on Rusty's nerves. Slowly Harper stood, seemingly in shock as she walked to the stage, then to the stairs on the side of the stage. The emcee helped her navigate them, and then she walked to Rusty.

"You two enjoy your date," Brooks said, his white teeth nearly blinding as he grinned.

Harper didn't respond.

Rusty wasn't sure what to do. He looked at Senior, who was clapping along with the audience. But all Rusty felt was humiliation. He held his arm out to Harper, and she slipped her hand through it. Cammi, the woman who had opened the curtain and led him on the stage, opened it back up and waved her hand at them to follow her.

Harper didn't say a word as they walked off the stage, and once Cammi disappeared, they were alone. She dropped her arm from his, seemingly still in shock about what had happened.

"Rusty, I . . ." She clamped her mouth shut. Then she said, "I'm sorry."

Pain slashed his heart. He hadn't known what to expect tonight, other than for the entire event to be excruciatingly uncomfortable for him. That was an understatement. He wasn't only hurt, though. He was angry. Not only had he been used, but he'd also been humiliated, even if no one at the gala knew. *I know.* That was enough.

"Congratulations, you two."

He turned around to see Brielle standing there, that same smirk on her face.

Harper stepped around Rusty and stormed to Brielle. Harper hadn't planned on bidding on

Rusty—until she saw how many women were bidding on him. Jealousy had slammed into her, and she'd raised her brochure. She could afford a thousand dollars—barely—especially for a good cause and especially to have Rusty for one night to herself, even if it wouldn't be a real date.

Then Brielle had pulled her stunt, and now Harper was in the hole for ten thousand dollars. Clearly Rusty was worth much more than that, but she didn't have ten thousand to spare. And when they finished bidding, he'd looked furious. He should be. She was interfering with his chance to find a woman he would hit it off with. She wasn't sure how to explain why she'd blocked him, other than tell him the truth, and she couldn't do that. And right now she needed to deal with Brielle.

"What's that supposed to mean?" she said to her through clenched teeth.

Brielle answered with another smirk.

"Harper, are you out of your mind?" Jack appeared next to Brielle. "Ten grand for that guy?"

Brielle turned to Jack, her smirk devolving into a scowl. "What do you care?" she snapped. "You said you didn't move back here for her."

"I didn't at first." He turned to Harper. "But I realize now how much she means to me."

"Is that why you betrayed me?" Brielle squared off. "You told her my plan."

"Of course I did!" Jack faced her. "Do you know how much trouble you could be in? You're lucky Harper's too nice to report you. Or stoop to your level."

"My *level?* What about you, bailing on our relationship and our partnership?"

"It wasn't working, and you know it."

Harper's gaze bounced back and forth between the two of them as they continued to fight. *Both of them are nuts.* She backed away and spun to talk to Rusty. Those two could duke it out for themselves.

But when she turned around, Rusty was gone.

Rusty climbed into his truck and peeled out of the parking lot, Harper's *"I'm sorry"* on repeat in his brain. Sorry that she'd bid on him? Sorry she'd spent so much money? Sorry she'd used him to get the upper hand with Brielle? *How about all three.* Not that it mattered. Once Brielle showed up, he'd been forgotten. And when the guy who had been sitting between the two women arrived, Rusty got out of there.

He drove with one hand as he yanked at the knot on his tie until it loosened enough around his neck to breathe. Why was he such a sucker? He should have just stayed home tonight. Then his heart and his pride wouldn't be a shattered mess right now.

He did know one thing: he was *done* with

women. For good this time. He'd be fine as a lifelong bachelor. It wasn't like they were an endangered species. Jasper Mathis had been single his entire life, and he was good. Crotchety sometimes, but he was also in his eighties, and he deserved some grouchy moments.

I have my own business, and soon I'll have a new house.

Rusty swore, something he never did. Harper was taking him to see the Miles Road land on Sunday. He'd call and cancel. No, postpone, because he would keep his word. Just not tomorrow. After what had happened tonight, he couldn't hack seeing her so soon.

But after he bought the property—and he would buy that property, especially after all this trouble—he was done with Harper Wilson.

After helping the rest of the committee clean up after the gala—and listening to everyone congratulate her not only for snagging one of the best-looking bachelors of the night but also being so generous—Harper left and headed straight for Rusty's. She pulled into his driveway, then cut the headlights. Her head pounded, and not from the champagne she'd gulped down earlier. What had she done? Her little nest egg was gone, and Rusty was furious with her. She had no one to blame but herself. She was ashamed she'd fallen into Brielle's trap and that Rusty had to see her sink so low. She had no idea how much of the hysterics he'd seen between her, Brielle, and Jack, but even a glimpse was too much. She owed him an apology and an explanation. She prayed he'd hear her out.

She got out of the car, and her heel caught on the sidewalk crack, almost sending her sprawling on the ground. Catching herself, she regained her balance and glanced around, hoping no one had seen what almost happened. The golden light from the seventies-era porch light fixture was on and illuminating the front yard. What had happened here? The overgrown bushes in front of the picture window were neatly trimmed, and the weeds that had grown in the sidewalk crack were gone. The lawn was mowed, and only a few dead leaves dotted the grass. Even the front stoop had been swept and the small windows on the door cleaned.

Did Rusty do all this?

She knocked on the door and waited, then knocked again when no one answered. When she'd left the gala, Senior was still there, talking with Cammi and some of the other women on the planning committee. But Rusty's truck was in the driveway, so she knew he was home. And when he didn't answer the door, she took one guess where he was.

A full moon was out tonight, so she could see where she was going. The yard was soft, and her heels dug into the dirt. Frustrated, she took off her shoes and left them there. She'd get them later. She went to the side of the house and unlatched an old steel gate attached to the crosshatch fencing. When she opened the gate, it squeaked. She paused, waiting to hear Rusty call out or come investigate who was entering his property. After a minute of silence, she walked into his backyard.

He was sitting on a lawn chair in the same spot they'd been when they stargazed together. But he wasn't looking at the sky. There was no point due to the bright moonlight that cast him in a silver shadowy glow. Instead, he stared straight ahead, then brought a bottle to his lips.

"Go home, Harper," he grumbled. "I ain't in the mood to talk."

She halted a few feet away from him. "How did you know it was me?"

"Heard the Merc."

Of course he'd be able to tell it was her car in the driveway. He knew the vehicle inside and out.

He took another long draw from the amber bottle and tossed it on the ground.

"Rusty, I'm sorry." She walked toward him, then stood by his chair, waiting for him to acknowledge her.

Finally he sighed. "I know. I heard you the first time. You can go now."

She'd never thought he'd be so harsh. "I want to explain."

He looked up at her. "What if I don't want to hear it?"

But she barely comprehended his words as she saw the aching pain in his eyes. Only then did she realize how much she'd hurt him. Knowing that he was suffering because of her foolishness pierced her heart straight through. *Oh, Rusty.*

He stared straight ahead again but reached down on the opposite side of his chair and grabbed another bottle from the six pack on the ground. He twisted off the cap and took a long swig. Oh boy, this wasn't good. She walked to him and grabbed the beer.

"Hey," he said, glaring at her. "What do you think you're doin'?"

"It's kind of pathetic to drink alone, don't you think?" She poured the beverage out on the ground.

"That's me," he said, picking up another beer. "Pathetic."

Oh, this wasn't going well. "You're not pathetic," she said softly. *I'm the pathetic one.*

He didn't respond.

She was getting nowhere with him tonight. She also didn't like this side of him. Brooding, silent Rusty was out of character.

Her feet froze as she tried to figure out a way to get him to talk to her.

He stood and looked at her. "I'll meet you at Miles Road tomorrow." Then he turned and headed for the house.

Miles Road? She'd forgotten all about their appointment to see the property. If he ended up buying it, she wouldn't have to deplete her savings. She'd written a check for five thousand before she left, saying she would have the rest of it for them next week. Since everyone involved with the charity knew Harper and trusted she was good for the remainder, she didn't have to bounce a check. Not yet, at least. And not if she earned a huge commission from the sale.

The screen door bounced shut, then fell off one of the hinges.

Harper made her way back around the house and picked up her shoes. She looked at the clean yard in front of her. He'd gotten a good start on the rehab. Although he didn't need the money to buy a new place, once he finished this house, she could sell it at a decent price . . . if Rusty would agree to let her sell it. That would make a dent in rebuilding her business, and she could build off both sales. Rusty would have the new house he wanted for him and Senior, and she would have both commissions. *Win, win.*

A dark-colored sedan pulled into the driveway behind Harper's Mercedes. The passenger-side door opened, and Senior stepped out. "See you next Saturday, Fran," he said before closing the door. He whistled as he turned around, then stopped when he saw Harper. "Everything okay?" he asked as she opened her car door.

She shrugged. "He's not happy with me right now."

Senior nodded. "That was quite the display," he said. "You and that other lady out biddin' each other." He walked closer to her. "If you ain't figured it out already, my Rusty's got a tender heart. Be careful with it." Without waiting for her to reply, he headed for the house.

Too late.

Chapter 20

W here are we going, Don?"

"It's a surprise. We're almost there."

Madge sat back in Don's Audi and forced herself not to jump to conclusions. He'd asked if he could pick her up after church and take her for a drive, and she'd agreed. He had promised he would be the husband she needed him to be, and he couldn't do that if she didn't give him a chance. *I have to give us a chance.*

He'd made promises before, but she had to admit that something felt different now. She couldn't quite pinpoint what it was. Maybe it was how relaxed he was right now. Not rushed or excited or pressing her to match his mood so he wouldn't be disappointed. He hadn't pressured her either when she had initially said no to him picking her up. He told her he understood and hoped she had a good weekend. Before hanging up, she'd changed her mind, and now they were on their way to wherever he was taking her.

When he turned down Central Avenue in Hot Springs and headed to the shopping district, she couldn't believe it. "We're going shopping?"

Don glanced at her, nodding. "Yep."

"But you hate shopping."

"And you love it. Besides, they have the Christmas decorations out."

"Already? We're just now getting to November."

"They put them out earlier this year. I know how much you enjoy them."

She did, especially when it came to decorating her house. She also helped decorate Amazing Grace for the Christmas season, but that wouldn't happen until after Thanksgiving, the normal time to decorate.

"Christmas was never your favorite holiday," she said.

He pulled into a parallel spot next to a row of shops. "Yeah, I'm a grinch around this time of year. Holidays were never much fun while I was growing up."

She frowned as he turned off the car. He never liked talking about his childhood, and he was so distant with his parents that she'd only met them a handful of times before they passed away a few years ago. He'd been cold and aloof at their funerals. Now that she thought about it, that was around the time he started pulling even further away from her and Harper. His behavior had affected Madge too. When her own mother died, she'd gotten so used to hiding her feelings, she hadn't cried at her funeral either.

Madge put her hand on his arm. "We don't have to do this."

He laid his palm over her fingers. "Yes, we do. You've always gone along with the things I wanted to do. It's past time I did the same." He opened the door, then paused. "I don't think I told you how much I like your new hair."

Suddenly self-conscious, she touched the sides. "You do?"

"Yes. You look beautiful." He stepped outside and shut the door.

Buoyed by his compliment, she got out of the car and marveled at the decorations she saw. The city had outdone itself, even though Christmas was more than seven weeks away.

"Where do you want to go first?"

She looked at him, searching for the faraway look she often saw when he was bored, or the impatience when he was in a hurry for her to finish something he deemed unimportant. Instead, there were sparks of excitement in his eyes, and he was looking at her the way he used to when they first dated. An ember of attraction she thought long burned out suddenly warmed her heart.

"Ice cream," she said.

He arched a brow. "You want ice cream? In this weather?"

"I'm in the mood for butter pecan."

Don grinned. "Then let's find you some butter pecan."

Later that afternoon, after they had spent

several hours eating ice cream, shopping, and getting coffee to go, Don took her home. As he pulled his car into the driveway, she gripped the Styrofoam cup. Would he ask to come inside? Or to stay the night? She wasn't ready for either.

He put the car in Park and turned to her. "I had a great time, Madge. Better than I've had in years."

Seeing the sincerity in his eyes, she said, "Me too."

"If it's all right with you, can I give you a call later in the week? Maybe we can grab a bite to eat next weekend. Or if it's too soon, I can wait."

"A call would be nice."

He smiled. "Thank you. I'll help you get your bags."

They got out of the car, and he took the three small bags out of his trunk and handed them to her. "I'll talk to you soon," he said, heading for the front of the car.

She nodded, stepping to the side as he got into the driver's seat. Then she hurried to the window and tapped on it with the back of her knuckles.

He rolled down the window, a questioning look in his eyes.

She leaned over and brushed her lips against his, not daring to deepen the kiss. "Thank you, Don."

He smiled, then nodded and rolled up the window. She waved as he pulled out of the driveway.

Today was a first small step toward . . . she wasn't sure exactly what. But she needed to savor this moment and not worry about the future. She also had some early Christmas presents to wrap.

On Sunday afternoon Harper arrived early to the Miles Road property after picking up the gate key from Brielle's office. Her weekend secretary had given her the key, and Harper was about to open the door to leave when she heard Brielle call her name. Rats.

She turned around and didn't bother to force a smile. "I'll return this as soon as we're finished."

"Good." Brielle walked toward Harper, a slight smirk on her face. "I wanted to let you know Jack and I worked things out."

"Okay." Those two were made for each other.

"We'll be moving back to Bentonville soon. I'll be keeping my office open here, though."

"Why are you telling me this?"

Brielle moved closer to her. "Because I won," she said in a low voice. "I always do." Then she turned around and left.

Harper rolled her eyes and walked out the door. What exactly had Brielle won? A fickle boyfriend? A business competition with Harper that she didn't even know about? For the first time, she felt sorry for Brielle. *That woman needs to relax.*

She left the Mercedes and went to unlock the

gate. She walked through it and into a large open space surrounded by trees that had lost half their leaves. This was gorgeous. It even smelled good out here—a fresh, earthy scent. She took in a deep breath. A few minutes later, she heard a vehicle coming down the road. As Rusty pulled over on the side of the road behind her Mercedes, she turned and watched him get out of the cab. Her breath hitched, as it always did when she was around him. He wore his work clothes, only this time instead of a ball cap he had on a black beanie with the garage logo on the brim. He hadn't shaved, and from the grease stains on his clothes she could see he'd come straight from work. He must have decided to work on the GTO, since the garage was always closed on Sundays. He even smelled like oil.

Swoon.

"Hi, Rusty." Years of practiced smiling came in handy right now. "Ready to tour the property?"

He nodded, his expression wooden. It remained that way as they walked the land, Harper pointing out different places where he could build his and Senior's new house. When they reached the pond, they both stopped at the bank. "What do you think?"

Rusty stared at the pond as if in deep thought. Kicked at a stray leaf. Then turned to Harper. "Where do I sign?"

"You don't want to see the rest—"

"No. I'm ready to buy it."

This was it. With one stroke of a pen—after going through all the legal documents, of course—her financial woes would be solved, and his and Senior's housing problem would be taken care of. Next step, selling Rusty's house. Piece of cake.

Her eyes met his . . . and she knew the truth. "You don't want this, do you?"

His brow quirked. "Yes. I told you I want to buy it."

She moved closer to him. "Do you? Or are you doing this to make Amber and Senior happy? Or to help me?"

"Both," he said without hesitation.

"What about you?" she asked. "What do you want?"

Harper had asked the million-dollar question, and he didn't know what to say. He knew what he *wanted* to say. *You. I want you.* But because he wasn't a masochist, he said, "I'm fine with whatever they want."

"I don't think you are."

He faced her, confused. "You're not makin' a lick of sense. Just give me the contract, and I'll sign it."

"No," she said, crossing her arms. "I'm not selling you this property."

Now he understood her game. "Because Brielle would make money off it?"

She frowned. "What? No. That's not the reason."

"But if I don't buy it, she loses the sale."

"There's plenty of people wanting to buy this place. She'll make money whether you buy it or not."

He scratched his chin, feeling the whiskers there. He hadn't bothered to shave or change out of his dirty work clothes after spending the morning working on the GTO instead of going to church. He felt a nag of guilt for missing the service, but he wasn't in the mood to deal with people. "You won't make any money, then."

"I'm okay with that."

"What about your business?"

"My business doesn't matter right now. Rusty, you don't want to move. I sensed it when you first told me about Amber moving away. You love your house. I don't want to convince you to do something you might regret in the future. Not even for a bank full of money."

He was floored. Up until this moment he'd been ready to buy this land and get started on building, telling himself he was excited about the prospect. But when she spoke the truth out loud, he knew she was right. Somehow she had figured it out before he did. "How did you know?"

"I'm very good at what I do. You need to tell Senior and Amber how you feel. I think you'll be surprised by their answers."

"I ain't sure about that. They're both awful settled on sellin' the place."

He followed her back to the gate, and she clicked the lock shut. Then she turned to him. "You owe me a date," she said, as calmly as if they'd been talking about the weather.

"What?"

"I had the winning bid, so you're obligated to go out with me."

She'd shocked him again. "Are you serious?"

"Extremely serious. Are you free Saturday night?"

He was always free on Saturday nights. "You don't have to do this, Harper," he said. "I won't hold you to the date. Let's just forget about it." How could he admit that he knew she and Brielle had used him? That he was acutely aware she didn't really want to go out with him?

"Oh no, we can't." She waved her index finger at him. "We have a *lot* to talk about. I'll call you later with the details." She walked to the Mercedes and got inside, then waved to him as she drove away.

He rubbed the back of his neck, still trying to figure out what had happened. He wasn't buying the property. He possibly wasn't moving at all. He was going on a date with Harper. He almost smiled, then stopped himself. It wasn't a *date*. It was a "date." And what did they have to talk about? Guess he would find out on Saturday. But he would keep his guard up and the time he spent with her short.

He climbed into his truck and dialed his sister's number. "Hey, Amber. Got a few minutes to talk?"

After Harper got home from dropping off the key at Brielle's, she called an emergency meeting of the CCs. That night they met at Knots and Tangles, and she spilled everything to her best friends, including what had happened at the auction and what went on with Brielle and Jack.

"You've been dealing with all that and didn't tell us?" Riley asked, looking a little hurt.

"We could have helped you," Anita said. Olivia nodded.

"I know. I thought I could handle everything myself." She grabbed one of the coconut macaroons she made yesterday. She'd managed not to do any taste testing while she baked three batches, so she took a little nibble. Mmm, pretty good.

Olivia sat back on the lime-green couch. "So what are you going to do about your business?"

"Never mind her business," Anita said. "What about Rusty?"

"You and Rusty." Riley grinned. "I can see it."

So could Harper. But could Rusty? She was less than sure. Still, there was only one way to find out, and claiming her date with him gave her an opportunity. That's when she would know if there was a future for the two of them. "I can't believe I'm even thinking about dating again. I was so sure I'd spend the next ten or twenty years focusing solely on real estate. And my friends," she added quickly. "Now all I want to do is relax, bake, go to church, spend time with my CCs, and—"

"Snuggle with Rusty."

Everyone looked at Olivia, who was the least romantic of the group. "What?" she said, holding out her hands. "Anyone can see how much you like him."

"You have this dreamy look when you say his name," Riley pointed out.

"Really dreamy." Anita sighed.

"Y'all are a mess!" Harper laughed.

"We're your mess," they all said in unison.

She wondered why she'd been so reluctant to turn to her friends earlier, instead of insisting to herself that she could handle things alone. "Will y'all help me plan my date?"

"Of course," Anita said. Riley and Olivia nodded. "It will be the best date you ever had."

Chapter 21

"You have to tell us what happens tonight," Anita said, adjusting the small candle in the middle of Harper's dining-room table.

"Yes," Riley added. "Every detail."

"Maybe not every detail," Olivia muttered, fluffing up the throw pillows on the couch.

Harper chuckled, although it was more from nerves than actual humor. She wanted to be casual and relaxed, and she couldn't think of a better way to do that than to cook him a meal at home, and now her girls were helping her set everything up.

It was almost five thirty, and there was a meat loaf in the oven, baked potatoes warming in the Instapot, and green beans and bacon simmering on the stove. Tiramisu sat under the dome on the cake stand.

"I think you're ready," Anita said, looking things over. Riley and Olivia moved to stand next to her near the fully set table. "Time for us to go."

"Are you sure you want to wear that?" Riley whispered to her. "You were the one who told me I had to dress up for Hayden on our first date."

Harper smiled. "I'm sure." She was wearing faded jeans and a baby-blue oversized sweater, no makeup, her hair in a high ponytail, bunny slippers on her feet, and her glasses.

"I didn't even know you wore glasses," Olivia said.

"You'll see them on me more often."

Her friends left, and she stood alone in her kitchen, her stomach a twisted knot. She hadn't expected to be so nervous about tonight, but she was close to diving into that tiramisu to soothe her nerves. She glanced at the clock. Six sharp. He should be here by now.

The minutes ticked by. Five after. Ten after. She paced the length of her living room. Was he standing her up? No one had ever stood her up before. But she was more discouraged than angry.

I got my answer before the date even started.

The doorbell rang and she jumped. *He's here.* She wiped her damp palms on her jeans, then touched the doorknob. With a deep breath, she opened it, and for the second time this week, she swooned. "Hi, Rusty."

"Hi," he said.

"Uh, come on in." She opened the door wider, trying not to stare at him, only to give up and give him her complete visual attention. *So sexy.*

"Sorry I'm late," he said as he walked in. He turned and tugged at his tie—the one she'd picked out to go with the rest of the suit he was wearing. "I reckon I overdressed. I wasn't sure what we were doin' tonight, and I didn't want to embarrass you if we were goin' somewhere fancy."

"Oh, Rusty," she said, going to him. "You would never embarrass me." She looked him up and down again. "Although I'm not mad about the suit. Far from it." Then she glanced down at her outfit. "I should go change," she said, starting to leave.

He touched her arm. "Don't. You look fine." Then he cleared his throat. "You look . . . beautiful."

Rusty held his breath, waiting for her response. He was late because he'd tried to sneak out of the house without Senior seeing him, but he should have known better. He also should have known that his grandfather would guess right away that he was going out with Harper. Rusty tried to play down that it was a date, but his grandfather would have none of it. "This is your chance, son." When Rusty tried to dismiss him, he said, "One of these days you're gonna have to risk your heart, Russell."

Rusty looked up at him. "You never call me Russell."

"I never had to get your attention so badly before. Listen here. Relationships are hard, no matter what anyone says."

"I ain't ever had a relationship before," he admitted. "Not one that lasted more than a couple dates, anyway."

"You've been hurt a lot, haven't you?"

Rusty shrugged. "Just by a girl or two. Three, maybe," he muttered.

"I don't mean that. I'm talkin' about your folks."

He looked at Senior. "They don't have nothin' to do with this."

"I'm not so sure. Like I said, me and your G'ma worried about you and Amber and how your parents leavin' you both behind would affect you."

Surprised at the pain flooding through him at the mention of their abandonment, he got up from the sofa. "Why are you bringin' that up again? I don't have any recollection of them. I was too young."

"But you knew they were gone and not comin' back."

He swallowed, unable to look at Senior.

"And those girls you dated. Did you ever think maybe you knew ahead of time things wouldn't work out?"

He spun around. "That doesn't make a lick of sense."

"Oh, I don't know. Ask the wrong woman out, you get the rejection over with right quick. Then it don't hurt so bad." He got up and left, leaving Rusty to ponder his words until it was time to pick up Harper.

Did he date the wrong girls on purpose? Senior

liked to watch this psychology guy's show in the afternoons, even though Rusty thought the doc was a quack, and this sounded like some kind of mumbo jumbo that doctor would say.

Then he thought about Sabrina, the girl he'd asked out in high school. She'd mentioned more than once that she'd had a crush on the tuba player in the Maple Falls band. And the woman with the boyfriend. Hadn't she told him from the start that they didn't have to go through with the date if he didn't want to?

Rusty fast-forwarded to the other doomed date he'd been on, and it was the same thing. The girl was unavailable. Yet he'd still gone out with her. He'd asked them all out. And when they rejected him, it hurt for a bit. But that was his ego talking. Not his heart.

Standing in front of him now, Harper's cheeks flushed, and she stared down at her bunny slippers. "Thank you," she whispered. Then she drew in a deep breath and said, "Can we wait on supper for a few minutes? I need to talk to you."

He tried not to let his mind go to Rejection City again, although it was hard not to. He nodded and followed her into the living room. They sat down; she perched at the edge of the chair. She tugged on the hem of her sweater. "I owe you an apology, Rusty."

Here we go. He stayed in place, though, and let her speak.

"I've made so many mistakes I don't know where to start."

He frowned. "I don't understand."

"The auction, for one. I shouldn't have pressured you to go. I was sure that you would have a good time, though, once you were there. And you might have if it weren't for me." She was stretching out the band of the sweater but didn't seem to notice. "You might have found . . . someone else."

"Someone else?"

"Someone to date. But I ruined it by letting Brielle get to me."

He listened as she explained how Brielle had sabotaged her business. "When she started bidding for you, I couldn't let her win."

"Because she's done you wrong," he said, hope slipping fast away.

"No. Because I couldn't stand the thought of you two together."

He shook his head. "That would never happen. She ain't my type."

"Who is your type?"

Rusty ran his suddenly damp palms over his brown trousers. Without realizing it, she had opened the door. But could he walk through it? Could he stand the agony if she didn't feel the same way? If she told him she wanted to be friends, it would rip his heart out.

But if he didn't say anything, he would be okay.

They would enjoy the evening—as friends—and then it would be over.

He wouldn't have to risk anything.

"Rusty?" she asked. "Are you okay?"

He gazed at her, taking in her makeup-free face, the strands of hair falling out of her bun, even the small food stain on the front of her sweater that he was positive she hadn't noticed yet.

She's worth it.

"You, Harper," he said, barely able to breathe.

"Me what?"

He leaned in close, his eyes never moving from hers. "You're my type."

Before he knew what was happening, she grabbed him by the tie . . . and kissed him.

Harper hadn't planned to kiss Rusty, but now that she was, she couldn't stop. She let go of his tie and put her arms around his neck as he kissed her back. *Delicious.* Then somehow, she ended up in his lap. *Even more delicious.* By the time they finished she couldn't catch her breath.

"Harper?" he said, looking confused.

"Yes?" She ran her fingers over his lips.

He smiled and kissed her again, his hand cupping the back of her head, then lightly brushing against her neck. When they parted he pressed his forehead against hers. "I can't tell you how long I've waited to kiss you."

"Not as long as I have to kiss you."

Lifting his head, he said, "What about that guy at the auction? The one sitting next to you."

"Jack? Ugh. He's my ex."

"But I saw you two together."

"We weren't together. He was trying to get back with me, though. That's why I hoped you would come inside, that night you saw us in my driveway. But I understand why you didn't." She moved off his lap but still sat close to him. She took his hand, needing to touch him. She didn't ever want to let him go. After she explained what had happened that night, she said, "I don't know if Jack is lying or Brielle is. Probably both. I don't care. I only care about you, Rusty. I think I have ever since you came over for supper that first time."

Relief crossed his features. "I reckon I should have taken a chance earlier than this," he said.

"I know why you didn't." She put her hand on his chest. "Someone told me you have a tender heart. Although I'd guessed that already."

He covered her hand with his. "I talked to Amber and Senior. They're fine with us keeping the house, as long as we add more room and make it accessible for Senior. That last part was Amber's request. You were right, I was surprised by their answers." He touched a lock of her hair that had come loose when they kissed and smiled at her crooked bun. "What are you gonna do about your business, though?"

"I'm taking a break." She smiled. "A wise, smart, and very sexy guy I know told me I need to relax more."

Rusty grinned. "I'm glad you're takin' some time for yourself. Then you'll be ready to tackle work when you go back."

"I may not go back. Or I might work part-time. Or find a completely different job. I want to do some more baking. Hang out with my friends. Maybe even learn how to crochet or knit." She chuckled. "I never thought I'd ever say that."

"Anything else?" he asked.

"I want to date my boyfriend, and I want to do that as much as possible." The *beep* of the Instapot went off. "Hope you're hungry," she said. "I make some mean baked potatoes. Well, the Instapot does."

He gathered her in his arms again. "I can wait." His lips hovered over hers.

She smiled. *Me too.*

Chapter 22

Madge brought the cup of Americano up to her lips, taking a tiny sip. The coffee at Sunshine Café was always exceptional, but she could barely bring herself to drink it. She set it down at the table and looked at the door.

"You're anxious." Under the table, Don gave her hand a squeeze.

"A little."

He frowned slightly, looking so handsome in a cobalt-blue pullover sweater. "Everything we're going to tell her is good, though."

"I know, and I'm not sure why I'm nervous." She glanced around the café, already decorated for Christmas even though Thanksgiving was in two days. Harper had texted both her and Don last night, saying she wanted to meet this afternoon for coffee. Don had called Madge right after answering the text, and they'd decided to tell Harper their news and agreed to meet at the café a little earlier than the designated time.

The door opened and Harper walked inside. She slid off the fingerless knit gloves Madge had made for her last year. This was the first time Madge had seen her daughter wear something she'd knitted for her, and she couldn't hold back her smile.

"Hello, you two," Harper said as she sat down at the table. She looked at them with a sly expression. "What a pair of lovebirds you are. I haven't seen you two sit this close in . . . Actually, I never have. It's amazing to see."

Madge exchanged a look with Don as he squeezed her hand. "We're glad you approve," she said seriously.

Harper slipped out of her brown leather jacket and hung it over the back of her chair. "I'm glad you could meet with me on short notice." When Anita started to come over, she shook her head. "Rusty should be here in a few minutes. I'll wait until he arrives. There's something I want you to know first." She looked at each of them. "I closed down my real-estate office."

"Temporarily?" Madge asked, stunned.

"No. For good. I'm not giving up being an agent, though. Just going to work part-time until I figure things out. I do have three clients that I need to work with first, but after that I'm going to shut it down and work from home."

"Does Rusty know about this?" Madge asked.

Harper nodded, then looked to see her father's reaction. When she had introduced her parents to Rusty shortly after they started dating, Don had given him the third degree. Rusty had handled it well, and they'd even gone fishing together before the cold weather set in.

"Are you going to have enough to live on?" Don asked.

"Yes. I already have a new income stream." Harper sat up straight. "I'm selling my baked goods here."

"Really?" Madge said.

"Is that going to be enough?" Don added.

"If I curb my spending and pinch my pennies, yes. My wardrobe will take a hit, but I was spending too much on clothes anyway. I also sold my Mercedes."

"What?" they both exclaimed at the same time.

"But that's your dream car," her mother said.

"It was. But dreams change. Rusty's letting me drive Lois until I get another car."

"Lois?" Don looked confused.

"Are you sure about all this?" Madge asked. She didn't care about Lois. She wanted to make sure Harper had thought through her decision. "You've worked so hard for your business, and you loved that car."

"Positive," Harper said, every syllable filled with confidence. "I love baking, and with the free time I now have, I can do something other than work until I fall into bed. Although I can't promise I won't give in to temptation and buy cute shoes every once in a while. Oh, there's Rusty." She waved for him to come over.

Madge watched as Rusty took off his beanie and finger-combed his hair, then stuck the hat in the pocket of his hoodie as he approached the table. When Rusty sat down, Don said, "What's a Lois?"

"2010 Accord. Treat a car right, she'll treat you right."

"I agree," Don said. "Felt that way about the planes I flew."

For the next two hours, the four of them talked, and Madge didn't even mind that Don and Rusty almost exclusively discussed planes and cars. Harper didn't seem bothered, either, and it gave Madge and her more time to talk about Harper's plans. By the time they had to leave, Madge felt more connected to her family than ever before and more optimistic about the future. Rusty was a wonderful young man, and she'd never seen her daughter so happy.

"We should make this a regular thing," Harper said.

Don helped Madge into her coat. "I agree. Once a month, for sure. If not more often."

"See you both on Thanksgiving," Madge said. They had made plans to meet at Madge's house for the holiday.

"I'll bring the pumpkin pie." Harper grinned.

With a last round of handshakes and hugs, they parted ways.

"They're pretty smitten with each other." Don glanced at Madge as he drove away and smiled. "Remember those days?"

"Yes." And now she could think back on them without resentment, without obsessing about what she'd lost or given up. But there was one thing she still needed to do. "Don?" she said as he slowed at a red light.

He brought the car to a stop. "Yes?"

She twisted her sterling-silver bracelet around her wrist. A gift from him for their twenty-fifth anniversary. Before today, she'd only worn it once. "I forgive you for the affair."

His head jerked toward her. "Really? You do?"

"Yes." The weight of pain and resentment enclosing her heart started to ease. "I also recognize my part in driving you away."

"Madge—"

"I know you want to take full responsibility. But that's not fair. I resented that you could follow your dreams while I had to give up mine. The truth is I don't regret staying home and raising Harper. Look how she's turned out."

The light turned green, and Don drove on, nodding. "Yes," he said, his voice thick. "She's amazing."

"I shouldn't have been so cold to you all these years," she said, her chest aching as she admitted the words. "I was punishing you, I think. I wanted you to hurt as much as I did."

Don didn't say anything on the rest of the drive home, and she wondered if she'd revealed too much. He pulled into the driveway but didn't turn off the engine. The headlights reflected off the garage door as he stared straight ahead.

After what seemed like an eternity, he spoke. "I did feel punished, Maddie. I would come home from being gone so long, and all I wanted was to be with my girls. But every time I walked through that door, I felt I'd done something wrong." He looked at her. "You weren't happy to see me. Eventually Harper wasn't all that happy to see me either. After a while I stayed away on purpose." His chest heaved. "I didn't believe I was good enough for you, or my daughter."

Madge hung her head. "I'm sorry," she said, tears forming in her eyes.

"That feeling of not measuring up wasn't all about you, though. Some of it's childhood stuff. I can see that now. Overbearing father, passive mother, among other things. Still, there's no excuse for what I did. I guess part of me wanted to punish you too. But we're over that now, aren't we?"

"Yes." She reached for his hand. Without hesitation he gently squeezed her fingers.

Fog obscured the car windows. She glanced at their clasped hands. "Do you want to, um . . . come inside?" Then she met his gaze, butterflies dancing in her stomach the way they had the first time they'd met. "You could also . . ." She swallowed. "You could stay. The night. If you want to."

Don paused, staring at the clouded window. "I want to," he murmured. "I can't tell you how much I want to."

"But you won't."

He looked at her. "It's too soon, Maddie. I don't want to repeat the past. When we do make love again, I want it to be when we're both ready to commit to our marriage."

His words pricked her. "Are you saying you have doubts?"

"No." He held her gaze. "You do."

She exhaled. She'd said as much, several times. She'd made it clear he had to prove himself to her. What she hadn't expected was to want him back so quickly.

"You're right." She smiled faintly. "And also wise."

"Thank my counselor."

"A counselor is only as good as his client," she said.

"Who told you that?"

"A counselor I once fired."

He looked surprised. "You went to counseling?"

"Briefly, years ago. The first two sessions were fine, but then he started pointing out my faults, and I didn't like that." She stared at her lap. "Maybe if I'd kept up with it, we wouldn't be where we are right now."

"Or maybe we would. It's impossible to know." He leaned over and kissed her cheek. "Good night, Maddie," he whispered. "I've only got so much self-restraint."

She opened the car door. He really was a special man. "Good night, Don."

He waved and drove away.

Madge turned and looked at the For Sale sign in her yard. She went over and pulled it out of the ground. "We're off the market," she said, then headed for the house.

"So when are you gonna see Fran again?" Rusty and Harper sat in his truck in the lot behind the café and had Senior on speaker phone. His grandfather had sent him a text while they were talking to Harper's parents in the café.

M iss you.

"Woo-hoo, you got yourself a girlfriend, and all of a sudden you're sticking your nose in other people's love lives."

Rusty laughed. "Just giving as good as I got." He glanced at Harper, and she scooted closer to him on the bench seat. "Seriously, when are you comin' back to Maple Falls? I need you to help me fix up your old bedroom."

"Next week after Amber moves," Senior said. "I'm so glad Austin found a house for them before Christmas."

"Me too. Do they need any help packing?"

"Naw. Amber said the movin' company's doing all that. She's also payin' them a little extra to pack me up, so you'll just have to load a couple things in your truck when you take me back home. Hey, I was thinkin'. How about you spendin' a few days here before they leave? It'll be nice to have you and Amber together for a spell. It's been a long time."

He couldn't remember the last time he and his sister had spent more than a day or two together since she married Austin. It would be nice to have some quality time with her and the kids before they moved. *I sure will miss them.* "I'd like that," Rusty said, glancing at Harper. She nodded. "Right after Thanksgivin', okay?"

"Sounds good."

They talked for a little while longer, then hung up. Rusty turned to Harper. "Will you be all right while I'm gone?" he said, winking at her.

"Oh, I guess I'll manage." She tapped him on the arm and smiled. "Are you up for a walk? The town has the Christmas lights up."

"Sure." He turned off the truck and opened the door for her. Then he took her hand and they walked to Main Street.

"I'm surprised they have them out so early," Harper said as they walked slowly down the sidewalk. The downtown businesses were closed for the night, and there was no one around.

Rusty reckoned they were all getting ready for Thursday's festivities.

"Hayden made sure to get that done," he said as they passed the café. "Quickel about blew his stack. I think he's seein' the writin' on the wall, though. Hayden's all but declared himself as a mayoral candidate in next year's election."

"Think he'll win?"

"I know he will."

They walked past Knots and Tangles, crossed the street, and continued past Petals and Posies, then stopped in front of #6. "It's still for sale," Rusty said.

"I know."

He looked at the building. "Sure you don't want to change your mind?"

Harper stood in front of #6 and stared at the For Sale sign in the window. Out of habit, she calculated numbers in her mind, tallying the costs of renovations. If she had purchased the building, she would have definitely repainted the facade. A crisp white, similar to her current office. Wait, her former office.

Rusty slipped an arm around her waist, and she gazed at him, the man she was falling more deeply for as each day passed. And she knew the answer to his question. She'd spent years investing in her career. Now it was time to invest in something else. "No. I'm not going to change my mind."

She put her head on his shoulder, having made a habit of wearing flats all the time, except for a few occasions. Her feet were thanking her for it, and her head had learned its place in the nook of his neck. "I want something different now."

He kissed the top of her head, and they stood in the cold, staring at the building. Hopefully the person who ended up purchasing it would do the town justice.

"You're positive?" he said.

"Yes, I'm positive."

"Okay, then." He faced her. "I'm going to buy it."

Her eyes widened. "You are?"

"Yes. Hayden and I had lunch with Tanner the other day, and we were talkin' about this buildin' bein' vacant for so long. I didn't say anythin' about you bein' interested in it at one time. But it got me thinkin'—since I'm not buyin' a new house or land, I might as well invest the money. I can't think of anythin' better than to invest in Maple Falls."

"Wow. I love that idea."

"I thought you might. With Hayden and Riley promotin' the town so much, I'm sure there'll be a small business or two that can use this space."

"This is wonderful!" she said, giving him a hug.

"I'll need a real-estate agent, of course." He smirked. "You wouldn't happen to know anyone, would you?"

She leaned up and kissed him. "As a matter of fact, I do."

Epilogue

Seven months later

M adge tightened the belt on her white bathrobe and walked out on the balcony of her hotel room. The Hawaiian breeze drifted over her short, damp hair. She placed her hands on the railing and closed her eyes, then smiled as she felt Don's arms slip around her waist.

"Best trip ever?" he whispered in her ear.

She turned around and kissed him, then leaned against him, his robe matching hers. "Absolutely."

He took her hand and led her back inside. Yesterday they had renewed their vows on the beach, with Harper and Rusty serving as witnesses. Then the couples parted ways. "What do you think the kids are doing?" she mused as she sat on the edge of the bed.

"I'm sure they're not thinking about us." Don walked to the table on the opposite side of the room and put some fresh fruit into a glass bowl. "And I don't want to think about them. I love 'em, but this trip is about you"—he gave her the fruit—"and me." He sat next to her.

She selected a plump strawberry and handed it to him as he put his arm around her. It had been a long road to get to this point in their relationship, and there were times when she didn't think they'd make it, particularly after she had started going to counseling with him. She'd had to face some uncomfortable truths about herself and her responsibility in their marriage. But they were both stronger afterward, and when he had asked her a month ago to renew their vows, she hadn't hesitated to say yes.

Don touched her chin and brought his mouth to hers. "You taste like strawberries," she said after they broke the kiss.

He smiled. "I love you, Maddie. Thanks for marrying me—a second time. Maybe in ten years we can do this again. But until then . . ." He drew her into his arms.

And the world melted away.

"I don't know about this, Harper."

She glanced at Rusty's bare toes gripping the slippery rock beneath his feet. Their hiking sandals lay nearby. "You'll be fine," she said. "It's just a waterfall."

"That's a mighty strong-lookin' waterfall."

She would have laughed if she didn't know he was genuinely scared. When they had arrived in Hawaii two days ago to celebrate her parents' renewing their vows, she'd promised herself she would fulfill one of her bucket-list items: standing under a waterfall. And who better to do that with than her husband of three months?

Rusty had bought #6 soon after he told her of his plans. For the next six months she had worked from home, mostly baking for the Sunshine Café and doing a few real-estate deals on the side. An antique store had moved into the bottom level of #6 in March, and the shop opened in May to great success.

But the highlight of the intervening months had been when she and Rusty married in a small ceremony at the church. They had kept the guest list to family and close friends, the way both of them had wanted it. The CCs and the BBs were there, of course, along with Senior and her parents. Amber, Austin, and their family had flown in from Colorado for the event, and her heart had swooned when she saw Rusty playing with his nephews and niece in the parking lot after the ceremony. Then she caught Senior watching them, too, happy tears in his eyes. Then she started crying, and her mother started crying, and soon everyone was bawling except for the kids.

It had been the perfect day.

Afterward she had moved into his newly renovated house. Living with Senior was an adjustment, but the extra addition on the back gave him his own living quarters with plenty of privacy. He only tried to butt into their business once or twice a week, something Harper didn't mind too much.

It was nice to be treated as part of his family.

"Just walk over here," she said, motioning for Rusty to move to the edge of the waterfall. It was a thirty-minute hike to these falls, and by some miracle they had the area all to themselves. But judging by the beauty of the falls and lagoon, they wouldn't be alone for long.

"What if I fall in?" he said, glancing at the waves in the natural pool below.

"Why are you worried about that?" She turned from him and let the misting water cool her face. "You're a good swimmer—"

His arm suddenly slid around her waist. He yanked her against him and lifted her off the ground, carrying her to the large rock behind the falls.

She squealed, then laughed as he set her down. Water thundered around them as Harper smacked him on the butt. "You had me going for a minute," she said.

He smiled and kissed her, his hands resting above the band of her bikini bottom. "Did I mention how much I like you in red?" he said, tugging her closer to him again.

"Why do you think I'm wearing this suit?"

Still in each other's arms, they turned and looked at the water falling in front of them. "I reckon I'm sold," he said, gazing at the falls. "You were right. This is definitely a bucket-list item."

She reached out her hand and touched the fresh, cool water, then smiled as she gazed at the man she loved. A good, genuine, kind man. Extremely sexy too. He was the best man she'd ever met, and he was hers.

She pushed him into the lagoon.

"Hey!" he sputtered when he came up for air. "You tricked me."

She crossed her arms and grinned. "Payback, babe. Payback."

Rusty laughed and held out his arms as he treaded water. "You're not going to leave me alone out here, are you?"

She shook her head . . . and jumped.

Acknowledgments

Real estate is a subject I know little about, but thanks to my sister-in-law, Karmen Daly, I learned a lot. Thanks, Karmen, for being patient and answering all my questions (and helping me brainstorm the plot too!). Big thanks to my agent, Natasha Kern, who always gives me encouragement and support. As always, thank you to my editor Becky Monds, who never fails to give me the insight I need to take the story to the next, and better, level. And a special thanks to her husband, Jerry, who came up with the perfect title for the book!

Thank you, dear reader, for taking another journey with me to Maple Falls. I loved writing Harper and Rusty's unlikely love story and Madge and Don's reconciliation. I hope you enjoyed their happy endings!

Discussion Questions

1. Harper is a workaholic. What advice would you give her to help her balance work with the other areas of her life?

2. Rusty has difficulty with change, but he also recognizes that it's necessary sometimes. Do you have trouble with change? If so, how do you deal with it?

3. Harper and Rusty are complete opposites, but they fall in love anyway. Do you believe that opposites attract, or do most couples you know have a lot of things in common? Why?

4. Madge separates herself from her friends at a time when she needs them the most. Have you ever distanced yourself from people in your life when you've been going through a difficult time? How did you reconnect with them?

5. Harper is very connected to her cell phone, something that's common in society today. Could you leave your cell phone at your house for an entire day? A week? Why or why not?

6. Harper wonders if she's hiding behind her makeup and fashionable clothes. What are other ways we hide our true selves from the world?

7. Rusty is confident in his professional life but has trouble with romantic relationships. Can you relate to his plight? Are there areas in your life that are easier to navigate than others?

8. Don almost lost his relationships with Madge and Harper because he had the wrong priorities. What can you learn from his mistakes and how he changed for the better?

9. Harper and her father finally learn the value of relaxing and having a balanced life. What do you do to relax?

10. Harper and Rusty, and Madge and Don, all had to take personal risks to find their happy endings. Have you ever had a time in your life where you had to do something personally difficult, and what made you take the risk?

About the Author

With over a million copies sold, Kathleen Fuller is the *USA TODAY* bestselling author of several bestselling novels, including the Hearts of Middlefield novels, the Middlefield Family novels, the Amish of Birch Creek series, and the Amish Letters series as well as a middle-grade Amish series, the Mysteries of Middlefield.

Visit her online at KathleenFuller.com
Instagram: @kf_booksandhooks
Facebook: @WriterKathleenFuller
Twitter: @TheKatJam

Center Point Large Print
600 Brooks Road / PO Box 1
Thorndike, ME 04986-0001 USA

(207) 568-3717

US & Canada:
1 800 929-9108
www.centerpointlargeprint.com